DAVID JACKSON is the author of eleven crime novels, including the bestseller *Cry Baby* and the DS Nathan Cody series. A latecomer to fiction writing, after years of writing academic papers he submitted the first few chapters of a novel to the Crime Writers' Association Debut Dagger Awards. He was very surprised when it was both shortlisted and highly commended, leading to the publication of *Pariah* in 2011. David lives on the Wirral with his wife and two daughters. Although he tells lies for a living, he has no big secrets of his own. But then he would say that, wouldn't he?

Also by David Jackson and available from Viper

The Resident
The Rule

NO SECRETS

DAVID JACKSON

VIPER

This paperback edition first published in 2023

First published in Great Britain in 2022 by
VIPER, part of Serpent's Tail,
an imprint of Profile Books Ltd
29 Cloth Fair
London
ECIA 7JQ
www.serpentstail.com

1 3 5 7 9 10 8 6 4 2

Printed and bound in Great Britain by
CPI Group (UK) Ltd, Croydon CR0 4YY

The moral right of the author has been asserted.

A CIP catalogue record for this book is available from the British Library.

ISBN 978 1 80081 021 1
eISBN 978 1 78283 973 6

MIX
Paper | Supporting
responsible forestry
FSC® C171272

For Lisa, Bethany and Eden

1

Front crawl.

Not her best stroke by any means, but at least she could keep her head down, eyes averted from the suffocating reality above.

'Backstroke!'

The echoing command was so forceful it gave her palpitations to ignore it. She continued to scoop armful after armful of air, legs scissoring furiously as she tried to imagine herself racing to happier times.

Turkey, on her summer holidays. Those days had been the best. Skin turning a beautiful caramel under the intense sun as she tore through her laps, delight at the shaved seconds on the wrist timer her parents had bought her for her birthday. Taking well-earned rests on a unicorn lilo, eyes closed behind oversized market-stall sunglasses as she sucked on the straw of a chocolate milkshake. And then back in the water, doing handstands or pushing down to the bottom for her dive-sticks, or toying with the massive blocks of ice that the grinning kitchen staff tossed in when the pool seemed almost fit to boil. And then, in later years, Romeo, the young Turkish pool attendant who had assumed the ridiculous foreign name in the hope of finding his true love, and had then sought it in a fifteen-year-old girl called Rosie rather than Juliet, who had also been overcome by dreams of discovering her soulmate in paradise.

The match was never to be, of course. Her parents had made that painfully clear to both of them. But she had relished the attention while it lasted, while the summer was filled with heat and haze and buzzing insects and exotic tastes and a mandarin sun blushing and spilling its glow across sparkling waters that spread farther than she could see or imagine.

She fought now to bloat her mind with those images, those memories. Tried to feel blistering heat, to hear joyous children chattering in foreign tongues, to revel in the warmth of the water slipping over her body as she powered through it.

Ah, yes, water. What she wouldn't give for water.

'Backstroke!'

She hesitated for a split-second, hoped he wouldn't notice and become angry again.

Arms arcing. Muscles growing tired. Shins and knees bruising. False fingernails splintering and tearing away as they snagged on the rough, unforgiving tiles. Her whole body aching and in need of buoyancy, the loving supportive arms of water.

A snigger carried to the remotest corners of the empty pool.

'Very good. You're learning. Simon says backstroke!'

She rolled obediently onto her back. Risked another glimpse of her new, unwelcome world. A shifting gloom, patches of grey sliding and merging. The only illumination provided by candles dotted all around the perimeter of the pool, their flames dancing and animating the vast cathedral-like chamber.

And then she picked out his shape. Saw how the many points of light seemed suddenly to be drawn to him, as if feeling obliged to highlight his presence. His shadow multiplied, creating an army of malevolent figures all around her.

She clamped her eyelids tightly shut again, and the effort squeezed out tears that scurried from the corners of her eyes and into the refuge of her ears.

She began moving again. Tried to become robotic, a clockwork doll. Incapable of provoking lust.

Was that what this was? Something . . . sexual? Something perverted and disgusting and—

She cut off the thought. It didn't pay to overthink. She had to stay in the moment, to remain focused, always with an eye out for an opportunity to get out of this alive.

But she felt so vulnerable under his gaze. She was eighteen now. A woman. And almost naked.

While she had cowered in the deep end, still bound, duct tape sealing in her cries and her pleas, he had sliced away her outer garments with a Stanley knife. She had stared wide-eyed at the blade as it sailed silently and effortlessly through the cloth, prayed for it not to do the same to her flesh. He had left her in her underwear, perhaps because it lent her the appearance of wearing a bikini.

She threw her arms back, dragged them along the tiles, kicked her feet, wondered what he was thinking up there, what he was getting out of this.

'Enough. Simon says stop.'

She lay perfectly still, panting with her efforts and the icy air that made it hard to breathe. She knew the rules now. They were established within the first few minutes. She could still feel the sting of the slaps she received until she got it right.

'Simon says stand to attention.'

She opened her eyes and got up from the pool floor. She did her best to stand rigid, ramrod arms at her sides, but the cold currents of air seemed to rush at her, invading her blood vessels and bones and sending violent tremors through her body. The skin on her thighs felt as pimpled as a table tennis bat.

She remembered this place well.

Primary school. Changing hastily in a tiny cubicle before someone could push open the door as a joke. Standing on the edge of the pool with her mates, giggling and comparing swimsuits and saying what a dork Kerry Lyndon looked in that hat. Chuckling at the shape of Mr Mahmoud in his enormous shorts, the dense mat of black hair on his chest that looked like it could house a family of rodents. Admiring the sveltness of Miss Palmer and hoping that she might look like that one day. And then jumping in, gasping in shock at the cold, but not caring, just laughing, just enjoying.

So different now.

The council had closed the building down about two years ago. No attempt to refurbish or repurpose it. Higher priorities than the development of the region's children. One less place for youths to spend their time profitably.

Ugliness. Without light, without water, without people, it was as ugly as sin. Like a Victorian asylum.

'I think we should have a break from swimming now. We'll come back to it later. What about dancing? Can you dance, Rosie?'

She wasn't sure how to answer. Everyone could dance, couldn't they? Everyone could bounce around in some fashion.

'A . . . a little.'

'I thought so. You look like a dancer. Do you have a favourite type of dance?'

She thought for too long.

'Rosie. I asked you a question.'

The menace of the implied threat pushed an answer out of her. 'Irish. I like Irish dancing.'

'Irish dancing, eh? All right, then. Let's see some. Go ahead.'

She took a deep breath. Thought, If I put on a good show, if I do everything he says, as well as I can, then maybe he'll let me go, maybe he won't hurt me again . . .

And she started her routine.

Irish dancing. She was good at it. Had done it most of her life, ever since her mother had dragged her to lessons at the age of five. Loved it. Performed on stage. Won trophies in competitions.

'NO!'

She stopped.

'What did I tell you? What did I fucking say? Did you hear the words? Did you hear the bit that goes "Simon says"? Well, did you?'

His fury was reflected in the high pitch of his voice. It worried her that he could switch from quiet intimidation to white-hot wrath in an eyeblink.

'N-no.'

'Are you a moron, Rosie? A retard? Did you understand my instructions?'

Too many questions. She wasn't sure whether to answer yes or no. 'I'm sorry,' she said.

'Sorry isn't good enough. You need to get it right. You need to prove to me that you can do what I say.'

'I will. I promise.'

Above her, he paced along the poolside, then halted suddenly.

'All right. One more chance. Dance.'

She remained motionless.

'*I said dance!*'

Nerves twitched, muscles tugged, but still she kept her pose.

'Just testing,' he said. 'Now, Simon says dance for him.'

She started up again, fought back tears of humiliation. The absurdity of it all: dancing solo in her underwear in an empty swimming pool. It ought to be funny, but it came nowhere near. It made her feel like the most insignificant forgotten thing in the universe.

Fear of what might come next threatened to overwhelm her again. As a distraction, she kept her eyes on one of the candles above. Its flame seemed taller, more powerful than the others.

That's me, she thought. Burning fiercely. I will get through this. I will overcome.

'Simon says stop!'

She came to attention again, eyes still on that flame. The dance had warmed her up a little, but she told herself that it was the flame's doing, sending her its heat, its life.

'That was impressive,' he said. 'You're a very talented girl. I need to find out what else you're good at.'

No, she thought. Make me swim. Make me dance. Anything. Just not—

'I think I'll join you now.'

It was as if he were a judge donning a black cap. Everything within Rosie tightened, coiling like serpents in a deadly embrace.

'Please, I—'

'Rosie! Did I ask you to speak?'

She clammed up. The shivering returned. Her fingers and toes flexed, her whole body preparing for titanic misfortune.

She watched the dark, demonic figure begin to climb down the iron ladder. Each footstep clanged and reverberated like a death knell.

She turned in desperation to her candle for answers.

In return, its flame elongated, then sputtered and went out, and a curl of smoke ascended to the ceiling like a departing soul.

2

Izzy was surrounded by her friends. Hundreds of them. All colours and sizes. Some tall and thin, others short and stout. Some serious, others frivolous. All beautiful and interesting, all wanting her hands on them.

Books.

They had been her close companions for as long as she could remember. Some she had read many times. When life grew dark and fearful, books were her saviour. Each had its own special place in her heart.

As a child, it had been a dream of hers to work in a bookshop or a library. It was an ambition condemned by her parents as unworthy. She could and would do much better, they informed her.

But now here she was. Behind the counter at the end of another day in a shop called Stern Words. And she was content.

The shop was split into two halves. On entering from the street you were faced with a good selection of new books and stationery items. To the left of the counter was a line of narrow pillars that marked the boundary of the other half of the shop, where all the second-hand books could be found. Izzy often played a game with herself where she tried to decide which section a new customer might head for.

Whatever their preferences, these customers came, browsed, bought and left. Mostly, they drifted up and down the aisles in silent contemplation. Sometimes they solicited her advice, which she always delivered with glee, but other conversation tended to be perfunctory. It hardly ever became personal, and that suited Izzy just fine. She had no intention of getting to know anyone else too well.

Melissa was one of those who fell into the category of people to whom Izzy felt too close. Not that she could in any sense be regarded as a friend, but that didn't matter. They had spent too much time together here in the shop. Bonds forged with no assistance from Izzy. That was how it worked, and there was nothing she could do to prevent it.

She glanced across at Melissa now. Only nineteen years old, and already on a slope that ducked under any decent future. She had left school with results that hardly merited the term qualifications, then fallen in love with a waste of space who put more money up his nose than into their relationship. To support his habit, she worked in the bookshop by day and a pub by night. She was already frazzled, but he continued to burn her.

Izzy had tried talking to her about it, but to no avail. Melissa had already accepted her fate as the instrument of her boyfriend's happiness. She claimed to be happy herself, but Izzy knew otherwise. Izzy constantly felt her pain, her confusion, and it tore at her insides.

The one thing they had in common was a love of books. For Melissa, this meant a steady diet of rom-coms and psychological thrillers. The times she really came alive were when talking to customers about novels she had recently read. The weight of her private life seemed to lighten at those moments, and customers were ignited by the fire of her enthusiasm. In those brief moments, gates opened before her.

There was still hope that she would step through them one day.

'Melissa?'

Melissa looked up from her book. 'What?'

'It's nearly five. You want to leave? I'll be locking up soon anyway.'

'You mind? I could do with going to the supermarket.'

'Couldn't Sean do the shopping?'

The question just slipped out. She knew she shouldn't have asked, but concern for Melissa's welfare had elbowed restraint aside.

Melissa's display of emotion was the merest flicker on her lips, but a pulse of anger – with her boyfriend, herself, the world – hit Izzy like a hammer blow.

'He's pretty busy at the moment. Trying to sort stuff out at the flat.'

A lie, and not even a good one. Izzy hated that she knew this with such certainty, but there it was. An inability to give others the benefit of the doubt came with the territory.

'Right.' To change the subject, she tilted her head towards Melissa's book. 'What's it like?'

Melissa transformed, brightened, became effusive. 'It's about this girl who's a prisoner in her own home. Everything she does is for her mother and father, who beat her when she gets things wrong. She's home-schooled, and not allowed to go out to meet other people. But then a new family move into the house opposite, and she can see the son in the window facing hers, and they find a way to send messages to each other—'

'Kind of a Cinderella story.'

'Exactly! And now the son wants to meet up with her, and I can't wait to find out what happens next.'

Izzy smiled. 'After that teaser, neither can I.'

Something curled up in Melissa again, like a short-lived flower. She grabbed her coat. 'I should go now.'

Izzy watched her leave, understood why a Cinderella story would resonate so deeply with Melissa. But Sean was not her

Prince Charming, and Izzy felt the void in Melissa's chest that told her that. The only interest that Sean would have in a glass slipper would be in selling it for drug money.

She checked her watch. Five o'clock now, but there were only two customers left in the shop and she wasn't going to hurry them.

Didn't make them less of a problem, though.

No, Izzy thought, that's not fair. They're not the problem. It's me. My problem, for me to deal with.

She watched them shuffle from shelf to shelf in the second-hand section. They always preferred the older books. They were pretty ancient themselves: Ronald at eighty-eight, and Edith two years his junior. Arthritis and other age-related ailments had bent and warped them, their sight misted, their hearing muffled, but still they enjoyed life and each other and reading.

They were regulars at the shop, came in at least once per week, and therein lay the difficulty for Izzy.

She had found their wavelength. Tuned into it precisely. Sometimes it was like that. With others, it might never happen.

She watched and soaked up their gladness at lives fulfilled. But there was something else, too. A hidden message behind the main melody.

The couple returned to a shelf they had visited earlier and took down a slim volume. There followed some muttering, the turtle-like nodding of heads, and then Ronald gently escorted his wife to the counter.

'Hello, you two!' Izzy said. 'How are you both?'

It was Edith who spoke first. 'Wonderful, thank you, dear. We've had some good news, and so Ronald here is buying me a book to celebrate.'

'Good news? What would that be?'

Ronald opened his mouth, but again Edith was first off the mark. 'He's had some problems. I won't go into detail, not in a bookshop, but anyway he's been for tests and, well . . .' She touched a hand to Ronald's arm. 'Go on, Ron, you tell her.'

'I got the all-clear,' he said. 'From the hospital. They said it's nothing a few pills won't sort out.'

'Isn't that marvellous?' Edith said.

'Fantastic. I'm made up for you, I really am. Now, then, what are we buying today?'

Ronald handed the book across. '*Pride and Prejudice*.'

'Always been my favourite,' Edith said, 'and this edition is so lovely.' She turned to her husband. 'I'll wait outside.'

They had always done it this way. They would choose a book together, and then Edith would step out while Ronald paid. She never wanted to know how much a book cost, as if the sordidness of a monetary figure might somehow sully its value to her.

When she had gone, Izzy picked up the book. It had a dark maroon cover, the title emblazoned on it in gold. She ran her fingers across the words, felt the love that had put them there.

'It's beautiful,' she said.

'Yes,' said Ronald. 'It is. But then most books are.'

'That's what I think, too. Your wife is a lucky woman.'

'To get such nice books, you mean? Or to have me as her husband?' He issued a soft chuckle.

'Both. You clearly mean the world to each other. You make my day every time you come in here.'

'Thank you. Yes. It was wonderful to get the news from the doctors. I can tell them to put a hold on that coffin they started making for me.' He laughed again.

'Let me gift-wrap it for you.' Izzy turned her back on him, but could move no further. She gripped the book firmly and stared at it, but the words on the cover began to melt and run into each other.

'Miss?' said Ronald. 'Are you all right?'

Izzy wiped a hand over her eyes and sniffed. 'Yes. Yes, I'm fine. I just need to find—'

'You're crying. Why are you crying?'

She turned to him again. No point in trying to hide it any longer.

Ronald craned forwards, his rheumy eyes seeking to confirm his suspicions. 'Was it something I said?'

Izzy took a breath. 'You didn't get the all-clear from the hospital, did you?'

He pulled back, as if propelled by her words. His jaw began working up to an objection, but then he softened again. 'How did you know?'

'I could just tell.'

'Was it that obvious? Because if Edith—'

'No, not obvious at all. Not to most people. I . . . I'm just good at picking up on things like that. Edith doesn't have a clue.'

He reached a hand to the counter, steadying himself. His sadness washed over Izzy, drowning her.

'How long do you have?' she asked.

'Not long at all. It doesn't frighten me. I've had a good life. But Edith . . .' He locked his gaze on Izzy again. 'She mustn't know. It would destroy her.'

'I promise I won't say anything.'

He smiled. 'They say you get wiser as you get older, but I think you're wiser than most. How old are you?'

'Twenty-three.'

'Twenty-three. I still remember when I was twenty-three. That's the year I married Edith. You married yet?'

Izzy laughed through her tears. 'No. No plans for that just yet.'

'A partner?'

'Yes. Andy.'

'Well, he's a very lucky man. And whether you two ever get

married or not, just remember one thing. It's all about keeping your loved ones happy. Nothing else matters, even if you have to make sacrifices yourself.'

'I'll remember that.'

He nodded. 'Better wrap this book. Edith will be thinking I'm having an affair in here.'

More laughter, wiping away the pain. Izzy quickly and lovingly parcelled up the book and handed it across.

'What do I owe you?' Ronald asked.

'Can this one be a gift from me?'

'No, I couldn't possibly let you—'

'Please. From me to you and Edith.'

Ronald's lip quivered, and his gratitude shone. 'That's immensely kind of you. Thank you so much.'

'It's a small gesture of my appreciation.'

'No. Not small at all. This is one of the greatest books of all time. It existed long before me and will be talked about long after I've been forgotten. A gift like that is precious.'

'Well, I won't forget you.'

He nodded again. 'Then my work here is done. Thank you, my dear.'

She watched him go, a crumpled man clutching something more than a book, more than a mere sequence of words on pages. He was holding love itself.

It took several minutes for Izzy to compose herself after that. Such episodes were exhausting, the effort of dealing with powerful emotions draining.

She locked the shop door and flipped the sign to 'Closed', then cashed up. Even after she had put in her payment for the book, the register didn't tally. It was short by twenty pounds. The last time it had been just ten.

Izzy sighed. 'Oh, Melissa. This has to stop.'

She put in another twenty of her own, a big scoop out of her meagre income.

And then she went home, her mind buzzing with memories of a devoted couple in the twilight of their life together.

3

Coming home was always a disappointment for Kenneth Plumley.

As a kid, he'd envied some of the tight, nuclear families he saw on television. There was something wholesome about them, unlike the shadowy chaos of his own upbringing. The houses – especially in American series – were always grand and beautiful, and when the father came through the door, there were wisecracks and laughter and hugs. And even when friction arose, it was always overcome by the end of each episode. By and large, those families slept well, ate well and lived well.

He'd wanted that. Sometimes the only thing that kept him going was the thought that, once he escaped childhood, he might be compensated by a loving wife and offspring of his own, and then he could restore the balance that seemed so tilted against him.

It hadn't worked out like that.

He turned the van onto the weed-infested driveway and took it around the back of the house. He killed the engine and lights but stayed put for a few minutes, staring dolefully at his life's accomplishments.

He'd be forty in a couple of months. *Forty*. Halfway through his life if he was lucky. In truth, probably dead or in prison well before then. And this was all he had to show for it.

He hated this house. Didn't matter, because Polina loved it, and he went where she led. It was on a country lane, a couple of hundred yards from its nearest neighbour. She'd said she wanted peace and quiet, even though she was always playing tacky pop music at maximum volume. It would make a great project, she'd said – echoing the estate agency speak for a property that was falling apart and hadn't enjoyed a lick of appreciation in decades.

The neglect hadn't dragged the house comfortably into his price bracket, though. Every penny he'd saved had gone into the deposit, and almost every penny he earned now went towards the mortgage. Pretty much anything left over was destined for the joint account – joint in the sense that he had been assigned the role of putting the money in while Polina assumed responsibility for taking it out again.

They'd had big plans for this house. Plans that had never materialised because of lack of funds and lack of willingness on Kenneth's part. Now it looked worse than ever. Paint blistered and peeled away like diseased flesh. Guttering was dammed with vegetation. Roof slates needed only the slightest encouragement from the wind to launch themselves like toboggans down the slopes. Doors and windows had sloughed away their protective layers and turned to sponges.

He could fix many of these things. In his job he had to be good with his hands. But he knew it would be purely cosmetic – like putting lipstick on a pig, as the saying goes. It wouldn't repair his life. The house looked like he felt.

He'd read a newspaper article about something called Seasonal Affective Disorder, and now firmly believed he was a sufferer. It was the middle of November, and the world seemed to be closing down. It was filled with darkness and dampness and oppression. Over the next few weeks, many would attempt to combat it with garish symbols of Christmas, but Kenneth felt that no amount of fairy lights could disguise the dreariness. If he had the option, he would hibernate until the spring.

Sighing, he climbed out of the shabby van and crunched across gravel to the rear door of the house. Heat mushroomed out as he opened the door. Polina liked to have the central heating at full blast at all times so that she could wander around in a T-shirt and skimpy shorts instead of dressing in warmer clothes like most cash-strapped people would.

The house seemed deserted at first. In the kitchen, Barclay the Alsatian heaved himself off his pet bed and waddled over, his claws clicking on the tiled floor like a slow tap-dance. He was old and he was fat and his creaky back legs looked ready to collapse under the strain, but he still knew how to demonstrate his loyalty and affection. The only one in this house who did.

'Hey, boy. You all alone? Where is everyone?'

On cue, he heard footsteps coming hurriedly down the stairs. When Polina joined him, her face was flushed and he could tell there was no bra beneath her vest top. He wondered if she'd even bothered with knickers.

Foolishly, he had believed the stories, because he had wanted to believe them. He had needed to know that, after all his failures in that department, he had finally found someone who desired him and wanted to be with him for ever.

She had jumped out at him from the internet images. He had grown suspicious of most of the women on there, many who seemed to be impossibly good-looking; he could see only pound signs in their eyes. But Polina had a homely appearance, a girl-next-door appeal. Attractive enough without being out of reach, and eight years his junior, she had made him feel like the luckiest man alive to be selected as the target of her affections.

He looked at her now. Pallid and dumpy. Puckered thighs and hips that tested the elasticity of her flowery shorts almost to break-ing point. A line of dark fuzz above her upper lip, and eyebrows that had been allowed to sprout like dandelion heads.

But she was all he had. And he clung to the gossamer hope that one day she might show some appreciation for what he had done for her. All he had to do was continue to be nice, to demonstrate his devotion. One day she would recognise his efforts and reward him for it.

'Kenneth! You're home! My movie superstar!'

The Russian accent was still strong. The one undisguisable pointer to her place of birth.

She flung her arms wide as she spoke, but Kenneth knew it was for dramatic effect. He had made that mistake before, zooming in for an embrace only to find her shrivel up and dodge his clutches.

'It was just the television. My fifteen seconds of fame.'

'Fame, yes. You are famous now. A hero.'

'Well, I wouldn't say that. I was just doing my duty.'

'Don't be modest. Some people, they would have said nothing.' She made the gesture of zipping up her mouth and throwing away the key. Kenneth thought it looked ridiculous.

He thought about what she'd said. About what others would have done. It was true: he could have said nothing at all and hoped they would never have delved any further. But that would have carried its own risks. At least this way, they were on a completely different scent, however fictitious.

More footsteps on the stairs, like a building rumble of thunder, and then Michael was in the kitchen, sidling up behind Polina as though she was his wife. He was shorter and slighter than Kenneth, but undeniably much more handsome – something to which Polina would happily testify. Kenneth gave a hard stare at the shirt tail that Michael had failed to tuck in, but received only a knowing smile in return.

He remembered Michael's arrival at the house vividly. He had come home late from work one evening, only to find him lounging on an armchair and stuffing his face with a Victoria sponge.

'What the hell—?' he had begun, but then the visitor had jumped out of the chair, proffering a hand.

'Hello, Mr Plumley. I'm Michael Danvers. Pleased to meet you.'

'Michael . . .'

'Danvers. As in *Rebecca*.'

'Rebecca?'

'The book. By Daphne du Maurier. I'm your new lodger.'

Kenneth didn't know what he was babbling on about. 'My what? What are you—?'

By that time, Polina had breezed in from the kitchen, bearing a tray of tea. 'He is our lodger, Kenneth. I told you.'

'No, you didn't. I don't know anything about this.'

'You do. We discussed this.' She put the tray down, then escorted him to the hallway, out of earshot of the cake-snaffling intruder. In a low voice she said, 'We decided it would be excellent way to make extra money.'

'No. *You* said it was a good idea. I didn't agree. And now we've got . . .'

'Michael.'

'Yes. Him. Where did you find him?'

'He answered advertisement.'

'What advertisement?'

'The one I put online. I have seen three people, and he is definitely the best.'

'Three . . . You've interviewed three people?'

'Yes. Two were very weird, but this one, I think he is suitable.'

'No, Polina. He's not suitable. He is very unsuitable. Get him out of here.'

It had been a futile argument, because Polina always got her way. The man who had introduced himself as Michael Danvers was duly installed as their lodger.

At first it seemed to work, and Kenneth became more accepting.

He and Michael would talk late into the night over a drink, or they would play a game or two of chess.

But then it all turned sour. Over time, Michael assumed part ownership of everything in the home, including Polina herself. Kenneth felt himself pushed further and further into the background, to become a servant, a lackey, an object of ridicule.

And he had sat back and allowed it. Because he was a coward, and always had been.

'When are you going in the jungle?' Michael now asked.

Kenneth glared at him. 'What? What are you talking about?'

'You know. *Celebrity Get Me the Fuck Out of Here*, or whatever it's called.'

Kenneth shook his head in despair. 'I'm not a celebrity. I just got on the telly for a few seconds.'

'That's more than most of us get.' He turned to Polina. 'Don't you think we should have a red carpet leading up to the front door now? Invite the paparazzi along?'

Polina giggled and then snorted loudly. She had a tendency to make that disgusting noise when she laughed too hard. Kenneth was oddly grateful that her outbursts of amusement were reserved for when she was in the presence of others.

'I like being married to a famous man,' she answered. 'It gets me very excited.'

'Oh yes?' Michael said. 'Did you hear that, Kenneth? Could be your lucky night.'

More giggling and snorting. Kenneth turned away from them and began to fill the kettle. No point in waiting for either of those two to offer him a cup of tea. He noticed that the sink was still full of dirty dishes. What the hell did they do all day?

No, he thought. Scratch that. I don't want to know.

'I'll have a brew if you're making one,' Michael said. 'So go on, then. Tell us what happened.'

Kenneth switched the kettle on and took two mugs down from the shelf. 'It's exactly what I said. No more than that.'

Michael wasn't about to let it slip away so easily. 'Don't play it down. You may have just saved that girl's life.'

Kenneth detected the sarcasm, and his anger flared like a match. He wanted to tell the pair of them to leave him alone, to stop probing. He hadn't saved anyone's life.

'Only if they find them. And only if I was right.'

'What do you mean? You're not sure? You said—'

'I said I *thought* it was her. It looked like her to me.'

Polina and Michael exchanged doubtful glances.

'So was it her or wasn't it?'

'I think so. It was some distance away.'

'And these blokes . . . Two of them, right?'

'I think so. I definitely saw the driver, but it looked like there was another guy in the back seat, next to the girl.'

He tossed teabags into the cups, then spooned in the sugar. He put an extra helping in his own, just for the hell of it.

'And the one you saw, he was an Arab?'

'He looked Middle Eastern to me. Not necessarily an Arab.'

'You think they were terrorists? ISIS? Why would terrorists—?'

'No, I don't think they were terrorists. I didn't say anything about them being—'

He stopped when he saw the twitch of amusement on Michael's lips. The bastard was taking the piss again.

Kenneth turned away, focused on the kettle. Willed the crappy thing to boil so he could just have a damn cup of tea.

He wondered again whether he'd done the right thing. Had he gone over the top? Middle Eastern types in a black sedan? Really? Had that level of detail been completely necessary?

'Well, I still think he is hero,' Polina said.

Kenneth drew a deep breath, then looked at her over his

shoulder. 'Thank you. I told them what I saw, that's all. Anyone else would do the same.'

'Yes. And you know what else you should do?'

'What?'

'You should phone up the terrorists and you should tell them that you have special set of skills, and that unless they release the girl, you will find them and you will kill them.'

The kettle was bubbling hard, shaking on its base. Kenneth concentrated on the noise and tried to allow it to drown out the uproarious laughter behind him. He couldn't look at them, couldn't share the proof that they had managed to cut him.

Why do I let them do this to me? he wondered. Why do I always let them win?

The kettle clicked off. He poured steaming water into the mugs. A drop splashed onto his thumb, and he let the pain sit there.

A hand reached from behind him and placed a milk bottle next to the mugs. As the hand withdrew, he wanted to clasp it and kiss it and whisper to her that he would do better if she would let him.

Instead, he finished making the tea. He passed a mug to Michael, resisting the urge to throw it in his face.

'We decided something,' Polina said. 'When we saw you on TV, we thought we should do something special to celebrate.'

He pictured them, next to each other in the bed probably, staring in disbelief at his wide face on their screen and then belittling his performance, just as they always did.

'Oh, yes? What do you suggest?'

'We thought a meal. A nice meal. Something different.'

He sniffed the air and found nothing, listened for the hum of the fan oven and found nothing.

'Out, you mean? A restaurant?'

Polina shifted her weight to her other foot. 'We thought maybe takeaway. Chinese. You like Chinese.'

Michael pulled something from his pocket and thrust it towards Kenneth. 'There you go, mate. We've written everything down there that we want. Get yourself something nice.'

Kenneth looked down at the list on the scrap of paper. Beneath that was a single ten-pound note. It was nowhere near enough.

'We'd go ourselves,' Michael added, 'only we've both been drinking, see. Which reminds me, we're getting a bit low on booze, so if you could just pop into the off-licence as well. Maybe get some bubbly, seeing as how we're celebrating.'

Kenneth nodded, then put down his mug and moved towards the door.

'No rush,' Michael said. 'You can finish your tea first.'

'That's okay. I'll go now, before I get too relaxed.'

The tittering began as soon as he reached the hallway. They hadn't even waited for him to leave the house.

In the van, he turned the ignition key and the engine coughed into life. He didn't drive away immediately but sat still behind the wheel, thinking about the way his life had gone and what he should have done to steer it along a different path.

There was anger there, yes, but it was overpowered by the bitter regret of not channelling that anger in productive ways. Everything he did seemed destructive now, to him and to others, and yet he seemed unable to prevent it. He wanted to be more assertive, more self-assured, but those qualities felt beyond reach. How would he ever climb out of the ditch into which he had willingly rolled?

The questions and the self-recrimination built up in his mind until it seemed his skull would explode with the tornado of activity.

'All right, stop it now,' he told himself. 'Take deep breaths. Count to ten. Relax.'

He closed his eyes, leaned back into the headrest. 'That's it. Be calm.'

And then: 'Simon says relax.'

4

The flat was small, but at least it was modern. It was also on the ground floor, which meant that Izzy and Andy got the yard. It had no lawn, but it was somewhere to sit out when the weather was nice. And the old couple upstairs were friendly enough.

I should count my blessings, Izzy thought. I have a roof over my head and someone to share my life with. That's all I need.

Sometimes it didn't seem enough to her, though. Sometimes it felt like the world was racing into the future without her.

She parked up her little Fiat 500 and went in through the front door. Beyond that were two further doors, the left one leading to their flat and the right one to the staircase going up to the other flat.

She pushed open her own door, which Andy never bothered to lock unless it was night-time, then took off her shoes and her coat. From the hallway, she turned left into the open-plan living room and kitchen.

'Hey!' she said, endeavouring to make herself heard over the roar of a food processor backed up by the film score from *Raiders of the Lost Ark*. Andy had a thing about movie soundtracks, which was okay until you'd heard the opening music from *The Godfather* five thousand times.

Andy turned, grinning. 'Hey! How's my little bookworm?'

'Turn the music down!'

'What?'

'I said turn the—'

Andy turned the music down. 'Sorry, I couldn't hear you.'

Izzy pointed towards the ceiling. 'You'll annoy the neighbours.'

Andy shrugged. 'They're probably deaf. Besides, I think they'd like this music. Old Herman looks a bit like Yoda, don't you think?'

'I sometimes wonder how he got that name.'

'What, Yoda?'

'No. Herman. I think he might have German ancestors.'

'Why, because Herman rhymes with German? Is that the logic you're applying here? Because, as reasoning goes, that's pretty lame.'

'I've just never met a Herman before. It's . . . unusual.'

'You know what's unusual? You. You're unusual. Now come here and give me a hug.'

They embraced, kissed. Izzy absorbed her partner's feelings and found happiness tinged with exhaustion.

'How was your day?' she asked.

Andy spoke while resuming preparation of the evening meal. Chicken bhuna by the looks of it.

'Well, nobody died, which is always a bonus, although I could have stabbed one guy with a scalpel with all the complaining he was doing.'

'What was his problem?'

'Druggie with a broken arm. Got stoned and fell off some scaffolding he decided to climb. Apparently nothing I did for him was right. Oh, and then there was a woman who somehow managed to embed a kitchen knife in her arse cheek.'

'How the hell did she do that?'

'Slipped on the kitchen floor while carrying the knife. She went down on top of it. Or at least that's her story.'

'You think there's more to it?'

'Personally, I suspect the husband. Proving it is another matter.'

'And not your job.'

'Nope. I just patch them up and drop them off at the hospital. What about you? Another day of high adventure and excitement in the land of books?'

'Hey, I'll have you know that a bookshop can be a hotbed of intrigue some days.'

'Really? You mean like when you see someone putting a book back on the wrong shelf?'

Izzy grimaced. 'I hate that. Sometimes I just want to tap them on the shoulder and tell them that's hardly the way to behave in a civilised society.'

'Then God help anyone you catch licking their fingers before they turn a page, or opening a book so much it breaks the spine.'

'They are definitely capital offences. The other day, a woman wanted her money back on a crime book. Her complaint was that she'd worked out who the killer was by the end of the first chapter, and so couldn't read any more of it.'

Andy frowned. 'Wait. If she only got to the end of the first chapter, how did she know who the killer was?'

'Exactly my question. She said she always jumps to the end of a book to see how it turns out, and if that's okay she reads the rest.'

Andy looked aghast. 'People do that?'

'I told you, you wouldn't believe some of the things that go on in my world. You paramedics have it easy.'

'Yeah, the only broken spines I have to deal with are in people. I don't know how you cope.'

'It's tough, but somebody's got to do it.'

Andy beheaded a pepper and twisted out its insides. 'How's the other one getting on?'

'Who, Melissa?'

'Yeah, her.'

'Hmm.'

'What does that mean?'

'I think she's been taking money again.'

'What? How much this time?'

'Twenty quid.'

'Twenty? Jesus, Izzy, you need to say something.'

'I don't want to drop her in it with Abel. She needs this job.'

'If she needed it so much, she wouldn't be stealing from her employer. Abel's going to work it out at some point anyway. He might be getting on a bit, but he knows how to run a business. He's had that shop for about a thousand years. He'll know if the till is short.'

Izzy lowered her head and knew instantly that Andy would click.

'Izzy? The till *is* short, isn't it?'

'Not exactly.'

'You covered for her, didn't you? You settled the balance.'

'Could you please put that knife down before I answer?'

'Izzy, I don't believe you! You can't keep saving that girl. We don't have much money as it is. Some months we can barely pay our own bills, let alone hand out cash to other people.'

'I know, and I'm sorry. But I like Melissa. She's just fallen in love with the wrong person. It could happen to anyone.'

'Tell me about it.'

The laugh told Izzy that Andy was joking, but still she felt guilty. She had very little income of her own, the majority of their outgoings coming from Andy's pockets.

'I'm sorry,' she repeated. 'I was just trying to give her a chance.'

'Well, if you're not going to turn her in, you need to talk to her.'

'Talk to her?'

Andy smiled. 'You say that like I'm asking you to commit murder. Yes, talk to her. Make her see the error of her ways.'

'I'm her colleague, not her mum. I'm not much older than she is.'

'What's that got to do with it? She's in the wrong, and we're the ones getting hurt for it. You've got a right to put her straight. If you don't, it'll only get worse.'

Izzy put on a mocking voice. 'A stitch in time saves nine.'

Andy looked baffled. 'What are you doing?'

'Something my own mum used to say in these situations. I've no idea what it means.'

'Me neither, but mothers are always right. Talk to her.'

'Okay, okay.' She went to the fridge. 'We got any of that wine left?'

'Uh-oh.'

'What does that mean?'

'It means, my little cherub, that there's something else bothering you.'

Izzy opened the fridge door and took out the carton of plonk. She shook it and gauged that it was about half full.

'Want some?'

'Go on, then. And then get whatever it is off your chest.'

She poured two glasses, slid one along the counter, took a big gulp from her own.

'There was this couple in the shop just before closing,' she said.

'Don't tell me. They got too excited reading *Fifty Shades* and started bonking in the DIY section, right?'

'Hardly. They're in their eighties.'

'Okay, so then they were casing the joint. They took all your first editions and escaped on their mobility scooters?'

'Andy, please! I'm being serious.'

'Sorry.'

'They're regulars. I've got to know them.'

Andy frowned again. 'Know them, as in recognise them? Or *know* them?'

'*Know* them. A little.'

'Ah.'

'Yeah.'

Andy resumed slicing and dicing. 'Go on.'

'He's called Ronald. She's Edith.'

'I can picture them already.'

'Right. They are such a cute couple. He's like the guy out of *Up*. Anyway, he's been keeping something from her.'

'At this point I have a queue of ready-made flippant remarks, but I will contain myself.'

'Good, because it's sad. He's dying.'

Andy put down the knife on the melamine board. 'Dying? How do you know?'

'They were talking about his hospital visit. About how he got the all-clear from the doctors.'

'And you did your thing?'

'It's not like I have a choice, Andy. I hear what I hear. I can't help it if it doesn't always match what people say.'

Andy abandoned the cooking and moved closer, glass in hand. 'You didn't . . . I mean you didn't—'

'Of course not. If there's one thing I hope I've learned in life, it's how not to hurt other people's feelings.'

'So what happened?'

'Edith went outside while Ronald paid. It's kind of a tradition of theirs. Ronald was talking to me, and then . . . and then . . . I just started crying.'

She found that saying all this raised the sluice gate again. Andy came to her, hugged her tight as if to help wring out the tears.

'It's okay,' Andy said. 'It's allowed.'

'But that's the point. It shouldn't be allowed. It seems so wrong. You don't understand how hard it is for me. I don't want people to be that transparent. I don't want to see all the clockwork inside them.'

'Did Ronald ask you what was up?'

'Yes, and I told him. And maybe that was wrong, too, but by that point I just couldn't hold back.'

'What did he think?'

'He thought he must be rubbish at keeping secrets, so then I had to reassure him that Edith knows nothing about it. He was so worried that she'd find out and that it would bring her world crashing down.'

'Then there's no harm done. You haven't interfered with their lives. You've obeyed the Prime Directive.'

'The what?'

'*Star Trek*. The crew of the *Enterprise* isn't supposed to interfere with the development of other civilisations.'

'That is such a typically nerdy response from you.'

Grinning, Andy moved back to the counter. 'I'll take that as a compliment. The point I'm making is that you did the right thing. You let Ronald and Ethel—'

'Edith.'

'You let Ronald and Edith live their life the way they want to live it. If he wants to tell a few white lies to prevent his wife from falling to pieces, then that's his right.'

'I know all that. I agree. All I'm saying is that sometimes it's tough working out the right thing to do.'

'With great power comes great responsibility. Use the Force wisely, Luke.'

'Who's Luke?' she teased.

Andy dipped a hand in the sink and flicked cold water at Izzy.

'Andrea!' Izzy shrieked, knowing full well that her partner detested being called by her full name.

5

It began when she was a baby.

Of course, she had no idea at the time, and neither did her mother. It was only in hindsight that the behaviour was explained.

Her mother would walk into the room. If she was upset or angry, Izzy would cry. If she was happy, Izzy would laugh. It was as simple as that. It was as if the baby knew.

There was one occasion, her mother later related, when they both began the day in perfectly good spirits. Izzy lay next to her on the sofa, smiling and giggling and blowing spit bubbles. The phone rang. Izzy's mother answered it. She heard that her father had died.

Izzy was the first to start crying.

When she was a little older, she would always know when to console her parents. One look was all it took for her to assess the situation, and then she would run over and give them a massive hug. Her mother and father put it down to coincidence. A little unnerving sometimes, slightly spooky on occasion, but nothing to get overly concerned about.

And then along came Jesus.

Izzy was only six years old when the school called her mother in. It was approaching the end of the autumn term. Christmas was looming.

Izzy didn't go to the meeting at school. She got her own private meeting with her mother later in the day.

'Hey, Izzy, how did school go today?'

'Good,' Izzy said as she pushed her toy bus up and down the rug. Although she didn't really feel that it had been good. A lot of people seemed to get annoyed with her.

'I hear you had a nice chat with Mrs Moore.'

Izzy nodded. She didn't want to relive her discussion with the headteacher.

'I talked to Mrs Moore as well. She said you were a bit unhappy about something. Is that right?'

'Don't know.'

'Well . . . she said you don't want to be a shepherd in the nativity play.'

'I don't. It's stupid.'

'Why is it stupid?'

'Just is.'

'Okay, well, you don't have to be a shepherd if you don't want to, but Mrs Moore said you got angry about it.'

Izzy said nothing.

'Is that right? Did you get angry with another teacher? With Mr Osbourne?'

Izzy wasn't sure what to say. She could feel her mother's frustration with her, and thought that if she owned up to getting angry with a teacher then her mother would get angry at her in return.

'Izzy? What did you say to Mr Osbourne?'

'Nothing. He said things to me.'

'What kind of things?'

'About Jesus and the Bible. He said he wanted me to be a shepherd, because the shepherds talked to the angel and then they went to see Mary and Joseph and the baby Jesus.'

'Okay. And what was wrong with that?'

'He . . .'

'Go on, Izzy.'

32

'He was lying.'

A long, painful silence. Izzy regretted her words, even though they were the truth.

'Lying about what?'

'Everything. About Jesus and the shepherds and the angel. It wasn't true. He said it all really happened a long time ago, but he was telling fibs.'

'Why do you think that, Izzy? Has somebody told you it's not true?'

'No.'

'Don't you believe in the story of Jesus?'

'I don't know.'

'Well, you didn't say anything about it when Mrs Everett was looking after the nativity play.'

'That's because Mrs Everett is different.'

'In what way? How is she different?'

'She . . . she wears a cross on her necklace, and she has a little Bible on her desk. She reads it sometimes when we're doing our work.'

More silence. Puzzlement.

'I don't get it. Why is it okay for Mrs Everett to talk to you about Jesus, but not Mr Osbourne?'

'I don't know! It just is!'

She couldn't explain it, not at that age. She wasn't equipped to appreciate personal belief systems. All she knew was that when Mrs Everett spoke, it felt believable, and when Mr Osbourne told exactly the same stories, they felt made up. Izzy didn't understand how it was possible for something to be real for one person and not another. How could something be true and false at the same time?

The conversation did not go much further, and within days it was forgotten about.

But then another controversial character repeated his annual appearance.

Jolly old St Nick.

As Christmas neared, the stories became incessant, the advice consistent:

You need to be good, otherwise Santa won't bring you any presents.

He has a list of all the good children and all the naughty ones.

He lives in the North Pole, along with the elves who help him make all the toys.

On Christmas Eve, he'll fly through the sky in his sleigh pulled by the reindeer, and then he'll slide down the chimney.

We'll need to leave a mince pie out for Father Christmas, and a carrot for Rudolph.

Let's write a letter to Santa, telling him what presents you'd like to get.

Each and every statement chipped away at the bond of trust between them. Izzy couldn't understand why they were doing this to her, why they felt the need to torture her like this. She clutched her concerns inside her, holding them tight in there because it seemed to be what was wanted. Her parents seemed to get such joy from it.

She broke on Christmas Day.

They had to wake her up, and seemed filled with disappointment that she hadn't come crashing into their bedroom and then leaping on them in hysterical excitement that the big day was finally here. She didn't tell them that she had spent much of the night awake, staring into the blackness and fretting, her developing mind bursting with foreboding.

'Shall we see if he's been?' they asked. 'Shall we go downstairs and see?'

She had hoped for change now that the day was here, but still the charade continued. She wanted to stay in bed, to remain under her duvet until this horrible day was over.

They practically dragged her out, the smiles and laughter at odds with the falsity of it all. They led her downstairs, gripping her tiny hands tightly in theirs. At the closed door of the living room came more teasers: 'What do you think? Do you think he's brought you anything? You've been such a good girl, haven't you?'

The door was opened. Under the tree, a mound of gaily wrapped bundles. Huge intakes of breath and expressions of wonderment.

Izzy stood and stared and bit into her bottom lip to stop it quivering.

'Come on, Izzy. Let's see what Santa's brought you. Look at this big one here. Wow! And the label, see? It's from Santa himself. He says you've been such a wonderful—'

Izzy flew out of the room and raced back upstairs.

It was her mother who came to her first. She eased the duvet back from Izzy's face and stroked away her tears.

'Oh, Izzy, what's the matter? It's Christmas Day. Why aren't you happy?'

So Izzy told her. Let it all out. Talked about how she was always being told to be truthful, and yet all around her people constantly fired lies at her. Lies about Father Christmas, lies about religion, lies about the Tooth Fairy, lies about whether her injections would hurt. So many lies.

Her mother did her best to reassure her. She talked about different kinds of lies: those that were meant to cover up bad deeds versus those that were meant to help people. She got into philosophical knots over the benefits of telling children about Father Christmas and fairies and elves. Izzy didn't understand all of it, but what she knew beyond doubt was that her mother's heart was in the right place.

But it was just the beginning. The older she got, the more she grew to realise that deception was such an integral part of the fabric of people's lives. She saw through their veneers, saw them for what they really were. Saw their greed and their hatred and their disloyalty and their treachery.

Some might regard such insight as a gift.

To Izzy it was more of a curse.

6

They sat on the sofa in front of the television, their meals on wooden trays on their laps. They had a small table they could use, but after a long day in the ambulance, Andy often preferred to slob out.

She passed some naan bread to Izzy, saying, 'Forgot to tell you something.'

Izzy swallowed a spoonful of curry. 'What?'

'You won't like it.'

'Well, now that your warning of doom has made it so enticing, I'm dying to hear it. What is it?'

'I said we'd go round to my mum's house on Sunday.'

'Can't. I'm busy on Sunday.'

'Doing what?'

'Making up excuses as to why I can't go to see your parents.'

'Not good enough, I'm afraid. We're going.'

'Do we have to?'

'We haven't seen them for ages. To be more precise, *you* haven't seen them for ages. They keep asking about you.'

'That's because they want to check I'm not up to no good. Your mum thinks I'm a witch.'

'No she doesn't.'

'She does. She thinks I've cast a spell on you, and that's the only reason you're not out chasing suitors who meet her minimum testosterone requirements. Plus, she specifically requested that we didn't go round for a meal when it was Halloween.'

'That was only because they had other plans. Anyway, you don't exactly go out of your way to seem less spooky.'

'What do you mean?'

Andy gestured at Izzy's attire of leggings and a hooded cardigan. 'Well, for one thing, you could try wearing something other than black.'

'I like black. Besides, black isn't a colour; it's the absence of colour.'

'Don't play with semantics. I like black too, but not *all* the time. In my mother's eyes, that's witchy.'

Izzy ate some more curry. The news had started on the television, but she wasn't paying much attention.

'What are we having?' she asked.

'What?'

'On Sunday. Please tell me it's not a roast.'

'Well, I would say that, but you're the worst person to lie to. My mum can only do roasts on Sundays. It's the law, like fish on Fridays.'

'No disrespect to your mum, but she needs to start breaking the law. Either that, or get a new timer for her oven. The police should look into using her beef as material for bulletproof vests.'

Andy laughed. 'Then you try asking for it to be all raw and bloody instead. That would really change her mind about thinking of you as a witch.'

Izzy gave up her protests. She didn't actually object to the thought of going to see Andy's parents if it kept her happy. Andy knew as much. It was that openness that kept them together.

She took a sidelong glance at Andy. Three years older, she was the most uncomplicated person Izzy had ever met. It didn't bother her in the slightest that she could keep no secrets from Izzy. In fact, she frequently admitted that she found it refreshing. No need to invent stories, to shroud herself in veils. She could just be herself.

Izzy had discovered that few people enjoyed being so exposed.

She had met Andy while drowning her sorrows one night. It had come after the end of Izzy's first and only year at university. One of her few friends from school had dragged her out in the hope of restoring a smile to her face. It hadn't worked. When they'd ended up in a nightclub, she'd been past caring. While her friend bounced around the dancefloor with her other mates, Izzy sat alone on a barstool, staring at some lethal concoction that had been placed in front of her. She was trying to decide whether to knock it back and then chuck it up again in the toilets, or find her way home and be sick at a more leisurely pace.

That was when Andy had shown up and turned a key in her head that changed everything.

'Girl versus drink,' she'd said.

'Sorry?' Izzy had replied.

'Girl versus drink. Like *Man versus Food*, but less idiotic. Your concentration levels are impressive. Personally, I think you've already overcome the mental battle to whup your opponent's backside.'

'Actually, this isn't my concentration face. It's my "Where the hell did I leave my brain?" face.'

'Okay, well you see that guy over there, the one who keeps look-ing this way while trying to impress you with his dance moves?'

'The one doing the windmill impressions?'

'Yeah, him. What do you say we extract his brain and use it as a spare while we try to find yours?'

And that had been it. From there, the conversation had poured out effortlessly. But while the words had flowed, so had the blood. It had surged through her veins and arteries, brought her alive, put her on a precipice that set her whole body pulsing with excite-ment. And, as if that were not enough, she had sensed it even more strongly in the other woman – a wave of attraction that Izzy couldn't prevent from drowning out the alarm bells threatening to cripple her.

'Didn't you go to that school?' Andy asked.

Izzy snapped back to the present and turned her attention to the television. A local reporter was doing a piece to camera. Over his shoulder, reflecting the glaring light, was a board at the school entrance: *Hemingway High School for Girls*.

'Yes. What's happened?'

'It'll be about that girl.'

'What girl?'

'The one that's gone missing.'

'I don't know anything about—'

'Hush! Listen.'

The reporter was nodding at something the studio presenter had just put to him. 'Yes,' he answered. 'It's now more than forty-eight hours since Rosie Agutter was last seen, and police are becoming increasingly concerned about her. They would urge anyone who has seen her or been in touch with her since then to contact them immediately.'

'Thanks, Tim,' the studio presenter said. 'But as far as we know, the last recorded sighting was there at the school?'

'That's right. Rosie had stayed after normal school hours to put finishing touches to some artwork she'd been doing for her A-level, and so all her friends and colleagues had long gone home. However, the school caretaker, a Mr Kenneth Plumley, thought he saw her leave the premises. Here's what he had to say when we caught up with him earlier today.'

On the screen, night became day. A stocky man with thinning hair came into view, the grey fluff of a microphone visible at chest level.

'Plummers!' Izzy said. 'He was the caretaker when I was there!'

The reporter said, 'You've told the police that you saw Rosie going out of the school gates on Monday evening. Is that right?'

The caretaker glanced nervously around him, as though checking for eavesdroppers.

'Well, I didn't know that at the time. It's a big school, so I don't know all the students by name. But the police showed me photographs, and it looked a lot like her to me.'

'And what was she doing?'

'She was next to a car, talking to a man in the driver's seat. Then she got into the back of the car next to another guy and it drove away.'

'Did you get a good look at either of the men?'

'Not really. I was quite far away. But as I said to the police, I thought the driver looked foreign. Like, maybe from the Middle East or something.'

'And the car? Did you manage to give a description of that to the police?'

Kenneth Plumley shrugged. 'It was big and black. Posh-looking. A Mercedes, maybe, or a BMW. I wasn't paying much attention. I wish I had now.'

The picture jumped back to the present. 'So there you have it,' the reporter said. 'Possibly the most recent sighting of Rosie Agutter. Obviously, police are anxious to trace the car described by Mr Plumley, if only to rule it out of their investigation, and would like anyone who drives such a car and was outside the school between five and six o'clock yesterday evening to get in touch with them.'

The report continued but Izzy had stopped hearing it. She lowered her spoon to her plate, her appetite suddenly gone.

'So what do you think?' Andy was saying. 'He said they looked Middle Eastern, so they obviously weren't her relatives. Why would she get in a car with them? Do you think they're holding her hostage somewhere? Izzy? Are you even listening to me?'

Izzy found it difficult to get her mouth to operate, and when she did, she could hardly believe what she was saying.

'He's lying.'

'What?'

'Plummers. All that stuff he told the reporter. It's complete bullshit.'

7

Andy was staring at her.

'What?' she asked again.

Izzy gestured towards the television. 'He was lying.'

'Wait. Which bit?'

'All of it. The car, the foreign-looking guy. It was complete bollocks.'

Izzy felt the stress bulging in her stomach. She wished she didn't know this about the caretaker. Wished she'd started watching a quiz programme or a soap instead of the news.

'Why would he be lying?'

'Well, lots of reasons. None of them good, that I can think of.'

Andy lost interest in her own food too. She lifted the tray from her lap and moved it to the coffee table in front of her.

'Are you sure about this?' she asked.

'Positive.'

'I mean, how do you know? When was the last time you even saw this guy?'

'When I was at the school. About five years ago.'

'Five years is a long time, Izzy. People change in that time.'

'They don't change their whole behaviour patterns. Some things stick with you for life.'

'Okay, I'm not trying to doubt you here, but all you've seen is a few seconds of him speaking on the telly. He's not even here in person.'

'Doesn't need to be. I know Kenneth Plumley, and what he just said was a load of crap.' Izzy took a swig of her wine. She needed something to calm her nerves.

'He's just the caretaker,' Andy said. 'How well did you get to know him?'

'Well enough. We weirdos stick together.'

'What does that mean?'

Izzy moved her own tray to the coffee table. She didn't like revisiting her time at school, but she had no choice.

'I wasn't liked at school. I didn't have many friends. To most people, I was just the freak with her head constantly stuck in a book.'

Andy put a hand on her arm. 'Aw, Izzy! That's awful.'

'It's okay. I didn't care, because I didn't like them either. It made things difficult at break and lunch times, though. We were forced to go outside, where we were supposed to mingle.'

'Yeah, you're not the best of minglers.'

'I'm not. So instead I used to try and find somewhere quiet to read, which wasn't easy. Some dickhead would always come along and disturb me. Anyway, there was this one time, I sneaked into this narrow passage between the workshop and the gym. Smokers' Alley they called it, because that's where the kids used to go when they wanted to light up. The head found out about it and ruled it out of bounds, so I really wasn't supposed to be there, but it was the only place I could get some peace. It was great. I went there day after day. Just sat on the floor and read. Until Plummers caught me.'

Andy grimaced. 'Shit. What did he do to you?'

Izzy threw her a deterring glance. 'Nothing pervy. He just saw me there, and he asked me if I was smoking, and I said no, and that I was really sorry and I wouldn't come back again. But then he just smiled and asked me what the book was.'

'And do you still remember?'

'Yes. It was *Of Mice and Men*.'

'And what did Plummers say?'

'He said he didn't read much, and he asked me what it was about. So I told him. He said it sounded really interesting, and he kept asking me questions about it. We must have talked for about fifteen minutes, but then the bell went. I told him I had to go, and I promised him I wouldn't come back there again, but then he said it was fine. He said I could come back as often as I wanted.'

'So you did?'

'Yes. Sometimes I didn't see him, but other times he asked me about my books, or he asked me to read out a page or two. He said he liked the sound of my voice.'

'Uh-oh.'

'Stop it. It wasn't like that. I think he was just lonely. He liked having somebody to talk to, and to be honest, so did I.'

Andy swivelled towards Izzy and drew her legs up onto the sofa. 'Okay, so next question. A really important question, given what we've just heard on the telly.'

'Go on.'

'You said he was weird. How weird? I mean, creepy weird? Abduction weird?'

Izzy cast her mind back, trying to recall not just her conversations with Plumley but also her feelings about him at the time.

'I don't think so. Not back then, anyway. He was quiet, introverted, but then so was I. I don't think he'd had much success with women, but he didn't try anything on with me.'

'How old were you when these little liaisons started?'

'I must have been about fifteen, sixteen. And don't call them liaisons. It sounds kinda sordid.'

'Sweet sixteen? And he didn't even have a twinkle in his eye?'

'I didn't say he wasn't interested, but no more than any other guy.'

'And you kept seeing him like this for how long?'

'The next couple of years, until I left.'

'And he never once made a move?'

'No. He was the caretaker for our school. He knew it wouldn't be right to come on to one of the students. And anyway, he had his own problems.'

Concern registered on Andy's face. 'What kind of problems?'

'He was – it's difficult to explain – he didn't have much self-esteem. He'd kind of accepted that no woman would ever find him attractive. He thought he'd be an eternal bachelor.'

Andy nodded. 'Okay. You know what I'm hearing here? I realise you're trying to paint him as some kind of gentle, shy bloke who wouldn't say boo to a goose, but frankly I'm starting to see him in a very different light. Low self-worth? Difficulty talking to women? Feeling that the world won't ever give him what he wants? Sounds like the ideal background for a serial killer to me.'

'That's ridiculous. I didn't pick up on anything like that from him.'

'Izzy, that was five years ago. He may have been rejected by women a thousand times since then. He may have joined a cult. He may have developed a taste for human flesh.'

'Don't say that. It's disgusting.'

'You're the one who said he was weird.'

'I said weird like me. Someone who doesn't fit in. An outsider.'

'Just like the ones who walk into their high schools with an automatic rifle. Not all of them, I admit – I'm hoping I won't wake up one night with you standing over me with a chainsaw – but that's beside the point. Throw enough shit at a person for five years, and it can change them.'

Izzy consulted her memories again. Plummers had been nice

enough to her. No inappropriate suggestions or sitting too close – nothing like that. But would she have wanted to be alone with him in a deserted park at night? Probably not. Could Andy be right about him? Could some awful event have happened that pushed him over a line?

She had to concede it was possible.

'All right,' Andy said. 'I'm going to ask you again, and I want you to think really hard before you answer. I know what you're capable of. I know how you can often see through people like they're made of glass. But just remember that you haven't seen this Plumley guy for five years. Your memory of him might not be as sharp as you think it is. So, given all that, how sure are you that what he just said on television was a lie?'

Izzy paused for what seemed an appropriate length of time, but her answer never wavered. No flicker of doubt intruded.

'He lied. I know it.'

'You're absolutely certain?'

'Absolutely.'

'Okay, so then my next question is what are you going to do about it?'

Izzy blinked. She hadn't expected a follow-up. He lied, that's it. Move on. Change channels. Let's watch a film or something.

'What do you mean?'

'It's a simple question, Iz.'

'Well then here's my simple answer. Nothing. I don't plan to do anything about it.'

'You've got to.'

'Why? Why have I got to?'

'Because a girl has gone missing. And right now, the police are spending a lot of their time and effort looking for a posh black car and a Middle Eastern driver that don't exist. And all because Plummers lied through his teeth on television. It's him they should be looking at, not going on some wild goose chase for sex traffickers or whatever.'

'Nobody has even mentioned sex traffickers.'

'No, but I bet lots of people are thinking along those lines after what your friend just said. The police included.'

'He's not my friend.'

'Then you shouldn't have to think twice about exposing him.'

'I'm not thinking twice. I just . . .'

'What?'

Anxiety was clawing at Izzy again. She hated pressure like this – pressure that nobody else ever had to deal with because they were isolated in their emotional bubbles.

'What do you suggest?' she asked. 'What am I supposed to do here?'

'Call the police.'

'And tell them what?'

'That you've just heard Plumley speaking on the news, and you believe he's telling a bunch of lies.'

'And when they ask how I know he's lying, what do I say then?'

Andy took hold of Izzy's hand. 'Iz, I know how difficult this kind of thing is for you. I'm not asking you to go into lengthy explanations. You don't have to tell them about your success rate on this kind of thing. All you have to say is that you used to go to that school, you got to know Plumley pretty well, and now you think he's telling porkies.'

'They'll think I'm nuts.'

'No, they won't. But even if they do, that's up to them. You'll have done what's right. Maybe it'll make them take a closer look at Plumley's story. And you know what? He could be perfectly innocent. He could be just an attention seeker. I'm sure the police hear stories like his all the time. But this is too important to ignore. You agree with me, don't you?'

Izzy took a deep breath, but it didn't seem to fill her lungs properly. She didn't want to do this, but she knew that Andy was right, the bitch.

'All right. I'll call them.'

'Good.'

'Tomorrow.'

'Izzy . . .'

'I will. First thing in the morning. Promise. Can we talk about something else now?'

Andy leaned in and kissed her on the cheek. 'Yes. We can talk about dessert. How about sticky toffee pudding?'

Izzy nodded, but her appetite remained at a distance. She suspected that sleep would evade her tonight as well.

It wasn't just the prospect of sounding like a fool when she called the police.

It wasn't even the fact that she was possibly the only person in the world who knew that Kenneth Plumley had lied.

It was that her furiously pinging radar was telling her that Plummers knew a lot more about what had really happened to Rosie Agutter.

8

Andy had to leave for work early, but before she went, she again extracted a promise from Izzy that she would contact the police.

Over a cup of tea and some toast with thickly spread marmalade, Izzy tried to build herself up to make the phone call. It was actually a good thing that she'd have to depart for work herself soon, as it put a time limit on her procrastination.

When she'd finished her breakfast and brushed her teeth, she picked up her phone and googled the number for Oakbury Police, because this wasn't an emergency, she didn't have a gang of masked men breaking her door down, it was just the passing on of a tiny nugget of information that probably wouldn't interest them in the slightest. Taking a deep breath, she called the number. The ring tone seemed to go on for ever, and she started to think they must be inundated at the moment, far too busy to be wasting their time on trivia like this, and perhaps she should just hang up and let them get on with more important things . . .

'Hello. Oakbury Police.' A woman's voice. Brusque.

'Er, yes. Hello. Yes. I think I've got some information. About a crime.'

'Is this a crime happening right now?'

'No. It's about the girl who went missing. Rosie Agutter.'

A pause, as if the name had triggered some kind of strict protocol to be followed, galvanising the woman into consulting her list of actions.

'Just a moment, please, and I'll transfer you to the team dealing with that.'

A couple of clicks, and then another voice, male this time. 'Oakbury CID. Can I help you?'

'Yes. Hi. My name is Isobel Lambert. I've got some information. About the missing girl. Rosie Agutter.'

'Okay. If I could start by taking a few personal details.'

He took her address and phone number, then said, 'Thank you. And what can you tell me about Rosie Agutter?'

'Well, strictly speaking, it's not about her. It's about the caretaker who was on the news. Kenneth Plumley. The one who said he saw Rosie getting into a car outside the school.'

'Okay. What about him?'

'He . . . he was lying.'

'What exactly was he lying about?'

'The whole thing. The car, the driver. Everything.'

'I see. And how do you know this?'

The big question. Get out of that one, Izzy, she said to herself.

'I know him. I went to that school. I could tell he was lying.'

'You could tell?'

She could hear the doubt in his voice, and she didn't blame him because if the positions were reversed her reaction would be exactly the same and she would be thinking, Jesus, not another wacko, why do they always crawl out of the woodwork on major cases like this?

'Yes,' she said. 'I'm pretty good at knowing when people are lying.'

'Right. Have you spoken to Mr Plumley about this case?'

'No. I haven't.'

'But you said you know him, so when's the last time you and he had a conversation?'

'About five years ago, when I was at the school.'

'Five years. And you haven't seen him or heard from him since?'

'No.'

A much longer pause, and then: 'Okay, that's great. I've got all that down on our computer. Thank you so much for your call.'

She was being fobbed off. Thanks but no thanks.

'But you will look into it? He really is telling lies.'

'We take every call seriously. Thanks again. I've got your details here, so we'll call you back if we need anything else from you.'

'All right. Yes. Thank you.'

'Bye now.'

The line went dead, and as certain as she was that her cheeks were burning brightly enough to light up the room, Izzy knew that the record of her conversation was being consigned to the folder labelled 'Cranks, Crackpots and Conspiracy Theorists'.

* * *

I did my duty.

That was what she told herself, every five damn minutes, which added up to a lot of times because this morning was lasting an eternity. The bookshop had seen only a handful of visitors since she arrived, and not one of them had been particularly talkative, not one of them had been considerate enough to try taking her mind off things. Even Melissa seemed unusually distant today.

I did my duty, she thought again.

I told them. What else could I have said? What more could I have done? I put it as plainly as I could. Kenneth Plumley is a liar. There. Only one way to read that. If the police don't want to follow up on it, that's their problem, and I can move on in the full knowledge that I warned them.

'You hear about the missing girl?'

Thanks, Melissa. Just what I need right now.

'Yeah. I went to the same school as her.'

'Wow. Did you know her?'

'No. I didn't mix with many of the kids below my year.'

Didn't mix with many of the kids in my own year either, she thought.

It was a disturbing question, though. She probably had seen Rosie at some point during her school life, without knowing it. Probably witnessed her laughing with her friends, discussing make-up and boys, skipping along the corridors, racing around the sports field . . .

Stop it!

But that's the thing, isn't it? Rosie Agutter isn't just a face on a television screen. She has a life. She's a living, breathing human being – at least, that's still the hope – with family who love her and are probably at this very minute sobbing buckets and praying for her safe return.

'I've got her Instagram up here. Look.'

Melissa swivelled the screen of the shop computer towards Izzy, who found herself drawn to it. The photographs showed her a bubbly, pretty girl, slim with long blonde hair, doing all the things girls of that age do. Well, most girls. Izzy didn't really go through that phase. The having-fun phase.

In one shot, taken in a bar, Rosie had a cocktail in front of her and was showing off two of her false fingernails, painted with tiny red roses. They obviously gave her an instant excuse for flipping her middle fingers at anyone who asked to see them.

'They're saying it's sex traffickers, did you hear?' Melissa said. 'What do you think they'll do to her? Do you think they've already shipped her out of the country? Or maybe they—'

'*Melissa!* Don't be ridiculous. It's nothing like that.'

Melissa looked hurt at this demolition of her pet theory. 'Well, what are they up to, then? Why else would a bunch of foreigners kidnap an English girl right outside her own school?'

Izzy was saved from further anguished discussion by the noise of the door being banged open. The shop's owner, Abel Stern, backed in clutching a large cardboard box of books. Izzy dashed around the counter.

'You need some help there, old man?'

He turned around and stared at her. He was as geometrically pleasing as his cardboard box: a squat oblong of a torso surmounted by a square head that was hairless save for two small white clouds that floated over his ears.

'Old man!' he said. 'I'm only sixty-two. To a mere embryo like you, that might seem old, but it's not. Not by today's standards. I could live another thirty, forty years, which is longer than you've been on this earth. What's more, I'm still as strong as an ox.' He carried the box to the counter and slammed it down. 'I can carry twice as many books as this. Three times. Been doing it most of my adult life.'

Izzy smiled. Abel was a wonderful man. He would never get rich running a shop like this, but he didn't care. He sold books because he loved them.

'You hear about the girl?' Melissa asked.

Izzy rolled her eyes. She had hoped she'd done enough to put Melissa off that particular topic.

'What girl?'

'The missing girl. From Izzy's old school.'

'What about her?'

'Well . . . she's gone missing. People are saying that sex traffickers took her.'

Izzy turned away, escaping the ridiculous discussion. Sometimes she hated social media.

The only certain truth was that a girl had gone missing, but everyone was gagging for a bigger, juicier story, and Kenneth Plumley had given them something to decorate like it was a Christmas tree.

The police will be sensible about it, she thought. They won't allow a single unsupported claim to occupy all their time and resources. They'll be looking into every other avenue.

Except maybe the one containing Kenneth Plumley himself.

Why would they? He's come forward, a fine and upstanding citizen. Why would they suspect he has anything to do with this? Because a young woman who works in a bookshop said so?

You tried your best.

But did you, though? Did you really? You don't think you could have pushed a little bit harder? There's a young girl out there somewhere. Hopefully still alive, but possibly not for much longer. Just a teenager. Frightened and lonely and wanting to go home.

And you think you did your best?

'I'm taking an early lunch,' she announced, grabbing her coat.

9

The walk to the police station took Izzy just over ten minutes. From the bookshop on Market Street she went to the Old Square – a name that had often puzzled her because there wasn't a New Square, and also because it wasn't a quadrilateral; it was more of an elongated oval. Benches dotted its perimeter, and at one end was the war memorial, now decorated with poppies. Every day at precisely eleven in the morning, an old soldier called Corporal Bert appeared, saluted, and observed a two-minute silence. He would continue to do this for exactly one month. Izzy knew it would be a sad day when he eventually failed to turn up for duty.

The Old Square was a pedestrianised area, and the side streets leading off from it formed the quaint part of Oakbury – antique and craft shops and pubs that called themselves taverns. At the northern tip of the oval, the more aptly named North Street housed many of the ubiquitous department stores and fast-food chains. Izzy avoided that route and instead weaved her way along narrow cobbled lanes towards the river. In front of the river was a park, and next to that was Oakbury Police Station.

Izzy had never been inside a police station before, and her heart was hammering as she approached the front desk. The uniformed officer there was gargantuan, with arms that were not only long but seemingly capable of snapping trees. She suspected there was a policy of putting humungous gatekeepers here to intimidate citizens who might otherwise consider frivolity. Like, say, those who might accuse someone else of lying without any evidence.

'Hello there,' he said, surprisingly jolly. Like a caricature of a roly-poly constable from a kid's animated series.

'Hi,' she said. It came out too timid, so she straightened her spine and said, 'I'd like to speak to the lead detective on the Rosie Agutter case, please.'

There. Couldn't be more assertive. Sometimes it's necessary to act confident.

She felt sick.

'You would, would you?' He was smiling now, which made her feel inadequate. 'And may I ask what it's about?'

'I have some information. Vital information. About the case.'

Vital. A good word. She had considered *crucial*, but that had seemed a step too far.

'Vital information, eh? All right, just a second.'

He picked up the phone in front of him and jabbed a couple of buttons. Then he said, 'Hi, it's Phil. I've got a young lady in front of me who says she has some vital information about Rosie Agutter . . . Yes, vital. That's the word she used . . . Okay, ta.'

He hung up, still smiling, and Izzy was already wishing she hadn't bothered.

Phil slid a large book towards her. 'If you could just put your name, address and phone number down here, then take a seat, someone will be right down to talk to you.'

Izzy entered her details, then crossed the floor to sit on one of the hard plastic chairs. She had been there only a minute when a door opened to her right and a man of about thirty stepped through, trailing one foot to keep the door propped open. He was wearing a grey suit and brown brogues, and one of his shoelaces had come unknotted. His tie wasn't properly done up either. His brown hair was formed from tight ringlets – the sort of hair that needed no attention, you could just jump out of bed and, *ta-da*, it would be ready for the day ahead. There was a smudge of what looked like ketchup in the corner of his mouth, as though he had just abandoned his lunch to race down here, which, if true, was quite sweet. Izzy imagined that there was always at least one flaw in his appearance at any time of the day – nothing outrageous, but just enough to lend him a little individuality.

He smiled and stretched out a hand. 'Detective Sergeant Josh Frendy.'

She rose and took his hand. 'Isobel Lambert. I'm sorry, did you say Friendly?'

'Frendy. Although I am also friendly.'

Izzy grinned. She liked that name.

He said, 'I believe you have some information for us?'

She noted that he didn't use the word *vital* again, which he would have done if he'd wanted to make fun of her, and she thought that was also sweet.

'Yes, I—'

'Come through.'

He pulled the door wide, stepping aside to allow her to pass before pulling alongside and escorting her up a concrete staircase.

'Detective Sergeant,' she said. 'That sounds important.'

He laughed. 'It's not. It's one step above dogsbody and several below noticeable.'

'Oh.' This was not what she wanted to hear. She had expected seniority. 'But you *are* in charge of the Rosie Agutter case?'

'Depends on how you define in charge.'

'Is there more than one way of defining it?'

'You're right, there isn't. So, no.'

'No what?'

'I'm not in charge.'

'But—'

'This,' he interrupted, pushing open another door, 'is the CID room. And over there, in the prime spot by the window with its glorious foliage, is my desk. Come and have a seat.'

She followed him across a grey carpeted floor. The room was filled with rows of desks, each with a computer. Several of the desks were occupied. Seated at one of them, a chubby-cheeked man in a heavily creased pink shirt looked up at her and smiled, but for some reason it felt like a trap and she didn't smile back.

Frendy appropriated the swivel chair from an empty desk and wheeled it over to his own.

'Park yourself there, and tell me what's on your mind.'

Izzy performed another quick survey of her surroundings. On Frendy's desk was the crumpled-up packaging from a burger meal, eaten only recently because she could still smell the grease. Next to that was a half-empty – those of a sunnier disposition might call it half-full – beaker of black coffee. It looked cold, but Frendy was already picking it up and gulping it with alacrity. Lined up along the wall, and partly obscured by the intrusive fronds of the jungle on the windowsill above, were several framed photographs of the detective with an attractive blonde woman. They looked incredibly happy together.

Widening her focus, Izzy became aware of the various noises behind her – the clacking of keyboards, the ringing of phones, the disjointed snatches of conversation peppered with expletives – and it all made her feel fathoms out of her depth. This was a world away from her humble, inoffensive little bookshop.

'Well,' she began, 'I'm not sure if you're aware, but I phoned up the station this morning. Your station.'

Frendy's blank look told her that either this hadn't been brought to his attention, or else he had regarded it as not worth a second thought.

'I'm sorry,' he said, 'but can I get you a coffee or a tea?'

'No, thank you. I want to get straight to the point, which is that I phoned up because there was something on my mind, and you might think it's totally trivial, but it was bothering me and I thought I had to say something, even if you don't want to do anything about it.'

He nodded, but quickly brought the coffee cup to his lips to hide his amusement at her awkwardness.

'Okay,' he said when he'd straightened his features again. 'Let me hear it.'

'Right. When I say this is about Rosie Agutter, it's not exactly. Well, it is and it isn't. It's more about Kenneth Plumley.'

'The school caretaker? What about him?'

'He lied to you. To the police, I mean. And the media. He made it all up.'

Frendy dropped any indications that he was finding this entertaining. 'Let me get this straight. You're saying that what Mr Plumley told us about seeing Rosie outside the school, and then her getting into a flash car with a Middle Eastern-looking gentleman – you're saying that none of that is true.'

She gave a single emphatic nod. 'Yes. That is what I'm saying.'

'All right. So the obvious next question is: how do you know this?'

She hesitated. She didn't want a next question, obvious or not. She wanted the detective to take her at her word and do something about it, like the public servant he was supposed to be.

'This is where it gets complicated. What if I said to you that I just know?'

'I'd tell you that I need a little more than that.'

'I thought you might say that.'

'Yes. Is this what you said in your phone call?'

'More or less.'

'Then you can probably see why news of it didn't reach my ears.'

60

'I suppose. Okay. What if I told you that I know Kenneth Plumley?'

'Do you go to Hemingway High?'

'Do I look like I go to Hemingway High?'

'Well...'

'I'm twenty-three. I left school five years ago.'

'You look younger than that. Take it as a compliment. You were saying?'

'He was there when I was there. We talked a lot. I got to know him pretty well. That's how I know he's lying now.'

Frendy chewed on his lip for a few seconds. 'I'm missing something. Have you met up with Mr Plumley since you were at school?'

'No.'

'You haven't seen him in five years?'

'No.'

'Spoken on the phone?'

'No.'

'Social media?'

'No.'

'But he said something back then? Something that contradicts what he said yesterday?'

'Not exactly. It's more ...'

'Yes?'

'His behaviour. The way he's acting. I'm good at spotting these things.'

'I see.' He sat back and put down his coffee cup. 'Okay, well, you've done the right thing coming in to see us. When you've gone, I'll type up what you've said and add it to our records. We'll see where that takes us.'

'You're not going to do anything about it, are you?'

'That's up to my boss. As I said, I'm just—'

'One step above dogsbody, got it. You're making a mistake.'

'A mistake?'

'Yes. Kenneth Plumley is lying. *You need to investigate him!*'

She sensed that the demand surprised him. She also sensed that her raised voice had attracted the attention of everyone else in the room.

'Look,' she said sheepishly, 'can we go somewhere a little more private? I'm finding this very intimidating.'

'And what would be the point of—?'

'Please. I need to explain something to you. Tell you why I know what I know. I can't do it here, not with everyone watching. Just a few minutes of your time. Please.'

Frendy considered the request. And then: 'I'll give you what's left of my lunch break. Follow me.'

He led her out of the CID room and across the corridor to another room. He knocked, checked it was empty, then beckoned her in. There were no windows here. Just a few chairs and a Formica-topped table supporting a big black box.

'Is this where you interrogate prisoners?'

'We don't interrogate anyone. We interview them.'

She pointed to the black box. 'Is that a recorder? Are you going to record this?'

'No, I'm not going to record it. You can speak freely here.'

Izzy settled herself onto another hard plastic chair, with Frendy sitting directly opposite her. Despite his apparent easy-going nature, she could see why anyone might crack under the pressure of being in a situation like this. If I were a criminal, she thought, I'd confess within the first few seconds.

'First of all,' she said, 'I want you to know that I'm not a weirdo and I'm not taking the piss. What I'm about to tell you will sound unbelievable at first, but you need to stick with it, okay?'

He nodded. 'All right.'

Here goes, she thought. Oh God, what am I doing?

'All the interviews you do, you must sometimes get a gut feeling about the person sitting in this chair, right? I mean, even if you have no evidence, you just *know* they're guilty.'

'Sometimes.'

'And that's your intuition working, backed up by years of experience.'

'I suppose.'

'Okay. Another example. You go home, and you see your wife, and all she says is—'

'My wife?'

'Yes. I saw the photos on your desk. I assume she's your wife.'

'Go ahead.'

'So you come home and you say hello and your wife says hello back to you and you know instantly if something is wrong. Like, if she's unhappy or upset or angry, you know immediately, correct?'

He thought longer about this one. 'Correct.'

'And that's because you've learned how to read her. You know how she acts when she's happy and how she acts when she's unhappy. You can see it even if others can't. Sometimes all it takes is a glance, and you know exactly how she's feeling.'

'Can we move on from me now?'

'Fine. We'll move on to me, because that's precisely what I do.'

'What is?'

'I read people. I pick up on their emotions. I have what's called highly developed empathic qualities.'

'That sounds very technical. How does it work?'

'I don't know. I just know that I'm better at it than most people. I've done a lot of research on the subject, and I think it's probably a combination of things.'

'Like what?'

'Well, body language, for one. Did you know that the vast

majority of interpersonal communication doesn't lie in what's said, but in the way it's said and how you behave when you're saying it?'

'I didn't know that.'

'Yeah. That's why people often misinterpret text messages and emails. They haven't got access to all the other signals they need to appreciate the full meaning. Like, suppose I do this . . .' She leaned forward, clasped her hands in front of her and looked directly into his eyes. 'That would tell you I'm really interested in what you're saying, or maybe that I'm attracted to you.' Then she added hastily, 'I'm not, by the way. That was just another example.'

'Got it.'

'On the other hand, if I do this . . .' She leaned back in her chair, crossed her legs, folded her arms and looked around the room.

'Then you're bored.'

'Yes! And if I tap my foot in the air like this, then I'm starting to get annoyed. You with me?'

'I'm with you. To be honest, those are all fairly obvious examples. What do they have to do with—'

'What I'm saying is that signals like that are *everything*. They can tell you exactly how a person feels, even if their words say the opposite. And yes, some of them are obvious, but a lot of them aren't.'

'So . . . you've studied these techniques. You know how to—'

'No. Not *studied*. I didn't learn how to do this from a textbook. It's just natural. I'm not even conscious I'm doing it, but I think I must be constantly analysing changes in the other person's mannerisms, their expressions, their posture, the tone of their voice, the way they look at me – maybe dozens of different things, all giving clues as to how their mind is working.'

He nodded slowly, his mouth downturned like an approving Robert De Niro. 'That sounds pretty impressive.'

'Yeah, well, it has its negatives too. The problem is I don't just *sense* the other person's emotions; I *feel* them. If they're sad, it brings me down. If they're angry, my blood starts to boil. After a while it can get exhausting.'

'I'll bet. So, bringing this back to Mr Plumley . . .'

'Yes. Lie detection. It comes as part of the package. Knowing how people feel means I can also tell when they're lying.'

'Anyone?'

'Most people.'

'I'm twenty-nine.'

'I'm sorry?'

'I'm twenty-nine years old.'

'And?'

'It was a statement that's either true or false. I was just wondering if you were able to tell me if I'm lying or not.'

It starts again, she thought. The tests. The parlour tricks. Why does it always have to be reduced to this?

'It's not as simple as that,' she said.

'I had a feeling it wouldn't be.'

The doubt once more. Glancing at his watch and wondering when he could stop all this nonsense.

'You're a police officer. You know about the polygraph test, right?'

'I know it's not allowed as evidence in a UK court of law.'

'It's not allowed in pretty much any court in the world, and that's because it's crap. It's unreliable, it can be affected by the subject's anxiety, and there are known ways to cheat it. That said, the methodology used is sound.'

'The methodology?'

'Yes. You have to start with a baseline. You need to know how the subject behaves in normal conditions – how they respond to questions which have a known true or false answer. Then you hit them with the big questions – the ones you really want the answers to – and you see how their reactions compare.'

'Yes, that's what you do in a polygraph test, but how does that apply to you? How do you set up the baseline?'

'By getting to know the person. The better I know them, the better my chances of knowing when they tell lies.'

'Couldn't they fake it, the way some people do for the polygraph?'

'Most polygraph tests work on metrics like respiration and heart rate, skin conductivity, blood pressure – a very limited set. I see a whole lot more than that, and that's why I'm better at it. It would be impossible for any human to take conscious control over all the things I somehow pick up on when I talk to them.'

'That's assuming your theory is correct – I mean, about how your skill works under the bonnet.'

'Yes,' she admitted.

'I don't suppose you've ever done any experiments on this, to see just how accurate you are compared to a polygraph?'

'No.' Another reluctant admission.

'So anything you say wouldn't be admissible in a court of law either? I mean, there's no scientific evidence that you're any good at this?'

'Not scientific, no. But I know it works. And I know that Kenneth Plumley lied to you.'

Frendy consulted his watch again. 'Look, this is really fascinating stuff, but I've got to get back to work.'

He doesn't believe me, she decided. He's not going to move me out of the crackpots folder, and I can't really blame him because he's looking at someone dressed like Morticia Addams who claims to have powers to see into people's hearts and who might as well be offering to read the coffee grounds at the bottom of his cup.

'Wait,' she said. She started to open up her shoulder bag.

'You don't have a bomb in there, do you?' he asked. He said it with a smile, but she got the impression he was on the edge of serious.

'No, just this.'

He leaned forward to get a better view of what she was holding.

'A pack of cards?'

'Yes.'

Parlour tricks. It's what they always wanted, and she hated it. But she was running out of options ...

She started to remove the cellophane from the box, already regretting the fact that the cards were adorned with a Harry Potter design, but that was all they stocked in the shop; and anyway, beggars can't be choosers when it comes to last-ditch attempts to help sceptical police officers solve crimes.

'Listen,' he said. 'I really don't have time for—'

'Two minutes. Please.' She shuffled the cards, then passed the whole pack to him. 'Pick a card.'

He fanned the deck, then took one out.

'Now put it face down on the table and give the rest of the cards back to me.'

He did as he was instructed.

'Great. Now, I'm going to show you some cards, and I want you tell me what they are. Ready?'

He nodded, and she started dealing cards.

'Seven of hearts,' Frendy said. 'Ace of diamonds, ten of clubs, three of hearts, seven of spades . . .'

Before he got too bored, she said, 'For the next few cards, I want you to lie to me, okay? Name any card *except* the one you see.'

'All right.'

As she resumed dealing, he said, 'Queen of clubs, six of diamonds, four of hearts . . .'

'Fine,' she said. She gathered up her cards, leaving only the one

Frendy had selected. 'Now, I'm going to ask you some questions about your card, and I want you to try to make me believe it's a different card.'

'You mean lie to you?'

'Yes.'

'Okay, go ahead.'

'Is your card a heart?'

'No.'

'Is it a diamond?'

'No.'

'Is it a club?'

'Yes.'

'Is it a spade?'

'No.'

'All right, now we'll do the same for the number. Is it an ace?'

'No.'

She continued through the card values. Frendy said yes when she got to six, and she stopped before she even got to the picture cards.

'That's all I need. Your card is the nine of diamonds.'

He turned the card over and gave her act his Robert De Niro seal of approval. 'That's a neat trick. How'd you do it?'

'It's not a trick. There was no sleight of hand or anything. You told me the card without realising it. When I was showing you cards and asking you to tell me what you saw, or to lie about what you saw, I was setting up your baseline. I was picking up on what you do when you tell the truth and what you do when you're trying to deceive someone.'

'And what's that? What is it I do?'

'I have no idea. Like I told you, I do it subconsciously. Maybe it's something in your voice, your behaviour, the time you take to answer – or any number of things. Whatever, it gave me enough information to tell me when you were lying as I was going through the suits and values.'

Frendy slid the card across to her, then leaned back in his chair. 'What exactly do you want from me, Miss Lambert?'

'I want you to believe me, and I want you to check out Kenneth Plumley. That's all.'

'You do realise that, even if he lied to us, it doesn't mean a lot. People lie to us all the time. Sometimes it's simply because they don't like us. Other times it's for attention, because they're sad individuals who will grab any opportunity to have a spotlight shone on them.'

'If that's all it turns out to be, then that's fine. Just promise me you'll take what I've said seriously, so that I can go to bed tonight knowing I did everything I could to help find that missing girl.'

He thought it over for a few seconds. 'I'll take it seriously.'

She smiled.

Because she knew he was telling the truth.

10

Josh Frendy wondered what the hell he was doing here.

He was parked up on the street outside Hemingway High School, directly opposite the gates, and he couldn't understand why.

She was nuts. Had to be. You only had to look at her to know that. She was like a mystic in a fairground tent, or someone who sold crystals and hobbit paraphernalia. And these powers she claimed to have? Utter bollocks. Nobody can do that. Okay, the card trick was neat, but it was no better than things he'd seen done by David Blaine or Derren Brown, and with a lot more pizazz.

And yet here he was, probably wasting time, and it was starting to irritate him that Izzy had sown just enough doubt in his mind to make him come here just so he could cross it off his list of Things To Double-Check. He was particular in that way, always having to be certain even when the information came from someone who seemed to be a complete loon. He had tried telling himself that it was no bad quality in a copper, but sometimes it drove him loopy.

His eye caught movement in the school yard. A door had opened in one of the single-storey buildings, and a man had stepped out.

It was Plumley.

He stood in the doorway, drinking from a mug. Seconds later, another figure came out of the building next to it: a young girl, dressed for PE in a T-shirt and shorts. As she ran across to the main school building, Josh thought that Plumley spent a disturbing amount of time watching her.

Stop it, he told himself. You're letting Isobel Lambert's baseless accusations get to you. The man's probably in a world of his own, not even aware he's looking in the girl's direction.

When Plumley disappeared back into his workshop, Josh got out of his car. He walked across the yard, listening to the sounds of young voices and thudding feet and squealing trainers from the gym, and then he reached the workshop door, ready to knock and announce himself, but finding that Plumley was suddenly there in front of him, a glinting craft knife in his hand.

He jumped slightly, as did Plumley, but something told Josh that the caretaker's display of surprise was fake, and that he really had meant to instil fear in whoever was daring to darken his door.

Thanks, Miss Lambert, he thought. You've really put me on edge with this guy.

'Mr Plumley,' he said. 'Detective Sergeant Frendy. We spoke yesterday.'

'Oh. Yes. That's right. Please come in.'

Plumley led the way to a long bench, its surface heavily scarred and pitted, where he put the knife down and climbed onto a wooden stool. As he took a stool opposite, Josh searched in vain for signs of any recent activity that might have required use of the craft knife.

'Is there any news?' Plumley asked. 'Have you found Rosie?'

'No. Not yet, I'm afraid. I just wanted to check a few things with you, if that's okay?'

'Of course. Fire away.'

Plumley didn't look worried. If anything, he seemed eager to help.

'We're having trouble locating the car you mentioned. So far, nobody else has come forward to say that they saw it too.'

'Okay.'

Still unflustered.

'Is there a possibility you may have been mistaken?'

'About the car? Well, like I said, I didn't have any reason to take much notice at the time. It was just a big dark saloon. Pretty new, I'd say. Other than that . . .'

'But you definitely saw Rosie Agutter getting into it?'

'Well, that's not what I said. I saw a girl who looked like Rosie to me, but I don't know all the students here. It's possible I saw a completely different girl. And it was dark too, you know. It gets dark so early now.'

'I see. And the driver? You said it was a foreign gentleman . . .'

'Foreign-*looking*, is what I said. He had dark hair and olive skin, but I suppose that doesn't necessarily make him foreign, does it?'

'No, it doesn't.'

Josh considered his next move. If it was Plumley's intention to send the police on a wild goose chase, he wasn't being very forceful about it. On the other hand, he might simply be backtracking because he was worried that police suspected his involvement.

'Mr Plumley, I'll be frank with you. A witness has approached us with a version of events that contradicts your own.'

'Contradicts? What do you mean? Contradicts it how?'

'I can't go into details. Let's just say that it's not possible for both accounts to be accurate.'

'I don't know what that means. Who is this witness? Are they calling me a liar? How the hell would they know what I saw or didn't see?'

A good question, Josh thought. Easy to answer, though. I can just tell him about my little visitor and about how she occasionally spoke to him five years ago and so now knows everything about him, and I could tell him about the card trick because that would really clinch it, that would definitely convince him to confess everything.

'I hope you understand that I have to ask these questions. Sometimes it happens like this, where we get different eyewitness statements that contradict each other. Usually, it's not malicious. Someone has made a mistake, that's all. It's our job to work out what the truth is, because obviously we don't want to start investigating things that don't need investigating.'

Plumley seemed appeased. 'I'm sorry. I thought you were saying— Anyway, you're right. Maybe I did make a mistake. Maybe the girl I saw wasn't Rosie. If that's the case, then I'm sorry to have wasted your time.'

'No. Not at all. Someone got into that car, right? What time did you say it happened?'

'After five thirty. Maybe a quarter to six.'

'Right. That's quite late for a student to leave the school. We've spoken to the art teacher, and she also confirms that Rosie left at about that time, so if it wasn't her you saw, then who was it? So far, we've got no other reports of any student being picked up in a dark saloon at that time, so yours could be the best lead we have.'

'Well,' Plumley said, 'that's why I came to you. I know I could have been mistaken, but I just thought . . .'

'Absolutely. You did the right thing.' He paused. 'So I can put this whole thing to bed, can I just confirm what happened after you saw Rosie?'

'After?'

'Yes. What did you do after that? Did you go home?'

'Not straight away, no. I had some more jobs to do.'

'Oh, okay. You work long hours.'

Plumley shrugged. 'It's a big school. There's always stuff to be done. These kids, they break things all the time.'

'Yeah, I can imagine. So you stayed longer. A few minutes more?'

'No. More like an hour.'

'An hour? Couldn't it have waited?'

'No. We had a careers fair starting early the next morning. I had to set everything up in the gym.'

'The building next to this one?'

'Yes.'

'So you weren't working in the main building, then?'

'Not on that job, no.' He paused. 'Is there a reason why you're asking all these questions? Am I a suspect or something? Has this witness you mentioned said something bad about me? Because not all the students here are saints, you know. Some of them would love to see staff members get into trouble, especially the ones who get told off on a regular basis.'

Josh wondered about that. Was this revenge on Isobel Lambert's part? Getting back at Plumley for something he did or said to her, even after all those years?

'No, nothing like that. I'm just trying to build a more complete picture of what happened that night. Just to summarise, then: you were setting things up in the gym, you saw Rosie leave, and then you carried on working until, what, a quarter to seven?'

'Yeah, about that.'

'Okay. But you said you work alone, right?'

Josh was thinking, You've got nobody to verify this, have you, Kenneth? You could have gone anywhere in that time, done anything.

'Usually.'

'Usually?'

'Yeah. Mrs Vernon is very particular about these things.'

'Mrs Vernon? The head?'

'Yeah. She likes to supervise things like that. She wanted it to look just right – flowers and placards and refreshments and that kind of thing.'

'Mrs Vernon was with you while you were working in the gym?'

Plumley nodded. 'Pretty much every minute. She's very hands-on. Even helped me carry trestle tables in from my van.'

11

Izzy tried to consign it all to the back corner of her brain for the rest of the afternoon. The few toe-curling minutes she had spent with Sergeant Friendly or Frendy or whatever the hell his name was had been worth it. Up to them what they do with it now, she thought. Not my worry anymore.

Her mobile phone rang just as she was locking up the shop. An unrecognised number. Probably a spam call.

She answered it with a wary 'Hello.'

'Miss Lambert?'

'Yes.'

'Hello, it's DS Josh Frendy here from Oakbury Police.'

Her stomach lurched. She thought she was done with the police. Why would he need to call her?

'Hi,' she said. 'Is everything okay?'

'Yes. Nothing to worry about. Just a courtesy call to let you know that you can put your mind at rest. I spoke to Mr Plumley this afternoon, and it was all just a misunderstanding.'

Izzy almost dropped her keys. 'What? A misunderstanding? What do you mean?'

'I mean that Mr Plumley isn't a suspect at this time, but I'd like to thank you for coming forward and—'

'No. Hang on. That's not right.'

'Miss Lambert, please be assured that I've checked this out fully, and I'm convinced that—'

'I'm coming to the station.'

A pause. 'I'm sorry?'

'I'm coming to the police station. We need to talk some more.'

'Er . . . actually, I'm not at the station. I'm on a break.'

'Then where are you?'

'If you must know, I've just arrived at a little café called Claudette's.'

'That's just up the road from my bookshop. I'll see you there in a couple of minutes.'

'I'm sorry?' he said again.

'Two minutes!'

She ended the call.

So much for it not being my worry anymore, she thought. I can't let it go at this. This can't be right.

She finished locking up and dashed up the road to the coffee shop. When she entered, she didn't see him at first, but he leaned sideways into the aisle and waved from the rearmost table. She smiled briefly, even though she didn't know why, then went to join him.

He stood up as she reached him, which she thought very old-fashioned and gentlemanly, and then they both took their seats. She saw that he had made a start on a jet-black Americano.

'What can I get you?' he asked.

'Nothing. I don't want anything.'

'If you insist on joining me in my break, you'll have to have something. That's the deal.'

'Oh. Well then, a cappuccino, please.'

'Okay. I'll ask the monkey to make you one.'

'The monkey?'

'The cappuccino monkey. Haven't you heard of them?'

'You're thinking of Capuchin.'

'Am I? Yeah, you're probably right.' He smiled as he said this, and she realised he was pulling her leg.

Frendy signalled a waitress and placed the order for her coffee.

'Something to eat?' he asked Izzy.

'No thanks.'

'I'm going to have the Black Forest gateau. They have lemon drizzle cake, if you're interested. You look like a lemon drizzle kind of person.'

'No thanks,' Izzy repeated, wondering what lemon drizzle people looked like.

When the waitress breezed away, Frendy said, 'So, Miss Lambert, what can I do for you?'

'Izzy. Everyone calls me Izzy.'

'Okay, Izzy. What can I—?'

'Can I call you Josh?'

'Please do.'

'Right. Good. Josh. The reason I'm here . . . barging in on your break . . .'

'Yes?'

'It's just that the thing I came to see you about today – well, that was a pretty serious subject.'

'Absolutely. And I told you I would treat it with the seriousness it deserves.'

'Yes. I know. But it's just that—'

She was interrupted by the return of the waitress, who was bearing two coffees and two slices of cake.

Izzy stared at the plate being placed in front of her. 'I said no cake.'

'Try it first,' Josh said. 'You can get angry with me only if it isn't the best you've ever had.'

She saw how he winked at the waitress, and realised that he was a regular here who had somehow passed her a message to supply cake despite any denials. Perhaps he had done it many times before. With many women.

She didn't know whether to be furious or grateful, and decided she would postpone that judgement until after she got the gen on Plumley. And also after she had sampled the cake.

'Anyway, as I was saying – this is a serious situation, and I just want to make sure that you've properly checked everything out.'

'And I have.'

'Yes, well . . . good. But, could you at least give me a little more detail?'

'Okay. Well, I spoke at length with Mr Plumley and, having done so, I don't suspect him of any involvement in the disappearance of Rosie Agutter.'

'That's not detail. That's just what you told me on the phone.'

'This is great gateau. You should try yours.'

'Why don't you suspect him? What did he say to give you the impression that he's as pure as the driven snow?'

Josh hesitated, then sighed.

'All right. I don't think I'm telling you anything that's confidential here, and if it gets me out of this interrogation . . . For one thing, Mr Plumley was too fuzzy about what exactly took place. He wasn't sure it was Rosie he saw, or even that the driver was foreign. To me, that's not someone who's doing his best to send us down the wrong rabbit hole.'

Izzy waved her fork in the air. 'Or . . . he doesn't want to sound too certain in case you've got something that blows his story apart. This way, he can back down gracefully if he has to.'

'Believe it or not, I considered that. But that's not all.'

'You do like a cliff-hanger, don't you?'

'I'm a detective. I'm in the mystery game. And in this particular game, Professor Plum has an alibi.'

'Plummers has an alibi? What is it?'

'He was setting up the gym for a careers fair when Rosie left the school and disappeared. He was doing that for at least an hour afterwards.'

'What kind of alibi is that? If he said he went to the moon and back at that time, would you believe it?'

'The thing is, he wasn't alone. Mrs Vernon was supervising.'

'Who's Mrs Vernon?'

'The headteacher. Apparently she's very particular about the refreshments. Nothing too cheesy, because of the smell.'

'Never heard of her. She certainly wasn't the head when I was there. Let me get this straight. Plummers told you that this Mrs Vernon was watching his every move at the time Rosie disappeared?'

'Yes. Your cake's going stale.'

'Forgive me for asking, but did you check this out with Mrs Vernon?'

'I didn't think it was necessary. He seemed honest enough to me.'

She went to protest, but stopped herself. *Queen of clubs*. Same delivery.

'That's a lie.'

'Yes it is. Good catch. Of course I spoke to her. She backs him up.'

Izzy stabbed her fork into the slice of cake, tore off a corner and thrust it into her mouth. She chewed energetically, driven by frustration, but then the flavours melted on her tastebuds and she mellowed.

'Good, eh?' Josh asked.

'I've had worse.' She downed another couple of mouthfuls and some coffee while she thought about what she had just heard. 'Wait a minute,' she said. 'If he was constantly under the watchful eye of this Mrs Vernon, how the hell did he manage to see Rosie getting into a car on the street outside? I've been in that gym, remember, even if I was rubbish at physical stuff; it has no windows.'

'I asked that, too. He took a smoking break. Went into the yard for a few minutes.'

'Well, there you go, then.'

Josh smiled. 'There I go with what?'

'You just said it: he was out of Mrs Vernon's sight for several minutes. He could easily have done something to the girl in that time.'

'Done what with her?'

'I don't know. Knocked her out or something.'

'So you're saying that he went outside for a cigarette, saw Rosie, went into a sudden fit of rage and decided to attack her?'

'It could happen.'

'And then what did he do with her? After he'd knocked her out?'

'Maybe he put her in the boot of his car. He must have had a car there.'

'He drives a white van.'

'Even better.'

'A van that Mrs Vernon helped carry trestle tables from.'

Izzy angrily speared her cake again. 'I'm doing your job for you here. You're the detective, you figure it out.'

'I don't think there's anything to figure out. Not as far as Kenneth Plumley is concerned.'

'You're giving up too easily. Maybe Mrs Vernon is mistaken about the timing. Or maybe she's covering up for him – have you thought of that?'

'Strangely enough, no.'

'Then you should.'

'Izzy, I think you need to admit defeat on this one. There's nothing there. Maybe Mr Plumley was lying, but—'

'He *was*.'

'Okay, fine. But that doesn't make him a monster. Maybe he's just a lonely guy who got caught up in his own fantasies. And, to be honest, it doesn't make that much difference. We're not going to be spending all our time looking for foreign abductors in a flash car. There's no real harm done. Besides, there are other reasons why I don't think he's involved.'

'What reasons?'

'I can't say.'

Izzy shook her head in despair. Josh had made up his mind, and nothing she could say would alter that. She knew for certain that Plumley had lied, but it wasn't just that. There was more to it. Problem was, she couldn't quite put her finger on it. Certainly couldn't translate it into words that would make any sense to the policeman.

'Can I ask you a question?' she said.

'Of course.'

She gestured to the table in front of her. 'You said this is a break.'

'Yes?'

'You're filling up on coffee and cake. That suggests you're not planning on going home any time soon.'

'You got me. I'm a glutton, for work and for cake.'

'Doesn't your wife object?' She saw his hesitation and immediately added, 'I'm sorry, that's none of my business.'

'No. It's okay. My wife and I went our separate ways.'

'I'm sorry to hear that.' She wanted to pursue it. Decided against.

'What about you?' he asked.

'Me?'

'Yeah. Married? Single? Pet budgie?'

'I live with my partner. Andy.'

'What does he or she do?'

Izzy smiled. She liked the way he didn't make assumptions. 'She's a paramedic.'

'An important job.'

'Better than being a bookseller, right?'

'Different. We need books too.'

He paused, and she sensed that he had other questions.

'What?' she urged. 'Go on, you can ask.'

'It's . . .'

'What?'

'It was the thing with the cards, back at the station.'

Something slumped inside Izzy. Why was this always so difficult?

'What about it?'

'I have to admit, my first impressions were that it wasn't that great. Not exactly a show-stopper. But the more I thought about it, the better it got in my head. It was so pure. No frills at all. I couldn't work out how you did it, unless the card was marked somehow. But it was a brand-new pack, still wrapped in plastic. There was nobody else in the room, no mirrors, no way you could have forced that card on me like magicians often do.'

'I told you it wasn't a trick.'

'No. But that only leaves the possibility that you actually read my mind.'

'That's probably a slightly exaggerated way of putting it.'

'I'm not so sure it is. But that brings its own problem.'

'Which is?'

'What you're claiming to have is basically a superpower. Why aren't you famous? Why doesn't everyone know about you?'

'Lots of reasons. First of all, don't build it into something it's not. It's not a superpower. I don't see inside people's heads. I'm just better at detecting signals that every one of us sends out, and only then when I've got to know the person.'

'So you don't know what I'm thinking right now?'

'You're probably wondering whether to have another slice of

cake, but that's just an educated guess based on your past con-
fectionary focus. Other than that, I haven't got a clue. Secondly,
I don't want to be in the limelight. I'm not a circus freak. My
mum wanted to get me checked out by psychologists when I was
younger, and I refused because I didn't want to become somebody's lab rat.'

'I can understand that.'

'Thirdly, having an ability like this isn't as wonderful as you
might think. I'm not after sympathy, but actually it's not easy
being me. I'd rather people didn't know I can do these things, so
usually I don't tell anyone.'

'Why? Why is it so difficult?'

She reached into her extensive grab-bag of examples and
brought out just one.

She told him about her father.

12

Izzy's father was an estate agent. At the age of seven, the sum total of her knowledge about his profession was that he helped people buy and sell houses. He co-owned the agency with Lance, and often Lance and his wife would come round for a meal. Occasionally, Izzy would be allowed to eat with them, even though most of the conversation went way over her head.

But to Izzy, there was a lot more to communication than mere words.

One Sunday, following a meal the previous night that had slid into a drinking session continuing long after Izzy had been sent to bed, she attempted to demystify some of the non-verbal messages she had intercepted.

'Mummy,' she said, 'why does Daddy like Caroline so much?'

It seemed such a simple question, and yet the storm of emotion it stirred in her bleary-eyed mother was intense.

'What? What do you mean?'

'I just want to know why he likes her so much.'

Her mother forced a smile onto her pale lips. 'Well, she's nice, isn't she? Don't you think so? I like her too.'

'Yes, but not in the same way.'

The smile collapsed. 'I'm not sure what you mean, Izzy.'

But she *did* know. Izzy could tell that she knew exactly what was meant, and that confused things even more.

'I don't know,' she said. 'He likes her. A lot. And she likes him.'

The fake smile again, followed by an even more hollow laugh. 'Everyone likes Daddy.'

'Yes, but . . . it's different. It's like . . .'

'Like what, darling?'

'Like they don't want other people to know about it.'

Her mother opened her mouth and then closed it again, but although words were failing her, she emitted a wave of uncertainty and fear that made Izzy relive the time she lost sight of her parents on a beach holiday.

'I . . . I'm sure that's not true. Lance and Caroline are good friends of ours. There's nothing secret about it.'

'But there is. Daddy has a secret and Caroline has a secret, but you and Lance don't know the secret.'

'Daddy and I don't keep things secret from each other.'

'You do. You both do. You told Daddy that the cat knocked his watch onto the floor and broke it, but that wasn't true.'

She saw and felt the surprise. Izzy hadn't witnessed the watch incident, but she'd known that her mother's explanation had been false.

'Okay, yes. Sometimes we don't tell each other everything. But I don't think that Daddy and Caroline . . .'

She didn't finish the sentence, but instead became suddenly filled with glaring doubt.

'I'm sure it's nothing,' she said finally, and then disappeared up the stairs.

Izzy thought no more about it until a month later. Another meal, but just the three of them this time.

'Daddy,' she asked, 'can we go to the cinema on Saturday? We haven't been for ages.'

The instant negativity was deadening.

'I can't, darling. Maybe next weekend instead.'

Her mother chipped in. 'Daddy's got to work all day Saturday.'

86

It should have been left at that. If no more had been said, it would have ended there. Everyone had said what they believed to be the truth. But then Izzy's father had to go and spoil things.

'I'm going to a conference in Birmingham,' he said. 'I'd much rather stay here with you, but I have to go to this.'

Izzy stared at him. 'No you don't.'

Raised eyebrows. 'Izzy, don't be like that. I've told you I'll take you to—'

'You don't have to go anywhere. And you're not going to Birmingham.'

She saw how her father glanced at her mother before continuing. 'I don't know what you're talking about. Now eat your meal.'

Izzy put her cutlery down, then sat back and folded her arms.

'You're a liar,' she said.

Anger now. But also a tinge of fear. 'Izzy, you're being rude. If you don't eat, you'll have to go to your room.'

'I don't care. You shouldn't tell lies.'

'I'm not telling lies. Why would I tell lies about going to Birmingham?'

'Because you always tell lies. You lie to me and you lie to Mummy.'

'That's not true. You're being silly now.'

'No, I'm not. You lied yesterday when you said it was Lance on the phone and it wasn't.'

Her father simply stared, and she could feel his fear mounting, but also a need to drown it in a fit of fury.

'Richard,' her mother said, 'what's she talking about?'

'Nothing. She's talking nonsense, and all because I can't take her to the cinema this week.'

'It's not nonsense,' Izzy insisted.

'Who was on the phone yesterday?' her mother asked.

'Lance, of course. He rings me all the time, you know that.'

Izzy's mother studied her daughter for a while before posing her next question. 'Are you sure it wasn't Caroline?'

'Caroline? Why would it be Caroline? Of course it wasn't.'

Izzy's mother turned to her again.

'It was,' Izzy said. 'It was Caroline.'

Once again to her father: 'And are you planning to see Caroline this weekend?'

Massive shock on his face, but Izzy's senses bristled at the falsity of it.

'Don't be ridiculous. Why are you even asking me that?'

'Are you?'

'No! What the hell is going on here?'

He was on the edge, about to go over. Struggling to block the echo of his emotions, Izzy closed her eyes tightly and lowered her head.

'Izzy,' her mother urged. 'Isobel!'

The crash of a chair toppling over as her father stood up from the table. 'I've had enough of this. You two carry on making up stories about me if you like. I'm going out for a drink.'

Through the roaring in her head, Izzy heard footsteps and then the slam of a door.

Tears, then. Immense sadness. Partly hers, but also her mother's. 'Izzy?'

She opened her eyes. Her mother was staring at her, searching her for answers.

'Is it true? Is Daddy going to see Caroline this weekend?'

Izzy said nothing for a while, then slowly nodded her head.

The marriage didn't last for much longer after that. Izzy's mother continued to use her as a divining rod, constantly probing her for verdicts on her father's thoughts and actions. He, on the other hand, became uncommunicative and unloving, afraid to show his emotions and of being caught in yet more lies. He grew increasingly resentful of his own daughter, feeling that she had been turned into a weapon against him.

Izzy was just a child, with the innocence and frankness that all children possessed. She said what she saw and felt. It took years for her to become properly aware of the part she had played in the destruction of her own family. And then the guilt set in like a rot.

13

'That's a sad story.'

Izzy downed the rest of her coffee. 'I've got a load more of them if you ever feel the need to get depressed.'

'You shouldn't feel responsible. For the breakdown of your parents' marriage, I mean. It wasn't your fault.'

'Maybe not. But when things like that keep happening to me again and again, it makes me want to stay away from people. I often wish I was just like everyone else.'

He looked thoughtful.

'What is it?' she asked.

'Nothing. I was just thinking about what you've told me.'

'Uh-huh. Can I ask you something?'

'Go ahead.'

'Are you disappointed in me?'

'In you? Of course not. In the outcome, yes, a little bit. A part of me was really hoping you were on to something.'

'You were hoping for a miracle worker.'

'Yes. I was clutching at straws. To be honest, I'd talk to anyone right now who can help me with this investigation, no matter how unconventional their methods.'

Izzy watched him, saw that he had changed. He had dropped the banter, the light-heartedness, and behind all that was a man who was dedicated to his job, who would move heaven and earth to find Rosie Agutter.

'I'm sorry I couldn't give you more. But I think if anyone's going to crack this, it's you.'

'Thanks. These girls, they—'

He stopped himself abruptly, and his internal alarm set off Izzy's own.

'Girls?'

'What?'

'You said *girls*, plural.'

'I was just talking about the work I do generally. Girls like Rosie go missing all the time.'

Izzy stared at him, and he avoided her gaze.

That wasn't what he'd meant. Not at all.

* * *

She thought about Josh all the way home. Thought about him while she changed into her slob-out clothes. Thought about him when she was chopping vegetables for a stir-fry. She wasn't as good a cook as Andy and had an extremely limited repertoire, but a stir-fry she could just about manage.

The thing was, he'd left a huge impression on her. A favourable one at that, which was something she experienced rarely these days. She'd never had a proper conversation with a police officer before, let alone a detective, and she'd been struck not only by how *normal* he seemed but also by his devotion to duty. If I ever need the help of a copper, she thought, I'd want someone like Josh.

When Andy arrived home, it became the first major topic of conversation once the wine had been poured.

'So, you told the cops, then,' Andy said. Izzy had sent her a text message in the morning, but nothing about more recent developments.

'Better than that.'

'What does that mean?'

'I didn't think they believed me, so I went in person to the police station.'

Andy's eyes widened. 'You did what?'

'Yeah, I know. Are you proud of me?'

'I'm always proud of you, but also a little amazed. How did it go?'

'Well, I met this really nice detective called Sergeant Frendy, and—'

'Sergeant Friendly?'

'Frendy. But he's also very friendly. Anyway, I told him what I knew, and at first I'm sure he thought I was nuts.'

'Which is a pretty good assessment, but go on.'

'Thank you for your support. Nuts I may be, but I'm also persistent. I turned him around.'

'You mean he's gay now?'

'Andy, be serious. We're talking about a missing girl here. I used my formidable powers of persuasion.'

Andy nodded sagely. 'The card trick.'

'Yes, the card trick. I think that's what clinched it.'

'Not to rain on your parade or anything, but how do you know it worked? What if he was just fobbing you off?'

'Good question. But I have an excellent answer.'

'Which is?'

'Which is that not long after our conversation he went to see Kenneth Plumley.'

'And you know this how?'

'He phoned me. And then we met up for coffee at Claudette's. They do an awesome lemon drizzle cake there. We should both go sometime.'

Andy raised a finger. 'Wait. You went for coffee? With a policeman you'd met for the first time today?'

'Yes.'

'I see.'

'What? What do you see?'

'He fancies you.'

'No, he doesn't.'

'He does. Did you tell him that you ride a different bus?'

'I did. I also made it clear that I'm currently in a relationship with the most wonderful woman in the world.'

'I'm glad you used our mutually agreed description of me, but he still fancies you. A cop taking a member of the public for coffee is not standard procedure. And you've seen the news reports. You know that policemen can be just as untrustworthy as anyone.'

'It wasn't like that. I gate-crashed his coffee break. He didn't invite me over.'

'Hmm. Okay, so what did he tell you about his visit to Plumley?'

'Nothing. It was a damp squib. Plummers just said he could have been mistaken about seeing Rosie Agutter. He also has an alibi for the time she went missing.'

'Okay, well, I guess that's that, then. When are we eating?'

Izzy had more she wanted to say, but Andy was already switching on the television and putting her feet up. Izzy moved to the stove and began heating up some oil in the wok.

The situation bothered her. She didn't know what else she could do, but it still didn't seem right to leave it like this. It felt like she was talking in a different language, as though she was pointing at Kenneth Plumley and saying, 'There! There's the guy you want!' but with nobody around her capable of understanding what she was saying.

She cooked and served dinner. They ate, talked about Andy's day, watched some television. When Andy went upstairs to soak in a bath, Izzy dug out the laptop and fired it up.

It didn't take long to find what she wanted.

Online news reports told her that, just over a month ago, a girl called Heather Cunliffe had gone missing in the nearby village of Fenchurch. The case hadn't attracted as much media attention as the current one because Heather hadn't got on well with her parents, and they had received texts from Heather's phone informing them that she was leaving home and didn't want to see them ever again. Ostensibly, she was just another runaway, and Izzy might not have given the story a second glance had it not been for two things.

The first was that, in the photographs of Heather, she looked very similar to Rosie Agutter. Slim, long blonde hair, dazzling smile.

The other was that the detective assigned to look into Heather's disappearance was one Detective Sergeant Frendy.

It was too much of a coincidence. There had to be a connection, or at least Josh believed there was one.

Was it possible, Izzy wondered, that Kenneth Plumley had taken *both* those girls?

14

His place had always been on the sofa. Always. Him on the left and Polina on the right. Not touching or anything intimate like that, but at least within an arm's length of each other. Plus, the sofa was in the perfect position for watching the television, which was what they normally got up to when they sat there, because heaven forbid they should snuggle up together.

And yet, here he was, relegated to the armchair, which was not only saggy and uncomfortable, but which pinged every time he shifted in his seat. Worse still, it was side on to the television, almost in line with it, making the damn screen almost impossible to see properly unless he craned his head to the side and gave himself a crick in the neck. Even the dog's basket was better placed.

He remembered the first time it happened. Polina looking up at Michael as he entered the room, and then saying, 'Kenneth, you should let Michael sit here. He is our guest,' and Kenneth relinquishing his seat reluctantly, not realising that it was a reconfiguration being set in stone.

He looked across at the pair of them now. The lights had been turned down to the point of near-darkness – something that never happened before Michael arrived on the scene – but he could still make them out in the glow of the television, could still see how close they sat to each other, thighs touching, the frequent fidgeting and sniggering. While they stared at the screen, he stared at them, and the more they enjoyed themselves, the darker his mood became, until he could endure it no longer.

He stood abruptly, stretched and yawned noisily, but the only response he got was the sudden decompression of a spring deep within the bowels of his vacated armchair.

'I'm taking Barclay out for his walk,' he announced, but even this drew only an unconcerned grunt from his wife.

Kenneth issued a short sharp whistle, and the mutt dragged itself out of its basket and limped after him into the kitchen. Old and befuddled it might be, but the dog was the only occupant of this house who showed him any devotion and loyalty.

Kenneth went out the back door and unlocked the van. He scooped Barclay up and lifted him onto the passenger seat, then walked round and climbed behind the wheel. He planned to be gone for some time, but he knew he wouldn't be missed. He could probably stay out all night and still not get a single question about it.

The woods were only five minutes' drive from the house. Barclay always came alive in those woods. The sights, sounds and smells seemed to provoke some primal instincts in the animal, stoking a liveliness in his gait that carried him scampering from tree to tree. It was a joy to witness in a creature so past its peak.

But that would have to wait. Right now, Kenneth carried on driving, the dog staring longingly out of the window at the beckoning trees. He continued on to the edge of town, to an area where there were no homes but only warehouses and shuttered shops selling carpets and wood and cars and tools. He turned onto the grounds of a large Victorian building and parked around the back, out of sight.

He stroked the dog's head and scratched behind its ear. 'Wait here, boy. I won't be long.'

He got out of the van and went to the back to grab a few things before locking it up and carrying the items to the rear door of the building. There were no other vehicles here, and no lights on inside. Nobody else was interested in this building now. It had been a hub of activity once, but a brash, modern upstart on the other side of town had taken its place, much as Kenneth's spot on the sofa had been stolen. One day, the council would do something about this wonderful old structure, probably by selling it off to private contractors to convert to apartments or something. For now, it lay forlorn.

He dug into his pocket and pulled out a large bunch of keys. He had developed a habit over the years of hanging onto keys that came into his possession, and also of making copies of keys that were not supposed to remain in his possession. You never knew when such a thing could prove useful. He had, for example, keys to practically every door, locker and cupboard in Hemingway School. If the staff there ever got on the wrong side of him and he was so inclined, he could cause them no end of trouble. He also had keys to a ground-floor flat he used to live in, and one day, when he was sure the new occupant was out, he had tried the keys out and discovered that the locks hadn't been changed. He didn't go in, but every time he walked past the place now, it gave him a thrill to know he had the power to enter it whenever he wished.

He unlocked the door in front of him – even the council hadn't bothered changing the locks since he had worked here – then strapped on a headtorch and went inside.

He paused when he entered the pool area, turning his head to play the light of his torch down the long rows of changing cubicles on either side. He could still picture the teenage girls at the poolside, their wet swimsuits clinging and emphasising. He had enjoyed working here.

But then he dipped his head, and the cone of light picked out the angular whiteness at the bottom of the pool, and the memories dissolved. There was a clean-up job to be done, and he could put it off no longer.

He stepped down into the shallow end of the pool, then followed the slope to the opposite end. When he reached Rosie's body, he dropped the tarpaulin he was carrying and spread it out next to her. He flipped Rosie onto the plastic material, then rolled her up inside. When that was done, he gathered up the ends and tied them tightly with string. With a grunt, he picked up the package and slung it over his shoulder before making his way out of the pool.

Once outside, he locked the building up again, then opened up the rear of the van and slid the body in. As he climbed into the driver's seat, he scratched Barclay behind the ear.

'Good boy.'

A few minutes later, he was driving back along the road through the woods. He checked his rear-view mirror: nothing behind him. He slowed, then turned off the road, easing the van just far enough through the trees for it not to be obvious to the occupants of passing cars.

He got out of the van. Barclay whimpered, desperate to follow.

'Keep your legs crossed a bit longer, boy. I'll be as quick as I can.'

He closed his door, then took a deep breath of the air, the musty odour of fallen leaves and damp bark unmistakeable. The sky grew suddenly brighter, and he heard an engine noise growing gradually in volume. But the car flashed past, leaving Kenneth smiling at his invisibility.

He opened up the back of the van, and the light from his head-torch flooded the interior. He grabbed the body, pulled it towards him and hoisted it over his shoulder again. Before he closed the vehicle up, he reached in and grabbed one other thing he would need: his spade.

He tramped deeper into the woods, which seemed to close up around him. The shadows cast by his torch made it look as though the trees were shifting and turning, disturbed by his presence. He could see the breath of his exertion as the body grew heavy. When he thought he'd gone far enough, he dumped the corpse unceremoniously onto the ground and rested a while.

With the edge of the spade, he parted the carpet of leaves, then thrust the blade into the rich moist earth. It satisfied him that it sank deeply and easily.

He began to dig.

It wasn't too difficult to shift the top few inches of soil, but then he hit tangled roots, slowing his progress. He sliced through them with the spade. He broke out in a sweat, and his muscles began to burn.

Simon says dig.

The words gave him fuel. They instilled a fury within him, driving him on.

A face materialised in his mind.

His mother's live-in boyfriend, later to become her husband.

Simon himself.

That fucking bastard.

Kenneth's mother was out. She was always out. She worked in a pub, and that meant she always worked late. But that was okay, because Simon, the new love of her life, would take good care of things while she was gone, wouldn't he?

Simon's face. In Kenneth's room now. His bedroom.

Shall we play a game? Simon Says. Because my name's Simon. You know how to play Simon Says, don't you? It'll be great fun.

Laughter. At least at first. Great fun.

And then …

Simon says take that off.

And then …

Simon says touch this.

And Kenneth is no longer sure whether this is fun or not. It seems weird. Simon's face is weird. He's not laughing now. His noises are strange and a bit scary.

But he's an adult, and he's taking care of the house, and Kenneth's mother has allowed this, so it must be okay, it must be right.

And then . . .

Simon says don't tell your mum. Because really bad things will happen if you do. Your mum will be very angry with you, and so will I, and you don't want to be punished, do you?

Kenneth dug with ferocity, his eyes stinging with the tears. He pictured Simon at the bottom of the hole, and he stabbed at it with all his might, ripping up roots as though they were entrails.

You bastard, he thought. You're to blame for this. It's your fault this girl is dead. Your fault I have to bury her.

And then it was done. The hole was ready.

Kenneth leaned on his spade and stared down into the yawning blackness.

He went to the girl, rolled her the few feet to the edge of her grave. One final push and she disappeared.

He started work with the spade again, but the task was easier now. Quickly he threw heap after heap of soil into the hole, then he stamped it down and covered it over with rotting leaves.

Stepping back, he was satisfied that the burial mound wasn't obvious. Nobody would find Rosie again.

Returning to his van, he put the spade away and then released Barclay. To be on the safe side, he steered the dog away from his recent handiwork. There was always the possibility that Barclay might chance upon the other grave, though, because even Kenneth had forgotten exactly where it was.

But he still remembered her name.

Heather Cunliffe.

15

She had to know for certain.

If there really was someone out there who had taken at least two girls, and might even have another one in their sights, then Izzy had to be sure it wasn't Kenneth Plumley. There was only one way to accomplish that.

Friday in the bookshop dragged. Business was brisk with people stocking up on their reading for the weekend, but it still dragged. Izzy's mind was filled with the enormity of her mission ahead, and she just needed to get it over and done with, despite all the ifs and buts. What if it all went wrong? What if it became dangerous, violent even? What would Andy say if she knew of her plans?

Well, that's an easy one, she thought. Andy would tell me not to be so fucking stupid, and to leave things like this to the professionals.

But she'd seen a professional. She'd seen Josh Frendy. And he was nowhere with the case. He was desperate for help. If she was capable of providing that help, then there was no choice.

Melissa dashed away at the first stroke of five o'clock. Izzy hurriedly sorted out the takings before locking up and running for her car. She worried that she might already be too late, which would mean that she couldn't try again until Monday. A lot could happen in that time.

The traffic was hectic at peak hour on a Friday. Izzy kept glancing at the dashboard clock of her Fiat 500, making the mental adjustments required to work out the correct time, since the clock was always way off.

It's Friday, she thought. He'll have gone home. Nobody hangs around on a Friday.

But then she arrived at the school and saw that the gates were still open, a van was parked on the grounds, and a light was on in the workshops. She breathed a sigh of relief, then almost choked on it when she realised that her mission could no longer be postponed. It had already begun.

She reversed the car back along the road and pulled in some distance behind a Vauxhall. Then she waited.

Twenty minutes later there was activity. Through the school railings she saw Kenneth get into his van and drive it out of the gates. She started up her own engine and put the car into gear, but then saw that the van had stopped on the road and Kenneth was getting out again and walking in her direction.

She felt a flutter of panic. Had he seen her? Was he coming to challenge her?

Of course. The gates.

Kenneth wrapped a chain around the gates and snapped a padlock in place, then got back in his van and drove off. Izzy set off after him.

She maintained as much distance as she could between them. When Kenneth approached a junction, she slowed down too, accelerating after the turn to get him in her sights again. At one point, a boy racer jumped into the gap ahead of her, and she had to slam on her brakes. She was tempted to sound her horn, but was afraid of drawing Kenneth's attention to what was behind him.

Izzy found the pursuit strangely exhilarating. She had never done anything like this before. Nothing remotely clandestine. She wasn't one of life's risk takers. Didn't do bungee jumps or roller coasters or surfboarding. She was someone who could find the jeopardy in a Disney animation too much to bear. But this was a thrill. This felt edgy.

And then the surrounding buildings thinned, and the roads became less well-lit and more deserted, and she started to wonder about the wisdom of the enterprise.

What if he knows? What if he's already seen me following and he's leading me into a trap? A cul-de-sac or something that he'll block off, and then he'll come at me with a wrench or whatever else he keeps in the back of that van. What will I do if that happens?

She shook her head. Didn't pay to think like that. It would be fine.

The narrow road she was on now didn't look fine. It looked downright spooky. Tall dark trees loomed over her on either side, as if they were watching and debating whether to pounce and drag her in with their long scratchy fingers. She'd never be found again if she ended up in there.

Focus, she told herself.

She stared at the tail lights of the van ahead of her in the distance and wondered how long this journey would take. She glanced at the petrol gauge, saw that she was low on fuel. Great. Nothing like the prospect of breaking down in the middle of nowhere for keeping the spirits up.

The van's brake lights flared and it took a left turn. Izzy did likewise and found herself on another country lane, quieter than the one she had just left. About a mile further along, she saw that the van was slowing and indicating as it drew level with a brightly lit pub.

Friday night, she thought. He's popping in for a pint. That's my plans scuppered.

But as the van turned, she saw that it wasn't entering the car park but heading up yet another lane just beyond the pub.

Got to be close to home now, she thought. What other reasons could there be for going that way?

She continued the pursuit, stretching the distance between them to avoid arousing suspicion. This road was practically deserted, with just the occasional cluster of cottages. Ahead, the van braked again. Kenneth didn't indicate, but performed a left turn anyway.

That must be where he lives, she thought.

She slowed the Fiat to a crawl while she debated her next move. She had wanted to know more about Kenneth, and discovering his home address had seemed a sensible first step in that direction, but she hadn't planned much beyond that.

I could knock on his door, she thought. I could pretend that my car's broken down and the battery in my phone is dead, and could I please use his telephone to ring for help? And then I could say, 'Don't I know you from somewhere? It's Mr Plumley, isn't it? It's me! Izzy, from school! What a coincidence!' And then he'd invite me in for a cup of tea and the use of his phone, and while I'm there I could snoop around and find a roomful of missing girls and I could save them all.

Sure, that'd work.

She jumped at the blare of a horn from behind her. A Range Rover overtook and was gone within seconds. Izzy pulled the Fiat onto the grass verge while she considered her options.

She had no options.

Best she could do for the moment was take a look at the house, see if she could learn anything from that.

She killed the engine, then got out and locked up the car. She didn't want to run the risk of taking it any closer in case it aroused suspicion. She pulled her collar up around her face and crammed a bobble hat on her head, because that's what spies do when they want to be inconspicuous.

She started walking down the verge. On either side, hedgerows separated the road from fields. She could see the lights of traffic in the distance. This was a very quiet spot. An ideal place to imprison teenage girls. Ideal to imprison her too, if this went tits-up. That was a comforting thought, especially as she hadn't told anyone she was coming here.

A wall came into view, fronting a property. She thought it must have been about here where Kenneth had turned in, but she wasn't sure. She walked on a bit further. It was a cottage, but with no lights in the windows and no other signs of life.

And there was a bigger problem. No van.

Izzy walked out into the middle of the road to get a better view of what lay ahead. It looked as though there was a dirt track on the far side of the next field, and then another house, bigger than this one.

Could Kenneth have driven that far? She didn't think so. She was convinced he had come off the road here.

Only one way to find out.

She went to the open gates. A driveway ran along the side of the house. The van could have gone up there and around the back of the property.

She started up the driveway. She'd decided that if she was spotted, she would politely ask if this was Howards End or The House at Pooh Corner or some such, and then apologise for getting the wrong address, hoping that Kenneth wouldn't recognise her in the darkness and after all these years and wearing her spy disguise.

She reached the cottage. Close up, she could see how neglected it was: paint peeling from the doors and windows; a doorbell hanging from a wire. Perhaps she'd been mistaken about where the van had gone. Plummers was a handyman. Would he allow his own home to get in a state like this?

She looked along the side of the house. There were no gates

barring her progress. Keep going or not? Perhaps just a little further, a quick peek.

She pressed on, along the side of the building. When she reached the back corner, she popped her head around it.

A white van, parked on a patch of gravel.

It was what she needed to know, but that would have to be it as far as intelligence gathering went for today. She turned to retrace her steps.

Lights came on at the front of the house. She heard loud voices. Her escape route was cut off, along with any means for talking her way out of this. Saying she was at the wrong address was one thing, but how the hell was she going to account for being in the back garden?

She looked around and saw a large wooden shed. She ran towards it. Somewhere behind her a dog started barking, and she thought, They've seen me, they've set the dog on me, I'm dead.

She hid behind the shed, then risked a peek around it. She could see into a kitchen at the rear of the house. A gigantic dog with gigantic fangs was standing at the French doors, staring back at her and voicing its desire to sink said fangs into a juicy calf muscle. A man – not Kenneth – appeared behind the dog, said something to it and dragged it away.

The voices were still debating on the driveway.

'I can't see it,' the male said. Izzy was sure that this one was Plummers.

'Stand here. You can see better from here. Shine the torch up.' A female voice. Foreign accent. Polish, maybe? Russian? Damn, this was getting more and more like a spy film.

'Okay,' Kenneth said. 'I see it now.'

'It is very dangerous, Kenneth. You must fix it.'

'It's not dangerous. The guttering's moved a bit, that's all.'

'That's not just a bit, Kenneth. It is nearly falling. Today a piece came off and nearly broke my head. Wait. I will show you.'

A pause, and then the slamming of the lid on a wheelie bin.

'See?' the woman said. 'It is metal. Heavy. It nearly killed me.'

'It's an iron bracket. It must have rusted through.'

'And the gutter, it is also metal, yes? So if it falls on us, we will be dead.'

'All right. I'll fix it.'

'Tomorrow, Kenneth. You always want to wait, but this cannot wait. You must do it tomorrow.'

'Fine. I'll go to Raynor's first thing in the morning and get a new bracket. Can we go back inside now? I need something to eat.'

'Yes. We can eat. What are you going to make?'

The voices faded. A door closed. The front of the house was plunged into darkness again. Any second now, the kitchen could be filled with people, and perhaps also the dog, and the dog would start barking again and they would all come out to find a strange young woman cowering behind their shed.

Izzy seized the opportunity and ran.

She ran back along the driveway, fully expecting to hear shouts and barking and snapping at her heels but getting none of that, and then hurtled through the gateway and along the lane, not stopping until she reached the little white bubble of protection that was her car. And it was only after she was safely ensconced inside and she finally got her breath back that she allowed a broad smile of satisfaction to break out.

Way to go, she thought. Mission Impossible accomplished. Tom Cruise, eat your heart out.

She now knew exactly where Kenneth Plumley lived, who he lived with, what the layout of his house and garden were like, and the registration number of his van.

But on top of all that, her next move had been handed to her on a silver platter.

She now had an early-morning appointment with Kenneth Plumley at Raynor's Hardware Store.

16

Izzy got out of bed at seven o'clock on Saturday morning. She would normally sleep in for at least another thirty minutes, but she'd already been awake for hours, her mind cycling through all the possible scenarios that might lie in front of her. She had texted Melissa the night before, advising that she would be a little late getting to the bookshop today, but even in her own head she had no idea what 'a little late' might mean. Kenneth had told his wife (*was* she his wife? And who was the guy in the kitchen?) that he would get to Raynor's 'first thing', but not everyone had the same definition of 'first thing'. To be on the safe side, Izzy had decided that she would get to the hardware store before it opened at 9.00.

Additional uncertainty surrounded how long the encounter would last. Worst case, Kenneth would rebuff Izzy's advances, make his excuses and race back home, bracket in hand, in which eventuality Izzy would probably get into work not long after Melissa. At the other extreme, Izzy pictured herself sitting in front of a pleasantly surprised Detective Sergeant Frendy, setting down her witness statement as to how she painstakingly bound Kenneth Plumley up in his own web of lies and convinced him to confess, thereby freeing the town and its surrounding region of a vicious predator. If that was how it went, showing up at the bookshop before the mid-morning coffee break would be unlikely, but surely Abel would be willing to forgive this tardiness of the heroic saviour in his employ.

Izzy managed to force down a cup of tea and most of a bowl of Rice Krispies. When she was washed and dressed, she said goodbye to Andy, who had the weekend off and was intending to spend the majority of it sleeping. Then she got in the car and drove to town, parking in her usual spot on the road opposite the bookshop, only a short walk from Raynor's.

That was when the nerves really kicked in, as all the scenarios lying between her two imagined extremes reasserted themselves. The scenarios that involved Kenneth becoming abusive or threatening or violent, or even simply causing a scene that would leave her humiliated and in tears. Was it really worth the risk?

And then she thought about Rosie Agutter and Heather Cunliffe and decided that yes, it was very much worth a little emotional turmoil.

She got out of the car, strolled up to Raynor's Hardware, just in time to see the owner opening up shop. Izzy stayed on the other side of the road, watching and waiting. Foot traffic grew quickly – all the early birds anxious to get their shopping done before it became too busy. She had to keep shifting position to get out of the way and maintain her view, and she started to worry that she would fail to catch sight of Kenneth.

But then there he was, ambling along like a person who didn't kidnap young girls, going straight into Raynor's like your average DIY guy.

Izzy crossed the street and took up position outside the barber's next door. Assuming that Kenneth would retrace his steps, he couldn't fail to come within inches of her. She took deep calming breaths, then shook her arms and flexed her fingers as though she was about to face up to a Wild West gunslinger.

'Izzy!'

She turned, saw a familiar face.

'It's me! Maya. From school.'

No, not now. Please not now.

'Maya! Yes. Hi. How are you?'

'Good. What about you? What are you doing with yourself?'

A glance towards the hardware shop. No sign yet.

'I work in the bookshop. Stern Words.'

'Really? I must call in there sometime. I don't get back here much now. It's a big world out there.'

Maya had gone to Oxford for her degree. Ended up in politics, which wasn't surprising since she had bored everyone at school to tears with her forthright political views. And now it sounded like she was already about to launch into a tale of how important she was to civilisation.

'Certainly is. We should definitely catch up.'

'Well, what are you doing right now?'

Another look towards the shop. She could see a figure at the counter.

He's paying. He'll be out here any second.

'Er, actually, I'm late for something.'

'Late? It looked like you were just standing here.'

The door is opening. He's coming out.

'Yeah, I was. That's why I'm late. See you, Maya. Gotta go.'

That's him. Coming straight towards me.

'Izzy?'

'Another time, promise.'

And then she was hurrying away from Maya, practically running, not caring how rude she must have seemed to her schoolmate as she concentrated on making a beeline for Kenneth Plumley, and then she was right on him, forcing him to make evasive manoeuvres that failed when she mirrored his movement and ploughed straight into him.

'Oh, God,' she said. 'Sorry. I'm so sorry.'

Kenneth had dropped the brown paper bag he was holding, and

as he bent to retrieve it, it suddenly occurred to Izzy that Maya might have recognised him from her schooldays and be tempted to turn this into some kind of shitty reunion. But when she glanced behind her, she saw that Maya had already marched away.

'Are you all right?' Izzy asked.

'No damage done,' Kenneth said. 'What about you?'

'I'm fine. I— Mr Plumley?'

He stared at her for a second, and then his eyes widened. 'Izzy? It's Izzy, isn't it?'

'That's me. Still just as clumsy as ever, apparently. I haven't seen you for ages. How are you?'

'I'm good.' He held up the bag. 'Just out on a little errand. My wife is sending me up a ladder to fix the gutters. To be honest, I think she's hoping I'll break my neck.'

Izzy laughed too hard. 'Wife? You're married now?'

Kenneth's face darkened slightly, and she got the feeling he was already afraid he'd said too much.

'Yeah. I'm a real grown-up now. What about you?'

'I have a partner, but we're not thinking of wedding bells just yet. Hey, do you fancy a quick coffee? It would be great to catch up.'

He frowned. 'I don't know. I should really get back and make a start on this job.'

But Izzy was already hooking her arm through his, playing all warm and friendly even though it made her sick to her stomach to get so close to a man who possibly liked nothing more than hurting young women like her.

'Come on. Ten minutes or so won't hurt. I'm dying to hear what's been going on at the school since I left.'

Kenneth looked around, as if for someone to rescue him, but there was no way she was letting go of him now, not after all the work she'd put into setting this up.

'All right,' he said. 'A quick coffee.'

'Great. Do you know Claudette's? They do amazing lemon drizzle cake there.'

'Sounds good. Lead the way.'

On the way there, she limited the conversation to trivialities, mostly about herself. She told him what she had done since leaving school, which was difficult to make sound remotely interesting, and also about the bookshop she worked in, which was even more difficult to dress up as glamorous. She was saving the interrogation of her suspect until she could stare him in the eye.

At such an early hour, Claudette's was quiet, with only one other couple present. For no other reason than she felt comfortable there, Izzy led the way to the table she had shared with Josh Frendy. As she took off her coat, a figure drifted across.

'Hello again,' said the waitress. 'Fallen under the spell of our lemon drizzle, have you?'

It was the same waitress as last time, and Izzy suddenly felt that coming here again might have been a mistake.

'Er, yes. Could I have it again, please? And a large cappuccino.'

Large, because that would take longer to drink.

'Certainly.' She turned to Kenneth. 'And for yourself?'

'Just a normal coffee. Small.'

'Anything to eat?' Before he could answer, the waitress turned to Izzy. 'He's not a policeman as well, is he? For some reason they always seem to go for the gateau.'

Shit, Izzy thought.

'Policeman?' Kenneth said.

'It's a joke. I'll tell you later.'

She felt his discomfort. This wasn't a great start.

'No cake for me, thank you.'

Izzy glared at the waitress in a way that told her that she should go away now, and the waitress dutifully obeyed. Looking at Kenneth again, she wondered how long to leave it before getting to the heart of the matter, the reason for all this. Had she buttered him up enough yet?

'So . . .' she said. 'You're married now. When did all that happen?'

'About three years ago.'

She waited for him to say more, but he seemed reluctant. It was almost as if he was ashamed of his marital status.

'Well, belated congratulations. What's her name?'

'Polina.'

'Pauline?'

'*Polina*. She's . . . she's Russian.'

'Yeah? How'd you meet?'

'It was . . . online. She flew all the way here to be with me,' he said with pride.

Ah, Izzy thought. An internet bride. She knew she shouldn't judge, but she judged anyway. The thought she couldn't stop passing through her head was that, for many people, seeking soulmates online was a perfectly reasonable approach, but that Kenneth, serial abductor that he probably was, undoubtedly had difficulty in interacting with women, and so his only solution for entering into a relationship of an acceptable kind was to have one shipped in from some remote corner of the world.

They chatted for another couple of minutes about old times. The coffee and cake arrived. They chatted some more. When Kenneth checked his watch, she took that as her cue.

'Hey,' she said. 'I just remembered. The girl I work with in the bookshop said there'd been something in the news about one of the girls at Hemingway going missing.' She had planned from the start to pretend that she hadn't seen the news report. She didn't want Kenneth making any connections between that and their 'chance' encounter this morning.

Kenneth shifted in his seat. 'Yeah. Rosie Agutter. She's a sixth-former.'

Goosebumps rose on Izzy's arms. There was something wrong with what Kenneth had just said.

'Do you know her?'

'Not well. I've seen her around.' He hesitated. 'Did you see me on the news?'

'You? No. You were on television?'

'Yeah. I thought I saw Rosie getting into a car outside the school on the day she went missing. I talked to the police about it, and then the television reporters.'

'Oh my God, you were the last one to see her?'

'Well, that's what I thought. Now I'm not so sure. It might have been someone else I saw.'

Damn. He was pulling back, like Frendy said he did with him. He wasn't being definite enough for her to detect the lies. She needed to pin him down.

'But what if it *was* her? Melissa at the shop said something about a foreign guy driving the car.'

Kenneth squirmed a little. 'That was probably my fault. I thought he looked Middle Eastern, but it was hard to tell. It was so dark, and they were so far away.'

Shit. This was going nowhere. She thought about posing more direct questions so she could get a better read on the situation, like *Did you take Rosie?* Or, *Is Rosie still alive?* But she couldn't think of any that wouldn't let him know she was on to him.

'I hope nothing bad has happened to her,' she said.

'Me too. She's a lovely girl.'

The goosebumps again. Why? What did he say?

And then she realised.

It was his use of the present tense. She *is* a sixth-former. She *is* a lovely girl. He wasn't feeling what he said. He wanted to use a different tense.

The past tense.

Meaning Rosie was dead.

Izzy struggled to prevent her face betraying her shock, to stop the grief overwhelming her. She wanted to say something, to blurt it all out. She wanted to call him a liar, a murderer, a monster.

Stay calm, she told herself. Keep control.

'I remember reading about another local girl who went missing,' she said. 'Must have been about a month ago.'

Kenneth drained his coffee cup. 'Yeah?'

'Yes. I think her name was Heather . . . Cunliffe or something like that. Have you heard of her?'

Kenneth shook his head and said, 'Can't say I have,' and Izzy knew instantly that it was a lie, that he knew exactly who she was and what had happened to her.

Kenneth checked his watch again. Said, 'Well, it's been nice talking to you, Izzy, but I should really go now. Polina will be thinking I've had an accident. I need to stop her claiming on the insurance.'

He laughed, and Izzy forced out a laugh too. 'Don't forget your bracket,' she said.

Kenneth picked up his brown paper bag from the chair, then looked at her curiously.

'How d'you know it's a bracket?' he asked.

'Oh . . . well, you said you were fixing the gutters, and that's definitely not a section of guttering.' She laughed again, but Kenneth didn't find it so funny.

'Take care of yourself, Izzy,' he said.

He walked away, and Izzy shuddered.

Not only because she had just had coffee with a serial murderer.

But also because his parting words to her had sounded more like a threat.

17

Andy's parents were in their fifties, which Izzy accepted wasn't that old really, and yet they had an attitude to life that seemed to hark back decades. They were nice enough, unfailingly hospitable, but Izzy could always sense an underlying discomfort that sat there simmering. Philip, Andy's father, dealt with it as fuel for inappropriate jokes, but his wife Fiona had no such outlet. There was a host of issues locked up in her diminutive frame, and Izzy could sense she wasn't coping.

'Dinner's on the table,' Fiona announced. 'Come and get it before it goes cold.'

Izzy felt the tension even in this apparently innocent prompt. A real worry there that a few seconds' delay in taking their seats could jeopardise the whole meal.

They filed through to the dining room, where a feast had been laid out on the table. Izzy and Philip sat on one side, Fiona and Andy on the other. Izzy always felt a bit awkward at this point in the proceedings, as though there might be an invitation to say grace. She wished for some music – anything to compensate for the embarrassing absence of conversation while they shuffled in their chairs and unfolded napkins across their laps.

She glanced at the immense plate of meat in the centre of the table. As she'd feared, it was roast beef, carved too thickly, the slices looking desiccated enough to suck the moisture from the air.

'Wine?'

Philip was looking directly at her, holding aloft a bottle of red. Izzy didn't care what it was as long as it contained alcohol, and she brought her glass up to catch a stream of the oxblood liquid.

'There you go,' he said. 'That'll put hairs on your chest.'

Izzy couldn't quite tell whether this was a dig at her sexuality, so she let it go and quaffed the booze instead.

'Don't stand on ceremony,' Fiona said. 'Help yourself. You look starving.'

Izzy didn't know what it was about herself that gave the impression she didn't eat enough. Fiona was always telling her she needed fattening up, as though they planned on serving her as a roast dish one day. Or perhaps they were hoping she would become so obese that their daughter would lose all interest in her.

She forked a slice of the arid meat onto her plate; then, catching the critical eye of Fiona, reluctantly took another. She tossed on a few roast potatoes that landed with an impact capable of cracking her plate, then spooned on some vegetable mush that looked and smelled as though it had been boiling overnight but would at least be soft enough to force down her gullet.

Unwilling to tackle this tour de force of culinary ineptitude without the aid of additional moisture, she scanned the table and spied only a single gravy boat. She nabbed it quickly and poured half of its gelatinous contents all over her meal, deciding that the others would have to fight over the rest or make some more, because her piece of cow alone was going to drink all of this and still be thirsty, and who decided it should be called a gravy *boat* anyway? Were there any other foodstuffs that were served in boats?

She waited while everyone else plated up, and noticed that Fiona took only one slice of meat, two tiny potatoes and a thimbleful of the vegetable concoction.

'Is that all you're having, Fiona?' she enquired politely.

Fiona fluttered a hand over her solar plexus. 'Little and often for me, because of my acid reflux. I shouldn't really be eating roast potatoes, because of the grease, but I'll be damned if I'm going to cut out every little thing that's slightly fatty or spicy. I mean, you've got to live, haven't you?'

Izzy nodded and looked across at Andy, who rolled her eyes.

'So,' Philip said, 'what have you two been up to today?'

He asked it as though they were two kids who'd been allowed to play out without adult supervision. Izzy was tempted to tell them exactly what they'd done before getting out of bed this morning, see how that dampened appetites.

'Nothing exciting. Andy and I did some—'

'Andrea,' Fiona corrected her.

And now Izzy really did want to give a blow-by-blow account of their earlier exertions, because for God's sake, did the contraction of Andrea's name seriously make her any less their daughter?

'Andrea, yes. We did some cleaning and tidying. A bit of shopping. That kind of thing.'

'I suppose you were out clubbing last night?' Philip said. 'That's how Fiona and I met, in a nightclub, all those years ago.'

Izzy had heard the story before. It tended to lead to reminiscences about the exploits of Philip and his mates in their attempts to attract members of the opposite sex, the key word being 'opposite'.

'Yeah,' she answered, 'that's how we met too. A bit of a quiet one last night, though. Just the two of us, snuggled up in front of the telly.'

She saw the nods and smiles, but also felt the unease in Andy's parents, who then immediately changed the subject.

'Andrea,' Philip said. 'How's the job going? Any gruesome tales to tell us?'

'Philip, please,' Fiona said. 'Not at the table. Andrea, the sanitised version, please.'

Izzy zoned out then, allowing Andy to do all the talking. Her mind returned to the thoughts that had been occupying it ever since the previous morning when she met Kenneth for coffee.

She was now firmly convinced that Kenneth was responsible for the abduction of both Rosie Agutter and Heather Cunliffe. She was also convinced that they were both dead.

That knowledge was a heavy burden, but what made it worse was that she couldn't share the load. She had thought dozens of times about calling Josh Frendy on his mobile – had even gone so far as to find his name in her phone contacts before changing her mind – but what would it achieve? She had no proof, no evidence. The only thing she could take to Josh was exactly what she had offered him before: her intuitive feeling that Kenneth was the guilty party. No amount of card tricks would persuade Josh to act on that basis alone.

She would need more. Something tangible. Hard, incontrovertible, damning proof.

Great, she thought. And how the hell am I going to get hold of that?

She recalled Kenneth's face as he left the coffee shop. His voice. *Take care of yourself, Izzy.*

To anyone else it might have seemed innocuous, but she had felt the menace there, the warning to stay out of his affairs.

Which meant he suspected that she'd been trying to trip him up.

She cast her mind back to her school days, to Kenneth as he was then. Strange, yes. And as private as a clam. But a would-be killer? What had happened to him in these past five years? He had managed to attract a wife, albeit one who might have been willing to jump on a plane for the first Westerner prepared to fund the air fare. Had she not been enough to satisfy his urges? Or had she somehow had the opposite effect?

Whatever; he was dangerous now, a killer of young women, and Izzy didn't fancy bumping into him in a dark alleyway. So how could she possibly investigate him while keeping him at a substantial distance?

She hadn't told Andy about any of this, not even about seeing Kenneth yesterday. Andy had thought it weird enough that she'd gone for coffee with a policeman; what would she think about her doing the same with a serial killer?

Serial killer? Really? Kenneth Plumley?

She didn't know what the formal definition of a serial killer was – there was probably some threshold on victim numbers that you had to pass to be considered eligible for membership of that particular elite – but in her book, anything more than one counted as serial. Which made her wonder just how many girls Kenneth had actually taken. Could they be counted on the finger of one hand? Double digits?

And when had he first taken an interest in this particular pursuit? Was he doing it when she knew him at school? While she was talking to him about the books she was reading, was he already plotting his next abduction?

There were limits to Izzy's powers, even with people she knew well. She couldn't just look at someone and divine their every secret thought or misdeed. And yet she was convinced that if Kenneth had harboured such dark desires back then, she would have picked up on *something*. She would have known that he was someone to be avoided.

Which brought her back to her earlier question. What had gone wrong in Kenneth's life in the five years since she had last seen him?

Izzy suddenly realised that all conversation at the table had stopped and that everyone was staring at her in expectation.

'What?'

It was Andy who answered. 'Mum wants to know if you think you'll ever go back to university to finish your degree.'

It was a typical question from Fiona. Its subtext was, *Look, Andrea, this girl clearly has no future prospects and you need to push her to one side and get on with life, preferably in the company of a red-blooded heterosexual male*. Izzy knew this even though she hadn't heard it directly, because in her experience most of Fiona's probing was laced with such discouragement.

Izzy furnished them with a suitably vague response and then returned to the arduous task of clearing her plate while struggling not to become lost in her own thoughts again. She forced herself to toss in the occasional contribution when it seemed appropriate, but she could sense that Andy was growing increasingly annoyed with her. She wasn't surprised when, at the end of the meal, Andy insisted that she and Izzy would do the washing-up.

'What the hell is wrong with you?' Andy said to her when they were alone in the kitchen.

Izzy shrugged. 'Nothing. Why?'

'Why? Because nobody can get a word out of you, that's why. I know my parents don't make scintillating conversation, but at least they're trying. Couldn't you make a bit more of an effort?'

'Sorry. I'm not with it today.'

'Not just today. You were like this yesterday too. Have I done something to upset you?'

'No, not at all. It's just . . .'

'What?'

'The Kenneth Plumley thing. It's still bothering me.'

'Who's Kenneth Plumley?'

'The caretaker at my old school. The one who—'

'Oh, him! I thought that was old news now.'

'It is, but . . .'

'You're doing it again, aren't you?'

'Doing what?'

'Obsessing about what's going on in other people's heads. You told the police about Plumley, then investigated, and it turned out there was nothing to it. You need to let it go now.'

'I know, but it's not as simple as that.'

'Why? Why isn't it?'

Izzy looked her partner in the eye and wondered what to answer. Tell her that she followed Kenneth to his house? That she eavesdropped on him from his own garden? That she then tracked him down at the hardware store, virtually manhandled him into a coffee shop and proceeded to extract an unspoken confession from him? Yeah, that would really contradict the view of Andy's parents that there were better catches to be had.

Besides, what would be the point? She had already reached the conclusion that the police wouldn't believe what she could tell them now, and that she had no practical way of taking it any further on her own. She was up against a brick wall.

'You're right,' she said. 'It's not my problem. Come on, let's finish these dishes so I can go and tell your mum and dad that we're thinking of going to Lesbos next year.'

18

Polina kept her eyes open throughout the lovemaking. Kept her gaze locked on Kenneth's face. Every gasp and every groan was meant for him. Kenneth felt he dare not look away or even close his own eyes as the tempo increased. She had ordered him not to, and he always did what she told him because she was his wife and he didn't want to risk losing her; he loved her, even though he sometimes hated her. She raised her arms and grasped the bedrail behind her, spread her legs even wider, told Kenneth how this was soooo good, asked him if he liked it too. Bedsprings squealed in time to the jiggling of her pallid flesh, her repetitive oohs and aahs forming a strangely hypnotic chorus. And then she was telling him yes, yes, yes, and she arched her back and stopped breathing, her mouth wide, her eyes wide, still staring directly at him, still looking into his mind as her whole body spasmed.

They collapsed in a heap then, body on body, still conjoined, and she asked Kenneth how he felt, what he was thinking, and he could say nothing, he could find no words, he could only look back at her. Because the truth was that he didn't know what he was feeling or even how he was *meant* to feel right now. Satisfied? Aroused? Enraged? What was the point of all this?

'I think you should go,' she said.

He obeyed at once. Michael, that is. The man who had just been fucking Kenneth's wife right there in front of him, while Kenneth sat on an old wingchair and observed from a distance like the sole audience member at an amateur dramatics performance, which was kind of what this was.

He watched as Michael withdrew and climbed off the bed, unashamed to exhibit his nakedness, mocking Kenneth with a display of virility he was unable to match. Michael pulled on a pair of boxer shorts and went to the door, pausing only to wink at Kenneth before making his way back to his own bedroom.

'Come here, Kenneth,' Polina said, beckoning.

He stood and stepped across the carpeted floor to stand over her. She lay on her back, her breasts uncovered except for a sheen of perspiration. He was wearing pyjamas and a thick dressing gown and slippers, and the contrast felt odd to him.

'You don't mind, do you?' she asked.

It seemed to Kenneth that this ought to be a ridiculous question. He suspected that things would never get this far in any other household. There would be violence, perhaps even death, before a situation like this would be allowed to develop. Any husband worthy of the status would not sit idly by while his wife cheated on him so blatantly.

But perhaps that was the point. He wasn't worthy. He couldn't give Polina what she deserved from a husband. Simon had seen to that.

Simon says watch what I'm doing now. WATCH!

'No,' he said. 'I don't mind. If it keeps you happy.'

'I'm still a young woman,' she said. 'Sometimes I need a man. You understand that, yes?'

'Yes,' he said, grasping her implication that he wasn't a real man. He was lacking. A failure.

'And . . .' She reached out a hand, untied the belt of his dressing gown, slipped her fingers beneath the folds of material. 'I thought maybe it would help you, too. I thought you might like to watch.'

He was aware of her touch on him and wished she would stop,

because it was having no physical effect, and that just made him feel even more of an abject failure, and he was also aware that what she'd said wasn't true – she didn't do any of this for his benefit, but for her own, because she got a kick out of being watched while she shagged a man who had no damn business being in their bedroom.

'Come to bed,' she said. 'We can try things. Maybe we will have success now.'

He considered the invitation. Considered the prospect of ever-increasing embarrassment and humiliation and frustration as she manhandled him, pulling and prodding and rubbing while his mind burst with images and sounds from his childhood – *Simon says stop crying, this is fun, for Christ's sake!*

He stepped out of arm's reach, retied his belt. 'I'm going down for some cocoa,' he said.

He left the room and plodded down the staircase. He put a lamp on in the kitchen, and Barclay gave a whimper of surprise and looked up at him. Kenneth switched the kettle on, then sat at the table and stared into space while he waited for it to boil.

It was at times like this, alone at night, that he worried most about himself, about what he was doing with his life, about his state of mind. He feared that he was heading for a breakdown. The idea that getting married would rescue him from his pit of despair had proven to be a disastrous miscalculation. He was worse off than ever. Trapped.

And now things had become more complicated, the way ahead more fraught. Polina's antics in the bedroom tonight were already being swept into the dark recesses of his brain.

That was no coincidence yesterday.

Izzy Lambert had run into him deliberately outside Raynor's. At the time it had seemed extraordinarily clumsy, avoidable even, but he had been willing to put that to one side. But then came the conversation, and for a while that too had seemed natural enough.

Until the questioning about Rosie. That sudden flash of memory about something her workmate at the bookshop had just happened to mention to her.

Bullshit.

She had known from the start. Probably seen the news report. She was just itching to drop that grenade casually into their little chat, see what devastation it caused.

And then – *and then* – to bring the Cunliffe girl into it as well! Did she think he was stupid or something, that he wouldn't see what she was trying to do?

But why? What was her role in all this? Why had she decided to help the police, and why were they willing to make use of her in that way?

Because that was what was happening. He knew that for a fact. When he walked out of the café yesterday, he didn't simply traipse down the road to his car, oh no. What he did was circle the block, wait until he saw Izzy leave, and then go back in there. He put on a pretty good act with that waitress, saying that he was hoping to catch Izzy still there because she'd given him the name of that policeman she knew and he'd already forgotten it and he was hoping to get some confidential advice from him, and did she have any idea what his name might be?

The waitress did know, and she told him, and he thanked her with a smile on his face, even though what he really wanted to do was scream the place down and overturn a few tables.

Josh Frendy.

The same cop who'd come to his workshop at the school. The same cop who'd put it to him that doubts had been cast on his version of events.

They were on to him.

How? How had that happened? Not just in connection with Rosie, but Heather too.

And another thing – how did Izzy just *happen* to be outside Raynor's as he was coming out? Nobody knew he was going there; he didn't even know himself until last night. She must have just seen him go in there, watched through the window as he bought the bracket, and then decided to turn it into an opportunity to quiz him.

But that was one hell of a coincidence, and he didn't like coincidences.

Too many questions. Too much to worry about. Polina hadn't stood a chance in that bedroom, not with all this shit constantly circling in his brain.

He had fond memories of Izzy Lambert. Images of her sitting on the ground in the sunshine, lost in her books. And their conversations! How her passion for reading, her love of stories, had come across so clearly. A strange and lonely girl, but with a good heart.

If she carried on like this, she would end up dead.

And that would be such a shame.

19

Izzy was thirteen when the new girl arrived at school, and she was instantly drawn to her. Her name was Ciara, and, like Izzy, she seemed to have difficulty making friends. In class, she always sat at the back, in the farthest corner, and made no attempt to contribute to discussions. At break time, she could generally be found standing by the railings, watching the other students playing and chatting and laughing. Her face was never brightened by a smile.

Izzy approached her one day. Went right up to her and introduced herself and asked her if she was settling in at school.

'It's okay,' Ciara said. 'I probably won't be here very long.'

'Why's that?' Izzy asked.

'Because we move every couple of years. My mum and dad like to buy a house, do it up, then sell it and move to a better one in a nicer area. We've been all over the country.'

'Where do you live now?'

'It's called Bramley Lane. Do you know it?'

Izzy nodded. 'That's a nice road. The houses are really big.'

Even though she hadn't got to know Ciara properly yet, she could detect the sadness in her. The poor girl was being shunted from pillar to post, unable to put down roots or make friends before being ripped away from them and transported to a new and unfamiliar location, and all so her parents could have a better lifestyle. It seemed so cruel.

'Do you read much?' Izzy asked.

Ciara nodded. 'I've read the Harry Potter books a million times.'

'Me too. What are you reading now?'

Ciara reached into her bag, pulled out a dog-eared paperback.

'Oh, I don't know that one,' Izzy said. 'Is it good? What's it about?'

And so a friendship began. One of the few true friendships Izzy ever had at Hemingway.

The first big lie came about a month later.

There had been smaller lies before then. Saying she had eaten when she hadn't. She was as skinny as a rake and clearly had issues related to food, but she hadn't taken it to extremes, not like some other girls Izzy had seen.

This one wasn't about food. She came in one day with her fingers strapped together. Told everyone she'd broken her little finger playing netball. Plausible enough. But not to Izzy.

'Looks painful,' she said to Ciara.

'It's okay,' Ciara said. 'It'll heal.'

'Did you really do that playing netball?'

'Yeah. What are the chances, right?'

'Million to one, probably. Maybe even higher.'

Izzy left it at that. She didn't want to come right out with it and call her a liar, not to someone who was pretty much the only friend she had.

But that was the problem. She had failed to nip it in the bud, and so it grew. Ciara started going off sick – a day here, a few days there. When she eventually turned up at school again, she would say it was period pain or the flu or some such. All lies, but her parents supplied her with the appropriate sick notes to explain her absence and excuse her from sporting activities.

And then one day Ciara showed up with her arm in a cast.

'I fell down the stairs,' she explained. She accompanied it with a laugh, as if to say, *Stupid me, I did it again!* And everyone else laughed along with her and signed her cast and thought nothing more of it.

Everyone except Izzy.

'How did you manage to fall down the stairs?' she asked when they were alone.

'I tripped. My dad calls me a klutz. I'm always doing stuff like that.'

'What did you trip on?'

'Just the carpet, I think.'

'The carpet?'

'Yeah.'

'Uh-huh. Ciara . . . is there something you want to tell me?'

'Like what?'

'I don't know. Anything. About stuff that's happening to you, at home maybe.'

She felt how Ciara teetered with indecision, how she wanted to open up and let it all out, but at the same time knew she couldn't do it.

'I'm not sure what you're going on about, Izzy.'

'Please, Ciara. You need to talk to someone about this. If not me, then somebody else. A doctor or one of the teachers.'

A flash of annoyance then. 'I've got nothing to tell them. I had an accident, that's all.'

Izzy was on the verge of crying herself. 'Please, Ciara. I'm your friend. I'm trying to help you.'

Ciara stared for a long, long time. Tears welling in her eyes, words bubbling up in her throat, just awaiting permission to be released.

And then a sniff, a tightening of the lips, the sense of everything being reined back in and imprisoned inside where it would fester.

'This isn't one of your fucking novels, Izzy. Leave me alone.'

She stormed off, took her cloud of hurt with her. Izzy watched her friend's departing back and felt the helplessness pressing down on her.

She spent the night lying awake, thinking only about Ciara and what she should do. At times she damned her gift and wished she could accept Ciara's story just as everyone else had. At other times she was supremely grateful for her unusual talent, because perhaps this was the best opportunity she had ever had to do some good with it, to right wrongs, to save her friend.

The next day she made an appointment for a confidential discussion with her form teacher, Mrs Gordon.

'First of all,' she said, 'I want you to know that this isn't about me. I'm fine. It's about my friend.'

Mrs Gordon's smile was beatific, and Izzy soaked up her genuine interest and desire to help. It bolstered her confidence that she was doing the right thing.

'Are you willing to say which friend it is?'

Izzy wanted to laugh at the way the question was framed, because she had only one real friend.

'Ciara.'

'What about her?'

'I think . . . I think somebody is hurting her.'

Grave concern furrowed the teacher's brow. 'What do you mean?'

'Her broken arm. And her finger that time. And all the times she's been off ill. I think somebody's abusing her.'

A long pause, because there was a lot to take in here, a lot to assess. 'Who do you think is doing those things, Izzy?'

'I'm not sure. Her parents, probably. Maybe someone else in her family.'

'Did Ciara tell you this?'

'No. She denies it.'

'Then what makes you think—?'

'I just know, okay? She's my best friend. She can't hide things from me.'

Another lengthy pause. 'Izzy, this is a very serious allegation. If you haven't got any proof, then—'

'I don't need proof. I know Ciara. I know what she's going through. Please, somebody has to help her. I can't do it by myself.'

She started crying. Mrs Gordon passed her a tissue and clutched her hand when she was done.

'What do you want to happen, Izzy?'

'Talk to her. Ask her about her injuries. Nobody ever comes right out and asks her. I think if they did – like a teacher or someone – then she might talk about it. Please. Before it's too late.'

Mrs Gordon mulled it over. 'All right. We'll bring her in and have a chat. But if she denies it again—'

'I understand. Really, I do. But we have to try. I couldn't stand it if something happened to her and I hadn't said anything.'

'Leave it with me, Izzy. Go to your next lesson. I'll sort something out.'

And she would, Izzy could tell. She was taking it seriously.

'Thank you. Thank you so much.'

She left, the tears flowing once more. It had been one of the hardest things she had ever done. A betrayal of sorts, but a necessary one, even if it meant that Ciara would never speak to her again.

Later in the day, the French lesson was interrupted by the arrival of Mrs Gordon, who asked if she might have a quiet word with Ciara. Izzy noticed how Ciara looked at her before leaving the room and felt a stab of guilt.

It was her final image of her friend.

When the home-time bell sounded and Izzy returned to her

form room to collect her things, she was asked by Mrs Gordon to stay behind for a few minutes.

'I thought you'd like to know,' Mrs Gordon said, 'that you were right. It wouldn't be proper for me to go into details, but we think there are things going on in Ciara's life that shouldn't be. She didn't come right out with it, but there was enough in what she told us for us to arrange immediate protection for her. She's safe now, and it's thanks to you. I'm sure it must have been difficult for you, but you did the right thing. A good thing.'

Izzy thought about those words for a long time afterwards. *The right thing. A good thing.* It made it easier to look at the empty desk in the classroom. Wherever Ciara was, she wasn't being hurt, and that was all that mattered. For the first time in her life, Izzy felt that she had done something really beneficial with her powers. It was a comfort that helped to salve the pain of her restored loneliness.

And then, two weeks later, Mrs Gordon called her in again.

She didn't need to say anything. Izzy instantly felt her pain, her distress, her reluctance to talk about this. Tears were staining Izzy's cheeks before a word was uttered.

'We heard some distressing news today,' Mrs Gordon began. 'I wanted you to hear it from me first, before the rumours started.'

'It's Ciara, isn't it?'

'Yes, darling, it is. It saddens me deeply to tell you that Ciara has taken her own life.'

Izzy sat and stared for the longest time, until the world turned blurry and the teacher's voice seemed a faint echo. When she blinked, she saw that Mrs Gordon had produced tissues for them both.

'Why?' Izzy asked. 'Why did she do that? She was safe. We saved her, didn't we?'

'That's what I thought, too. Ciara left a note. She said she couldn't bear to live with the shame of everyone knowing what had been going on in her family. And even though life had been so cruel to her, she desperately didn't want to go into care.'

Izzy took this in, spat out her immediate thought. 'It was my fault. I caused this.'

'No, honey, no. That's not true. This is why I needed to break the news to you. I had a feeling you might react like this. But you're not responsible for what happened to Ciara. If anyone's to blame, it's her parents, for the way they treated her for years.'

'But I told on her. I broke up her family.'

'You told the truth, and anybody else in your shoes would have done the same. She was being abused, and you stopped that happening. You had no way of knowing where that would lead.'

'If I'd said nothing, Ciara would still be alive. She'd still be my friend.'

'Perhaps. Or perhaps her abuse would have grown so bad that it would have killed her anyway. Please, Izzy, don't beat yourself up about this. You did the right thing.'

They talked some more. Mrs Gordon did her best to console her, told her she would contact her mother, arrange for Izzy to see the school counsellor. And when Izzy came away, that phrase was ringing in her ears again.

The right thing.

It didn't feel like the right thing.

It felt like she had taken Ciara's life with her own hands.

20

Izzy spent much of Monday morning thinking about Ciara and about the numerous other episodes in her life that had gone disastrously awry. It seemed to her that every time she tried to put her powers to good use, some supernatural overseer punished her for daring to rise above her station. So what was the point of a gift like hers if it led only to misery? Did nobody think about that when they were handing out abilities willy nilly?

She had dared to believe that the Kenneth Plumley situation might finally be her chance to prove herself wrong, to discover that she really was capable of making a positive difference, an improvement. But no. She couldn't even get off the starting block.

She wondered if she should take it as a hint. Perhaps someone up there was saying, *Look, I'm making this as difficult for you as I can because you'll end up in the creek without a whatsit, just like you always do. For your own good, don't rock the boat. You want to start eating forbidden fruit, you'll pay for it, and believe me it's not the first time I've said that.*

It was time for a break – from the shop and from her mood. She looked across at Melissa and said, 'I'm going for a coffee.' Didn't even bother to ask if Melissa wanted one too.

She went into the room behind the counter. It contained a small kitchen area and a table and some wooden chairs, but what Izzy most liked about it was that there were lots more of her friends here. Not people friends but book friends, the friends that nobody else seemed to care about. Precariously tall piles of second-hand books everywhere you looked. It was like an ever-shrinking maze, but Abel wouldn't stop bringing them in and piling them high in the vain hope that one day the shelves in the shop would magically clear themselves of enough room to house them all.

Izzy put the kettle on and navigated her way carefully around the room, idly picking up books at random in an effort to entice her mind down from its unceasing treadmill. When the kettle had boiled, she made an instant coffee, then sat and began reading the last book she had grabbed, without even checking what it was. It was an ageing hardback, its cover in tatters. Its first sentence read: 'He lay flat on the pine-needled floor of the forest, his chin on his folded arms, and high overhead the wind blew in the tops of the pine trees.'

Shit, she thought.

She flipped it closed, studied the fading lettering on the spine. *For Whom the Bell Tolls*, by Ernest Hemingway.

Hemingway. Like the school. The school that she had attended. And Ciara. And Rosie. The school where Kenneth Plumley still worked.

Shit.

She pushed the book away. So much for distractions.

She decided to go back into the shop, chat about something frivolous with Melissa.

She got as far as the doorway. Melissa was just closing the till, her other hand pushing something into her back pocket.

'Everything okay?' Izzy asked loudly.

Melissa jumped, whirled. 'Yeah. Fine.' She gestured vaguely toward the street. 'Just sold another copy of that new diet book everyone's going crazy for. Tempted to try it myself!'

Izzy glanced through the front window. There was no sign of

any customer, and even if one had recently left, Melissa had taken a hell of a long time closing the till following the transaction.

She continued to stare at Melissa. Guilt emanated from the girl like heat from a radiator. Izzy had no proof, though. If she had walked in a few seconds earlier, she might have caught Melissa in the act, but she couldn't accuse her now, not on such flimsy evidence, even if she had no doubt about what had just transpired.

Melissa turned away, slunk back to her chair. Izzy made herself count to ten before resuming her own place behind the counter, but she was still fuming – not just about Melissa, but also about all the other crap that had stormed back into her head with a vengeance.

Fuck this heightened empathy shit!

For the rest of the day, Izzy and Melissa hardly spoke. Izzy kept throwing accusing glances towards her colleague, while Melissa studiously pretended not to notice, which only served to raise Izzy's blood pressure even more.

When closing time rolled around, Izzy felt no relief, and she had no intention of allowing this matter to disturb her sleep tonight.

'Before you go,' she said, 'do you mind helping me to cash up?'

Sudden fear in Melissa. 'Why? You always do the cashing up when we're both here.'

'I know. Just thought it would speed things up a bit.'

'We haven't been that busy today. I don't really think it's a job for two people.'

'I don't agree. If we both did it, we could check each other's figures.'

'Why would we do that?'

'Well, you know, in case of mistakes. A few times lately the amounts haven't tallied.'

Melissa stared. 'Uh-huh.'

'So I just thought, if we went through it together—'

Melissa dismissed the suggestion with a wave of her hand. 'I don't think we need to do that, Izzy. Besides, I have to get home.' She started to head towards the stock room.

'Are you worried about something?'

Melissa halted. 'What do you mean?'

'The cash. The amount in the till. Is something about it bothering you?'

'Don't be ridiculous. Why would it—?'

'Because that's the signal you're sending out. Is the till going to be light again today?'

Melissa put her hands on her hips. 'Izzy, are you accusing me of something?'

'I don't know. Should I be? Several times lately the till has been short. I've been making it up out of my own pocket because I don't want either of us to get into trouble.'

Melissa's features hardened and she shook her head. 'I'm not listening to this.' She disappeared into the back room.

Izzy trailed after her. 'Melissa, please. I'm not trying to start a fight here, and I'm not going to grass you up. I just think we need—'

'Grass me up! For what? I haven't done anything. What are you talking about?'

'The money! Ten pounds here, twenty there. How much was it today, Melissa? Thirty this time?'

'Oh, fuck off, Izzy. I'm going home.'

She grabbed her coat, but Izzy remained in the doorway, blocking her exit.

'We have to talk. This can't go on. I've been covering your arse, but I can't afford to keep doing it.'

'Just get out of my way.'

'I will when we've talked about it. Is it your boyfriend? Is he making you steal for him?'

'I'm not— Jesus, will you listen to yourself? Making up all this shit about me. You're crazy. I haven't done anything.'

'Then you won't mind turning out your pockets.'

'What?'

'Your pockets. If you're innocent, you won't mind turning them out, will you?'

Melissa stood open-mouthed for a few seconds. 'I'm not doing anything for you, Izzy. You're not the fucking police. Now get out of my way!'

She marched straight towards Izzy, who didn't budge. Before Melissa could slam into her, Izzy raised her arms and pushed Melissa away, harder than she intended, and Melissa back-pedalled into one of the book piles and fell hard, bringing a cascade of books down on top of her.

Izzy stepped forward, wanting to apologise.

'You bitch!' Melissa yelled. She jumped to her feet, and for a split-second Izzy thought she was about to get into her first fight since her early teens, all scratching and hair-pulling and screaming. But Melissa was now armed with a book, which she threw straight at Izzy.

Izzy batted it away and shouted 'Melissa!' but another book came her way and then another. Izzy circled the room, seeking refuge, but the bombardment increased in severity, missile after literary missile, some going wide but others finding their mark and bursting apart in explosions of fragile pages. Izzy's last resort was a desperate counter-attack, and she grabbed the nearest tome and hurled it in Melissa's general direction, only to see it smack into the corner of a bookcase and flap chaotically to the floor like a bird that has stunned itself on a pane of glass.

And then she saw the figure standing in the doorway, and she felt the colour drain from her face; saw how Melissa also stopped dead, her next salvo still clutched in her hands. The sudden intense silence was broken only by a lone page see-sawing its way to the graveyard of books beneath it.

'What are you doing?' Abel asked. His voice was not raised or tinged with anger, but soft and pained, which somehow made the offence he had just witnessed even more shocking.

Justifying their actions was beyond Izzy. All she could manage was, 'Abel, I'm so sorry.'

Abel stepped forward into the devastation, staring at his crippled books and experiencing an immense sorrow that saddened Izzy to her core. He crouched and picked one of them up, and the cover came away in his hand.

'Why?' he asked.

Izzy looked across at Melissa, whose eyes were wide in fear that Izzy might sacrifice her.

'Abel ...' she began, but couldn't formulate anything further that wouldn't sound pathetic and hollow.

'Get out,' Abel said quietly. 'Both of you.'

There was no point in arguing, and Melissa was already running out of the door. Slowly, Izzy collected her things, took one last look at Abel hunched over his broken treasures, and then left.

She cried all the way to her car. A mix of shame, anger and desperate unhappiness drove out the tears. Self-pity made itself heard when she got behind the wheel. The number of people in her circle of friends and acquaintances was tiny, and it seemed to her that she had just reduced that count by a substantial percentage. She had totally mishandled the situation with Melissa, who would probably never speak to her again. Not that they were likely to meet again, given that Abel would surely sack both of them in the morning.

Poor Abel! What had she been thinking, throwing books like that? Such wanton vandalism appalled her. She deserved to lose her job.

She started driving home. She needed someone to hold her and comfort her. She needed Andy. And then Izzy realised that her partner was working a late shift, and that the only thing she was heading towards was an empty evening in an empty flat with a microwave meal and cheap plonk to dull the pain, and it felt like a prison sentence.

Anger erupted again. This was all the fault of Kenneth Plumley. He was like a black cloud floating above her, darkening her mood, sucking all the joy out of her life. If it wasn't for him and what he was doing to her, she would have come into work today with a spring in her step, keen to be with books and readers and Melissa and Abel. If she had broached the subject of Melissa's stealing at all, it would have been with much more humanity.

But no. Kenneth was there, always there, scratching at her thoughts, refusing to let her heal.

At the first roundabout, an impulse took control of Izzy's arms, causing her to miss her turning and come back on herself.

Her new destination was Hemingway High School.

21

She parked in the same spot as she had on the previous occasion. From there, she could see that Kenneth's white van was still on the school grounds.

She waited, and wondered what she was doing here.

He'll just go home, she thought. He'll get in his van and I'll follow him all the way to his crummy cottage, and that'll be my evening wasted.

The mood she was in, she didn't care. She would repeat this every night if that was what it took. At some point, he would do something incriminating – maybe even lead her to where he was keeping Heather and Rosie, dead or alive. She just had to stay on his back.

A girl came out through the school gates, clutching a stack of folders to her chest and staring at her phone. She walked away from Izzy, then halted in front of the school sign down by the main entrance, still studying her screen.

Kenneth appeared five minutes later. As before, he manoeuvred the van onto the road, padlocked the gates and began driving away. Izzy fired up her engine, put it into first gear.

The van had stopped again, just up the road.

Izzy craned her neck, but couldn't quite make out what was happening. Had Kenneth forgotten something? Was he about to come back to the workshop? She turned off her music and opened the window, but by that time the van was driving away again.

And that was when she realised that the girl was missing.

She had been standing there, right there by the sign, where the van had stopped, and now she was gone.

'No, no, no . . .' Izzy said. She started to pull out, but then a huge delivery lorry came round the bend behind her, preventing her from moving while it squeezed past, travelling at about five miles an hour, and all she could do was fall in behind it, trailing after it while she waited for an opportunity to overtake.

'Come on, come on,' she said.

The lorry's brake lights came on, and Izzy put her foot down and sped past it, forcing an oncoming driver to perform an emergency stop that caused him to lurch forward in his seat. He leaned on his horn and yelled something as she drew level, but her attention was already on the road ahead – the road which no longer contained a white van.

'Shit! Where did you go?'

She accelerated to the junction, then slammed on her brakes. She looked up and down the busier main road. Which way had he gone?

She chose the route that would take Kenneth back towards his house. That would be the most likely. Even if he wasn't going all the way home, he would take the girl to somewhere that felt familiar to him.

She put her foot to the floor again and stirred the lever up through the gears. The little Fiat didn't have many horses under the bonnet, but this wasn't a fast road and she eventually managed to close the gap with the vehicle ahead. Three cars in front of that was a white van.

Has to be him, she thought. Has to be. But what if I lose him again? Maybe even permanently. A girl's life is at stake here. And what if I don't lose him? What if I manage to head him off and he gets violent? What then?

She decided she needed help.

Taking one hand off the wheel, she dipped it into her bag on the passenger seat and found her phone. Eyes flicking between the view ahead and her phone, she managed to locate Josh Frendy's mobile number in her contacts. She rang him and put it on loudspeaker.

'Hello?'

'Josh? Josh, it's me. Izzy Lambert.'

'Hi, Izzy. How are—?'

'Listen, I don't have time to talk. I'm following Kenneth Plumley. He's got another girl.'

'What? Izzy, what are you—?'

'He's abducted another girl. From the school. He's got her in his van now.'

'How do you know all this?'

'I saw it with my own eyes. I'm serious, Josh. I'm following him, but I'm scared I'm going to lose him. I don't know what to—'

'All right, listen to me, Izzy. Stay calm. Where are you?'

'I'm on Falmouth Road, heading east.'

'Okay, good. You said you can see the van?'

'Yes.'

'Can you see its registration number?'

'No, but I already know it.' She recited it to him.

'Great. Stay on the line, I'm sending help. Keep your distance and don't do anything heroic, but if he changes direction, let me know. Okay?'

'Okay. Yes. Please hurry.'

The phone went quiet, but she could see that the connection was still open. She drove for another couple of minutes, almost afraid to blink in case the van disappeared from view.

Approaching a roundabout, the van indicated a left turn. Izzy waited for it to complete the turn before she put on her own indicators.

'Josh, are you there?'

'Yes, I'm here. Are you okay?'

'I'm fine. The van has just gone left onto Warwick Road.'

'Got it. We're closing in, Izzy. Keep your distance from him.'

'I will.'

She took the turn, and saw that there was now only one vehicle between her car and the van. A few hundred yards later, the van turned right but the car in front of Izzy continued straight on.

'We're turning right. I don't know the road name. Gimme a sec . . .'

She slowed to catch sight of the street sign.

'Utley Avenue. We're on Utley Avenue.'

'You're doing great, Izzy. If he stops, just pull in and wait for us to get there.'

She didn't answer, but kept her focus on the van's tail lights. Its brake lights came on, and Izzy slowed her own car to maintain the distance.

'I think he's stopping! No, wait! He's doing a left turn.'

She followed again, but this time couldn't catch the road name.

'I don't know what this road is called. It's about the third turn on the left from Utley Avenue. And—'

There was no sign of her quarry.

'I can't see him! I can't see him!'

'It's okay, Izzy. Don't panic. We're almost there.'

She stopped at the cross junction, looked both ways. No sign of Plumley in either direction. On a whim, she went left, flooring the accelerator pedal again. This was a quiet residential area. Nobody around to ask about a van. She went right, then left, going back to her original route. Still no large white van. She decided she must have made the wrong choice, so she went back on herself and then the other way at the cross junction.

'I can't fucking find him!' she screamed into the air.

Ahead, the only vehicle lights she could see belonged to a dark Mini. She threw her car left and rocketed it towards the last house.

'Herbert Street. I'm on Herbert Street. About to go left.'

She didn't give way at the junction, but took a chance and hurtled around the corner at full pelt.

The headlights were blinding.

Izzy slammed on her brakes, spun her steering wheel to avoid a collision. Her car went into a tailspin, and even though she managed to dampen most of the car's momentum, she still felt the crunch as its side struck the front of the oncoming van.

Kenneth Plumley's van.

And then she was out of the car, diving round to the passenger door of the van and yanking it open, seeing that the seat was unoccupied and yelling at Kenneth, 'Where is she? What have you done with her?' She had no thought of her own safety now; the cautionary words of Josh had already been forgotten. Instead, she raced to the back of the van and unfastened the doors, saw that the rear was also empty. *Where is she?*

And then Kenneth was out of the van, coming towards her, and still she felt no fear. She closed the gap, got in his face, slapped her hands against his chest and shoved him, her own face contorted as she called him a perverted bastard and demanded to know what he'd done with the girls, what the fuck had he done?

And then the air was filled with wailing and pulsing blue light and voices, and hands grabbed her and dragged her away, even though she implored them to listen to her, to stop this man, to force the truth out of him and then lock the sick fuck away for the rest of his miserable life.

22

The uniformed police officers were courteous and kind, and they sat her in the back of their car while they gently probed her with questions. But what frustrated Izzy was the extent to which they did not seem to appreciate that she had just handed them on a plate one of the most serious offenders this region had ever seen. And while she could accept that Josh Frendy hadn't exactly spread news of her prowess far and wide among his colleagues and that she was therefore having to go over old ground repeatedly for these officers, what she couldn't accept was her view through the car window of Kenneth Plumley's interrogation, which as far as she could tell consisted of a fairly casual chat with an unconcerned policewoman.

'Why aren't you arresting him?' she asked. 'He'll lie to you. You mustn't believe his lies. Don't let him get away with this.'

'Don't worry about him,' the officer behind the wheel said. 'My colleague there is getting his side of the story. Let's just focus on—'

'But that's what he'll give you – a *story*. Don't believe a word of it. He lies through his teeth.'

'As I say, let us talk to him. We'll get to the truth.'

But the tone of his voice felt patronising. She saw him exchange glances with his partner in the passenger seat, and she knew how little they thought of her. They believed she was delusional, a waste of police time.

Another car pulled up and a man got out. Josh Frendy. He went to Plumley's van first and had a brief conversation with the police-woman, then came towards the car in which Izzy was sitting. Seeing Josh headed their way, the driver got out and met him for another catch-up, then both came over to Izzy. The driver opened the rear door.

'Come on out, Izzy,' Josh said. 'Let's have a chat in my car.'

She climbed out and allowed Josh to escort her to his saloon. As they passed the van, she saw Kenneth Plumley glaring at her.

'Josh, you need to arrest him. He took the girl. I saw him. He took all the girls.'

'Okay, Izzy. We'll talk about this in the car.'

She jabbed a finger towards Kenneth and yelled across the street. 'I know what you did. They've got you now, you bastard!'

'In the car,' Josh said, more firmly now.

She sat next to Josh. He started the engine.

'Where are we going?'

'Just around the corner, away from here.'

'Wait. Why? Why do we need to do that? You shouldn't leave him with those officers. I'm not sure they believe what I told them.'

Josh said nothing. He just moved the car a couple of streets and parked up again.

'What's going on, Izzy?' he asked.

She stared at him in disbelief. 'What do you mean? I told you on the phone. He abducted another girl from the school. He somehow persuaded her to get into his van, and now she's disappeared. He's put her somewhere. It can't be far from here. You need to start searching, or make him tell you.'

'You're right,' Josh said. 'She isn't far from here. She lives in that house there.' He pointed to a small terraced house across the street.

'What?'

'Kenneth Plumley gave her a lift home. He often does on a

Monday. The girl stays late for extra help with her French, and if Plumley leaves before her parents can get to her, he takes her home.'

Izzy continued to stare. 'What? No, that can't be right. He took her, just like he took Rosie.'

'No, he didn't. We've checked at the address. She's sitting at home now, listening to music in her bedroom.'

Izzy didn't know what to say. She felt embarrassed and stupid.

'What I want to know,' Josh continued, 'is why you were following him in the first place.'

'You know why. I told you about his lies.'

'Yes, and I told you that I'd checked up on it and found there was no evidence to back your claim. So why couldn't you leave it at that?'

'Because you were wrong. Because he did take Rosie. And because . . . because he also took Heather Cunliffe.'

She saw the shock on his face, felt it reflect back onto her.

'What do you know about Heather Cunliffe?'

'She disappeared, just like Rosie did. I did an online search. You investigated that case too. You believe the same person was responsible for taking both girls, don't you?'

Josh was silent for a moment. 'You've been busy, haven't you? What makes you think Kenneth Plumley abducted Heather?'

'What makes you think he didn't?'

'There's no evidence *anyone* abducted her. She sent text messages to her parents saying she was leaving home.'

'Yeah, but you never believed that, did you? You think someone took her. And you also think the same person took Rosie. That's why you used the word "girls" in the plural when we were in the coffee shop. Why do you think it was the same person?'

Josh shrugged. 'Similarities between the girls, I suppose. Similar age and looks. The way they both vanished into thin air. Nothing concrete.'

'Intuition? A bit like what you think I do?'

'I guess.'

'All right. So why does your intuition tell you it can't be Kenneth Plumley?'

'Because of the school. Why would he go to all the trouble of trying to cover his tracks with Heather Cunliffe, like faking text messages from her, and then draw attention to himself by taking a girl from his own school and going on TV about it? That doesn't make any sense.'

'Maybe. But he's still guilty.'

'How can you be so sure?'

'I asked him.'

A stunned silence. 'You asked him? When did you ask him?'

'Saturday morning. I bumped into him in town.'

'You bumped into him. Just like that. You expect me to believe that?'

'It's the truth.'

'Uh-huh. And then what? You just said to him, "Hey, Kenneth, did you abduct Heather Cunliffe?"'

'Not exactly. We went for a coffee, and then—'

'Wait, wait. You went for coffee? With the man you believe goes round abducting young women?'

'It was necessary. Anyway, I didn't accuse him or anything. We were talking about his appearance on TV, and I just happened to mention there'd been another abduction recently, and I asked him if he'd heard anything about it.'

'And?'

'He denied it, of course. But he was lying again.'

'Your spidey sense?'

'Yes.'

'I see. Izzy—'

'And that's not all. There was other stuff he said. I got the impression that . . .'

'Go on.'

'I think they're dead, Josh. The two girls. I don't think he's keeping them alive somewhere.'

She felt his pain, but then an immediate flash of anger. 'Izzy,' he said. 'You have to stop this.'

'Stop what?'

'This . . . this *campaign* against Plumley. I'm a police detective. I have to work with facts and evidence. I can't do anything with this stuff you're giving me, no matter how much you believe it's true.'

'It *is* true. You don't think I'm just making it up, do you?'

'I don't know what to think. All I know is that I've got a busy caseload, which includes trying to find Rosie Agutter, and I could do without you landing yourself in trouble for harassing a member of the public.'

'A member of the public? He's public enemy number one, Josh. He's—'

'Enough, Izzy! For your own good, stay out of this and let us do our job.'

She stared at him for a while, then turned to look straight ahead through the windscreen.

'Fine, then. Pardon me for interfering with your precious police work. Could you take me back to my car now, please? I'd like to go home, while you have a nice chat with your new friend Kenneth. Maybe you can take him for some lemon drizzle cake.'

'Izzy . . .'

She refused to look at him, and when he gave up and started the car, she wished today had never happened.

23

Izzy was first to get to the bookshop on Tuesday morning. Andy had arrived home in the early hours, and was fast asleep when Izzy left. Sometimes she hated the way Andy's shifts got in the way of their home life. She really needed a companion at the moment.

Once she had unlocked the shop and put some lights on, she went straight to the back room. Abel had tidied it up, insofar as this room could ever be called tidy. Not a damaged book or torn page in sight. Despite the lack of evidence of casualties, she cringed at the memory of the warfare that had taken place here.

She returned to her place behind the counter. The shop door opened. Melissa entered, walked straight up to Izzy. Izzy prepared herself for round two.

'I just want you to know,' Melissa said, 'that I'm sorry. Really, really sorry.'

Izzy could see the tears forming in Melissa's eyes and felt the sting of them in her own.

'I'm sorry too,' she answered. 'I should never have come down on you like that.'

'No, you were right. I did take some money. Things have been hard for me lately, and—'

'You don't have to explain.'

'I do. You deserve an explanation, especially as you've been covering up for me. I'll pay you back, I promise.'

'You don't have to do that.'

'I want to. I will. And I want you to know that I've left Sean. I broke up with him last night.'

'You did? How did he take it?'

'He got angry, made some threats. The usual Sean approach.'

'Are you worried about what he might do?'

'Nah. I'll just stay out of his way. I've moved back to my parents' house. Sean was a bad influence on me, and it took me too long to see it. So . . . this is me turning over a new leaf.'

The tears were flowing down Izzy's cheeks now. 'Come here,' she said, and went around the counter. She flung her arms around Melissa and pulled her in tight. 'I'll help you,' she said. 'If you need anything, you only have to ask.'

Abel came through the door about half an hour later. Izzy and Melissa froze and awaited his pronouncement. He stood a couple of feet in front of them like an old colonel inspecting his troops.

'Have you two sorted out your differences?' he asked.

'Yes,' Izzy said. 'Yes, we have. It won't happen again.'

He nodded. 'Then that's good enough for me.'

He turned to walk away again, and Izzy stepped forward. 'Abel, I'll pay for the books. Just let me know how much.'

He smiled. 'You know as well as I do that it's not about money. Those books are irreplaceable. What I do here, I do for love, and I think that's true of both of you, too. It's why I employ you. What you did last night was unforgivable, but unless I'm a terrible judge of character, I'm sure you've already felt the pain of your crime.'

'We have,' Izzy said.

'Yes,' Melissa said. 'So . . . do we still have a job?'

Abel looked at each of them in turn. 'For as long as you need it.'

Izzy wanted to cry, and she felt that Melissa did too. But these would be happy tears. Today was going to be a much better day.

* * *

Abel left the shop after about an hour. At lunchtime, Melissa also left to do a little shopping. Izzy served the only customer in the shop, then went to the back room to make a coffee, only to hear the door open again before she could even reach the kettle. She returned to the front of the shop, a welcoming smile already in place.

Her smile withered when she saw who had dared to come here. Kenneth Plumley.

He looked very different from when she had gone to the café with him, and even from last night. He seemed more ragged. His eyes drooped as if from exhaustion or the effects of drugs, and there was a nervous twitch in his upper lip.

'What do you want?' she demanded. 'How did you find me?'

'You told me,' Kenneth said. 'Remember? On Saturday, when you *accidentally* bumped into me. You told me where you worked.'

'Okay, so you know where I work. That doesn't explain what you're doing here.'

He rotated his head slowly, taking in his surroundings. 'It's a bookshop. I might want to buy a book.'

'So buy one and get out.'

'I like to take my time. Bookshops are for browsing, aren't they? I'm browsing.'

But he didn't move, and his eyes remained focused on Izzy. There was danger in those eyes.

'My colleagues will be back soon,' she said. 'You should leave.'

His smile was humourless. 'You've changed so much, Izzy.'

'And so have you, Kenneth. So have you.'

'You used to be such a quiet girl. Studious. Always with your head buried in a book. You wouldn't have said boo to a goose back then.'

'And you wouldn't have attacked teenage girls.'

The twitch in his lip became more pronounced.

'Yes, about that. I think we need to clear the air.'

She shook her head. 'Clear as a bell as far as I'm concerned. Now, are you going to leave, or do I need to phone the police?'

'You think they'll listen to you after the way you behaved yesterday? You're making a fool of yourself, Izzy.'

'Well, I'd rather be a fool than a monster. Say what you've got to say, and then get out.'

She hoped she sounded tough, but her heart was fluttering around her chest and the bones in her legs had turned to rubber.

'You're mistaken about me. I haven't done anything wrong.'

His nose might as well have been growing, his lies were that patent.

'I don't believe you. You know what happened to Rosie Agutter, and you know what happened to Heather Cunliffe.'

'I don't, Izzy. You're wrong.'

More bare-faced deceit. Every word was helping to establish his guilt in Izzy's eyes. She needed no further proof.

'Are they alive?'

'How would I know?'

She shook her head. 'This is going nowhere. I'd like you to leave the shop now, please.'

He stepped closer to the counter, pressed his paunch into its edge in what seemed almost an obscene gesture. He leaned forward as if to divulge a secret. Izzy wanted to move backwards, but didn't want to reveal how frightened she was.

'I'm worried about you, Izzy.'

'You don't need to worry about me. I'm fine.'

'Well, that's true for the moment, but I was hoping you'd see sense. You shouldn't be making accusations about me.'

'Is that a threat?'

'A threat. A promise. A warning. Stop what you're doing, Izzy, or you'll get hurt. I wouldn't want to see you get hurt.'

His menace infected her, made her a shadow of him. 'Listen to me, you fucking pervert. I don't know what happened to you to make you like this, and I don't care. I'm not a schoolgirl anymore. I will fight you. You come near me, and I will rip your balls off. Until then, I won't stop hassling the police until they investigate you properly for what you've done. That's also a threat, a promise, a warning. Do you understand me?'

He straightened up, as if electrified by her counter-attack. She sensed real fear in him, and uncertainty as to how to deal with it.

'You're making a mistake, Izzy. A huge mistake.'

'My biggest mistake was becoming your friend, Kenneth. I thought I knew you.'

'You don't know anything,' he said with a sombre sadness. 'Nothing at all.'

He left the shop then, his shoulders hunched as he lumbered down the street. Izzy's legs finally admitted defeat, and she collapsed onto a chair. She felt a surge of pride at having stood up to the bully, but also concern that she might have just made things a hundred times worse. Perhaps it would have been better if she had just said yes to his demands, even if she planned to ignore them. Had it really been necessary to antagonise him like that?

It had largely been beyond her control. His lies, his guilt had filled her with loathing. His attempts at intimidation had pumped aggression into her. It was all a part of her condition. She was a human mirror for emotions both positive and negative.

She let out a long, slow breath of relief, then buried her face in her hands as she contemplated what she had done.

When the shop door opened again, she leapt out of her chair.

'Miss me?' Melissa asked.

24

He stood in the doorway of a butcher's that had just closed for the day. He wore a thick padded coat, his hood up. He blended into the shadows.

He had a perfect view of the bookshop from here. It was nearly quarter past five. She would be leaving soon.

It's her own fault, he thought. She should have kept her nose out of it. Too late now.

Simon says never tell.

He wondered what Polina would think if she knew he was here now, contemplating extreme violence. What a difference that would make to her opinion of him.

The bookshop lights winked out. End of a long day. End of a short life.

She came out onto the street. Turned her back to him while she locked up.

He readied himself, unsure as to which way she would go, where she had parked her car. He watched as she waited for a gap in the traffic and then hurried across. He backed deeper into the darkness, but she walked away from him. He emerged. Hands deep in pockets, he followed.

She turned down a narrow one-way street. He picked up the pace until he rounded the corner. She was just metres ahead. She had taken out her phone and was chatting away, oblivious to her surroundings. One car went past and then there was emptiness.

He had expected a long pursuit, but this was perfect. He wasn't going to get a better opportunity.

Simon says keep our secrets.

He pulled the length of metal pipe from his coat, closed the gap just as she reached the mouth of an alleyway.

He struck. Side of the head. Her phone shattered and pieces spat across the pavement. She went down, whimpered. He struck again. Stillness.

He raised the pipe once more, ready to crack her skull open like an egg . . .

And then he hesitated.

He looked around. No witnesses. His intention had been to end it here, but now other ideas were tugging at him, familiar urges wresting control. She wasn't really his type, but this was too good an opportunity to squander.

He dragged her into the alleyway and hid her still body behind some bins. Then he went to fetch his vehicle.

He hadn't finished with her yet.

Simon says let's have some fun.

* * *

She came to, her head pulsating. She brought up a hand and found warm, sticky wetness on her scalp. She wondered where she was, what had happened. She had been walking to her car . . .

This wasn't the street. There were no sounds, no lights.

'Hello?' she called. *'Hello?'* Her words echoed in the blackness.

She sat up, and her skull felt ready to explode. She wanted to vomit.

'Hello? Is anyone here? I need help.'

It was cold here, so cold. And yet not a whisper of a breeze.

A click. A brief spark of light. Then another click and the

fire took hold. A lighter. It was brought to a candle and its glow reached out to her.

Her confusion multiplied. Four walls and a floor that seemed to slope at a ridiculous angle. What kind of room—?

Wait. Not a room. A swimming pool. She was at the bottom of an empty swimming pool.

Click. A new flame. More light. Why these candles?

'Hey!' she called out. 'What's going on? Why have you brought me here?'

As she turned to follow the figure moving to the next candle, she slid her hand across the bottom of the pool. Her fingers found something. She picked it up, held it close to her face to scrutinise it in the gloom.

It was a false fingernail, decorated with a red rose.

That was when the panic took over and she started screaming.

25

Josh Frendy hated this aspect of the job. Most parts he really enjoyed, but this one always got him down. He had seen a lot of things over the years, gruesome and terrible things that would give many people nightmares for long afterwards, and they no longer bothered him; he could detach himself from them. He had quickly learned the art of treating a corpse as just a piece of meat. It was essential in his line of work. The jokes, the banter at crime scenes, were all a part of the defence mechanism that protected him and his colleagues from irreparable mental damage.

This, though – the delivery of bad news – always involved people from outside the job, people who would cry and wail and get angry and depressed, people who would break down in front of him. People who would remind him what it was to be human in the face of loss.

Strangely, it was the ones who said nothing that affected him most. The ones who accepted the news as if it was something they heard every day. Their blank expressions haunted him because he knew that they were hiding the pain of the acid bubbling inside them. At some point, hours or even days later, they would have to acknowledge it, and by then there might be nobody there to catch them as they fell.

He parked up at the address Izzy had supplied when she had first walked into the police station. It was a pretty terraced house, small and cosy. A wooden bench in the tiny front garden. A light above the glossy red door. Lights on behind the shaded downstairs windows too.

He prepared himself for what he was going to say. Was cautious optimism an option here? *She hasn't been seen since she left the bookshop several hours ago, and her car hasn't moved, and her phone is in pieces nearby on the street, and there are traces of blood in an alleyway that may be hers. But on the other hand, there's probably a perfectly reasonable explanation, so please don't get too worried about her at this stage.*

Yeah, that'll work.

Shit. I'm overthinking. Let's get this done.

He got out of the car. Unlatched the little wooden gate. Went to the door and rang the bell for the downstairs flat. Its sound was pleasant, like wind chimes.

He tried to remember if Izzy had told him the name of her partner, but it evaded him. Would she be home now?

Movement from inside. A porch door being opened. A fuzzy, blurry-edged shape beyond the frosted glass.

A bolt was drawn back and the front door was pulled open. Josh looked into surprised eyes.

'Hello, Izzy,' he said.

26

'Missing? What do you mean, she's gone missing?'

Izzy had looked at Josh standing there outside their flat, and her first thought had been, My God, he's finally listened to me and arrested Plummers. But that dissipated the instant she saw his face and felt what he was feeling. And now here they were, inside the flat, and Izzy's alarm was growing with every passing second.

'Melissa didn't make it home this evening. She didn't go to her parents' house and she didn't go to her boyfriend's.'

'They've split up.'

'So I understand. She was also supposed to be working as a bartender at The Knight's Arms tonight. She hasn't turned up there either.'

Fingers of dread closed over Izzy's heart and squeezed it. She started towards the sofa, where she'd left her mobile.

'I have her number on my phone. I'll try calling her.'

'No. Izzy, you won't be able to get through to her.'

She stared at him, stunned by his words. 'What do you mean? What aren't you telling me? She's only been missing a few hours and you're already knocking on doors? That's not how you normally do things for missing persons, is it? Not unless— What's happened to her, Josh?'

'We found her phone. It wasn't far from her parked car. She was in the middle of a call to her parents when it was cut off. She was telling them she was on her way home, so it looks like she had no intention of wandering off at that point.'

'She didn't even make it to her car? Oh, my God. What else?'

Josh was silent, his expression pained.

'What else, Josh? I can read you like a book. There's something else you haven't told me.'

'There were . . . possible signs of a violent struggle.'

'Oh, Jesus! She's hurt. Melissa's hurt. You have to find her, Josh. You have to move quickly.'

'We are. Because of the unusual circumstances, we're treating this as a high-priority investigation. Right now, I need you to stay calm and answer some questions, okay?'

Questions, yes. Questions were good.

'Okay.'

'When did you last see Melissa?'

'Just a few hours ago. At the bookshop.'

'At closing time?'

'Yes.'

'Who left the shop first, you or her?'

'I did. I went at five o'clock. Melissa was still there.'

'I see,' he said, but she sensed a lot more in those words. Something of concern.

'What?' she asked.

'We've spoken to the shop's owner. Mr Stern. He told us that *you're* the one who usually locks up when you're both there.'

'Usually, yes. This time was different.'

'Any particular reason?'

She hesitated. She didn't want to tell him about Melissa's stealing. She had asked Melissa to cash up and close the shop as a gesture of faith, to demonstrate her belief in her colleague now that she wanted to change her life. It was meant to be something beautiful. She didn't want to corrupt it. And anyway, it wasn't relevant.

'I thought I'd give her the experience. She doesn't get to do it very often.'

'You trust her?'

'Implicitly.'

'You don't think it's possible she's been involved in any criminal activity?'

She stalled. Did he already know about the cash?

'Why do you ask that?'

'Her boyfriend. *Ex*-boyfriend. He's known to the police. I just wondered if you might have heard about her getting mixed up in anything illegal.'

'No, nothing like that. She's a good girl, Josh. She just has bad taste in men.'

'Yeah, well, that's not uncommon. How well do you know her?'

'Well, we don't mix socially or anything, but we get on okay. She's—'

'But well enough to be aware of something going on in her life?'

'Like what?'

'Her relationship with her ex-boyfriend? Possible threats against her?'

Izzy realised that Josh already knew the answer to this, presumably from talking to Melissa's parents.

'Yes, she did mention that.'

'What, that he was making threats?'

'Yes, but that's got nothing to do with this.'

'What do you mean?'

She began pacing the room. 'He was waiting for her, outside the shop. That's how he got to her.'

'Who? Who are you talking about?'

'Kenneth Plumley, of course. Who else?'

'Plumley?'

'Yes. Don't you see? It's a message. He did this to hurt me, to warn me off.'

Josh came towards her. 'Izzy, this isn't about Kenneth Plumley. It's probably got nothing to do with the disappearance of Rosie Agutter, either.'

She rounded on him. 'Are you blind? Of course it has. It's all connected.'

'There's no evidence for that. People go missing all the time, and there's hardly ever a connection with other disappearances.'

'You believe there's a link between Rosie and Heather.'

'Yes, I think there might be. But Melissa doesn't fit their profile at all. She doesn't look anything like them, and there were no signs of violence in those previous cases. They also weren't associating with known criminals in the way that Melissa has been. You're filling in lines between the dots that shouldn't be there simply because you have a thing against Plumley.'

'No, I'm doing it because he told me this would happen.'

Josh stared at her. 'What are you talking about?'

'It's . . . it's my fault. Kenneth Plumley told me to keep my nose out of it, and I refused. I said all the wrong things, and now poor Melissa—'

'Wait. When was this? When did he warn you?'

'Today. Lunchtime.'

'In the shop?'

'Yes. He came in when Melissa was on a break. He tried to bully me, told me to stop saying things about him. I said I was going to do everything I could to prove he was abducting young girls, and now—'

'Sorry, Izzy. I know I'm repeating myself, but I want to get this absolutely straight. You are saying that Plumley came to the bookshop at lunchtime today and threatened that if you didn't stop trying to blacken his name, he would hurt you or someone close to you.'

'Yes, more or less.'

'More or less?'

'Well, I can't remember the exact words. I was panicking. But yes, it was along those lines.'

'Why didn't you call the police?'

'After what happened yesterday? Would anyone have listened to me?'

Josh didn't reply directly. He said, 'I'll talk to Plumley. Tomorrow I'd like you to come in and give a statement. Are you willing to do that?'

'I'll do anything to get Melissa back. He took her, Josh. It was him. He knows where she is. You have to believe me.'

'Okay. Stay calm. I'm sure we'll find her. You need to relax. Is your partner here?'

'Andy? No. She's on lates.' She headed towards the fridge. 'I need a drink.'

She filled a glass from the wine carton and threw most of it back in one gulp.

'I'm sorry,' she said. 'Do you want one?'

'No, thank you. I don't drink.'

'I'm not an alcoholic, you know.'

'No, I didn't think you were.'

'And I'm not crazy either. Plumley did this. He took Heather, he took Rosie, and now he's taken Melissa. You have to stop him.'

* * *

After Josh had left, she continued to drink. Sleep was out of the question. Hell, even just sitting still for longer than two minutes was a feat in itself. So she drank until her eyes stopped talking to each other.

This was too big for one person. Which was how it felt, no

exaggeration. Isobel versus the world. Nobody listening or believing.

She didn't know what time it was when Andy finally came home, and frankly she didn't care. She needed her.

Andy looked as surprised as she was exhausted. Izzy knew it was unfair of her to land this on her partner now, when all Andy wanted was sleep, but this couldn't wait. The weight was too heavy.

'What are you doing up?' Andy asked.

Izzy went to answer, but all that came out was a sob, followed by a flood of tears.

'Hey,' Andy said, rushing to her. 'What's the matter? What's happened?'

They hugged. Izzy cried some more, then tried to produce sensible sounds not mangled by the tears and the alcohol.

'It's Melissa. She's gone.'

'Gone? You mean sacked? Did you have a fight over the money?'

'No. Gone. Disappeared. Abducted.'

'Abducted? What do you mean? Izzy, what's happened?'

It came out in a jumble then, about talking to Kenneth in town, about chasing after him when she thought he had taken another girl from school, about his threats in the bookshop – although she didn't mention following him to his home and hiding in his garden, because in hindsight even she found it hard to believe she'd taken such a risk.

'You did all that? Jesus, Iz. What the hell were you thinking? You can't go round playing private detective like that. It's fucking dangerous.'

'I know that now! He's taken Melissa.'

'How do you know?'

'I told you. He threatened me. He tried to warn me away and I practically told him to go fuck himself.'

'That doesn't mean he took Melissa.'

'You're as bad as Josh. Of course it does. It's his warped way of sending me a message.'

'Why would he do that? I mean, God forbid anything should happen to you, but if he wanted to get back at you, why didn't he just abduct you?'

'Because it would be too bloody obvious, wouldn't it? I'm the one who's been slinging mud at him. If I disappear, the finger points squarely at him. The police would be all over him like a bad rash. That's the last thing he wants. This is his way of saying, "Look, Izzy, this could just as easily have been you."'

Andy's head-shaking was redundant, because Izzy could feel the doubt radiating from her.

'I don't know, Iz.'

'Well, I do. He's taken her and it's all my fault and I don't know what to do about it and—'

Andy cut her off with another firm embrace. 'Hush now. You've had a lot to drink. You need a good night's sleep. We both do.'

Izzy sniffed wetly. 'I don't think I can sleep.'

'You have to let this thing go. The police are on it, right? Let them do their job. If you're right about Plumley, they'll get him, but that's all the more reason for you to stop antagonising him. I really don't want to see you get hurt, Izzy.'

Izzy nodded, deciding to say no more about it.

Because what was the fucking point?

Even through the alcohol-induced haze she knew for certain that the woman who loved her more than anything else in the world didn't believe a word she had said about Kenneth Plumley.

27

Here we go again, Josh thought. Parked in exactly the same place outside the school. Eyes on the workshop while he waited for the yard to empty.

It was first thing Wednesday morning. The school bell had just been rung, and the last of the students were filtering in through the doors. The silence was eerie after the previous cacophony of laughter, chatter and yells, the yard now a grey desert blotted only by a crisp packet rolling along in the breeze like tumbleweed.

She's nuts, he thought. I've said it before and I'll say it again. She's nuts. It has to be all in her head. The whole thing is too crazy for it not to be.

And yet there was no denying that another young woman had gone missing. A woman who worked alongside Izzy. The connection was too strong to ignore. She had made a complaint, an allegation, and it had to be followed up. That was his job.

But he still thought she was nuts.

He got out of the car and strolled across to the workshop, prepared this time in case Plumley jumped out of the shadows again with another sharp implement in his hand.

But he found Kenneth at his bench, reading the newspaper and drinking from a mug. Not cutting up a body or sniffing female underwear. Just a regular guy in a regular work setting.

'Mr Plumley,' he said.

Kenneth looked up from his paper as though he had been caught napping. 'Oh, hello. Detective . . . Friendly, isn't it?'

'Frendy. DS Frendy.'

'Yes. Hello again.' He stood up. 'Is this about the incident with Izzy?'

Josh was taken aback. Was there something in what Izzy had said?

'The incident?'

'When she ran into my van with her car. That's quite a dent she made.'

'Oh, no. That's for your insurance companies to handle. But it's related.'

'Oh? In what way?'

'Ms Lambert has made certain allegations about you.'

Kenneth sighed. 'Yes, I heard her. She seemed a bit . . . off her head. Accusing me of abducting girls. Honestly, I don't know where she got that idea.'

'Yes, well, since then she has made another claim.'

'Another one?' He laughed. Actually laughed. 'Go on, then. What is it this time?'

'She says you came to see her at the bookshop where she works yesterday lunchtime.'

He nodded. 'Yes, that's right.'

Again, Josh felt wrong-footed. 'Would you mind telling me the purpose of your visit?'

Kenneth shrugged. 'It's no big secret. I just wanted to clear the air with her. We knew each other well when she was at the school. I thought we'd be able to have a reasonable discussion, as friends. I wanted her to know that I had nothing to do with the things she was accusing me of.'

'How did you know where she worked?'

'She told me, after she *accidentally* bumped into me on Saturday.'

'You don't think it *was* an accident?'

He smirked. 'You'll have to check with her, but it seemed fairly deliberate to me.'

'Why would she do that?'

'Again, I think Izzy is probably the best person to answer that.'

'All right. So, this conversation yesterday. It was good-natured?'

'Well, not exactly.'

'What does that mean?'

Kenneth took a deep breath. 'Izzy didn't want to listen to reason. Didn't matter what I said in my defence, she wasn't interested. She just kept accusing me, saying terrible things about me.'

'What kind of things?'

'That I was perverted. That I had a thing for young girls. I'm a happily married man. I would never do stuff like that. It disgusts me.'

'So what did you do when she said all this?'

'Not much. What could I do if she wasn't willing to listen? In the end, I just gave up and walked out. I was pretty upset about the whole thing. Still am, if you want to know the truth.'

Josh nodded slowly. 'Mr Plumley, what you've just told me is a little different from Ms Lambert's version of your meeting yesterday.'

'Really?'

'Yes. She said that you went there to warn her off, and that you actually threatened her with harm.'

Kenneth's eyes widened in alarm. 'No, no. That's ... that's not what happened at all. Oh, my God, that's what she said? That's so wrong.'

'So you didn't issue any threats?'

'No. Absolutely not. I don't know why she's doing this to me. What have I ever done to hurt her?'

Josh watched him for a few seconds. His incredulity, his anguish seemed genuine. What was he to believe?

'Mr Plumley, when you went to the bookshop, was there another woman there with Izzy?'

'No. The shop was empty.'

'Do you know that she has a work colleague called Melissa Sawyer?'

'No. I don't think Izzy even mentioned her. Why do you ask?'

'We're concerned for her welfare. She went missing after leaving the bookshop yesterday. Nothing has been heard from her since then.'

Kenneth stared while he processed this information.

'Hold on,' he said finally. 'Is she saying – are *you* saying – that I had something to do with that?'

'The suggestion has been made.'

'By Izzy? And you believe that lunatic? You've seen what she's like with me. She's crazy. This is all— I don't believe this.'

He was becoming agitated now, pacing up and down the workshop.

'Mr Plumley, please stay calm.'

'Stay calm? How am I supposed to stay calm? Is this how it's going to be now? Every time a woman goes missing, you're going to interrogate me about it? And all because of the nonsense coming out of Izzy's mouth? Why do you even listen to her?'

Because she does great card tricks, Josh thought. Which is all it comes down to when you think about it. Without that, her claims are pretty outrageous.

So why do I listen to her?

'If what she's saying isn't true, why do you think she would make all these things up about you?' was the best he could offer.

Kenneth chewed on his lip, as though preventing it from shaping words queued up behind it.

'Mr Plumley?'

'I don't like to say.'

'Well, I don't think this is something you should keep to yourself. Some pretty serious allegations are being made here. If there's something you know that could help us . . .'

'She . . . Izzy had a thing for me.'

'A thing?'

'An infatuation. A crush. Whatever you want to call it.'

'When? At school?'

'Yeah. I don't know why. I mean, I know I'm not exactly George Clooney. But Hemingway is an all-girls school. There are a lot of hormones there, if you get my drift. Some of the girls can get a bit flirty.'

'And Izzy got flirty with you?'

'Well, a little more than that.'

'Could you be more specific?'

'She started getting very suggestive. She was always reading books, you know, and sometimes . . . sometimes she would insist on reading bits out to me. Like, the naughty bits.'

'Sex scenes?'

'Yeah, that kind of thing. *Lady Chatterley's Lover* and some Jilly Cooper novels. Even *Fifty Shades of Grey*.'

'I see. Did she do anything else?'

'Yeah. She'd talk about wanting to try out some of those things, wondering what it felt like. She asked about me. About my . . . my vital statistics, if you know what I mean?'

'And what was your response?'

'I told her she had to stop it. It was completely wrong. I made it clear that I had absolutely no feelings for her in that way, and that there could never be anything between us. That really pissed her off.'

'She got angry?'

'Not just angry. Furious. I mean, off her head. She said she was going to start spreading rumours about me, telling everyone I tried to touch her. She really upset me. I thought we were good friends until then.'

'So how did it end?'

'I called her bluff. I was scared that she'd go through with her threats and I'd lose my job, so I said I was going to talk to the head of school about her if she carried on. She stopped coming to the workshop after that.'

Josh was silent for a moment. This was putting a whole new slant on things.

'Mr Plumley, do you know that Izzy is gay?'

It didn't faze him. 'I don't know what she is now. Back then, though, she was a very confused, weird girl with no friends. In fact, she's still confused.'

'Why do you say that?'

This one he found more surprising. 'Well, look at what she's doing. She's stalking me.'

'That's a very strong word to use.'

'I don't care. It's accurate.' He paused. 'Look, I really didn't want it to come to this, but she's forcing me to defend myself. Like I told you, she didn't just bump into me on Saturday morning. She knew exactly what she was doing. She even knew what I'd bought in the shop I'd just left. She was obviously spying on me.'

'And I asked you why she would do that. She left school five years ago. Why would she suddenly start harassing you now?'

'Because of my TV appearance.'

'Explain.'

'She obviously saw it and it opened up old wounds. I know how ridiculous that sounds, and even I didn't believe it at first, otherwise I wouldn't have agreed to go to the café with her. I was really hoping she'd grown up a bit. And at first it all seemed okay, we were having a nice chat. But then she started to get weird.'

'Weird how?'

'Well, saying nasty things about me. Saying that she hadn't forgotten about how I'd turned her down at school, and now she had a chance to get even.'

'Did you know what she meant by that?'

'No. So I asked her. She said she could make my life hell about the Rosie Agutter story, that she could go around telling people I had something to do with it.'

'She said that?'

Kenneth nodded. 'The atmosphere turned pretty sour then, so I just got up and walked out. I was pretty upset that she still felt that way about me, but I tried to put it out of my mind. I really didn't think she would go through with what she said. You'd have to be really screwed up to do something like that, right? But then she goes and crashes her car into my van and starts screaming at me in the street. You saw her. You saw how batshit crazy she was. The girl is off her rocker.' He paused for a moment, and Josh could see that his hands were trembling. 'I'm sorry,' he continued. 'I didn't intend to say any of this. I hoped that if I ignored her, she would just go away, but she made it clear that wasn't going to happen. When I went to see her in the bookshop, it was because I thought I had to give it one more try. I asked her to let bygones be bygones, but it just seemed to pour fuel on the fire. And now she's blaming me for yet another girl going missing. Surely you can see how obsessed she is, can't you?'

Josh didn't answer the question, but he had to admit that Kenneth was making a pretty good case.

'One more thing,' he said. 'Melissa Sawyer was last seen in the bookshop, shortly before closing time. Do you mind if I ask if you can account for your whereabouts between five and six yesterday?'

'Between five and six? Sure. I was here, like I am every weekday.'

'You were here till what time?'

'About half past six.'

'Anybody vouch for that?'

'Yes, actually. Same person as last time.'

'Mrs Vernon? The school head?'

'Yeah. She couldn't get her car started. She asked if I could help her.'

'And did you?'

'Yeah. Took a while. There were all kinds of weird warning lights on her dash. I didn't think I could do anything for her, but you know what it was?'

'What?'

'She has keyless ignition and the battery had gone in her key fob. I found a new battery and it was right as rain.'

Josh nodded slowly.

'You can check with her if you like,' Kenneth said. 'I won't be offended. And after that, why don't you go and ask Crazy Izzy what *she* was doing between five and six yesterday?'

28

It was weird not having Melissa around. Abel had taken her place behind the shop counter, but it wasn't the same.

Izzy was certain that the police were doing everything they could to find Melissa, but she didn't find it reassuring. No matter how many times she tried telling herself that Melissa had probably got into a fight with her druggie boyfriend, Kenneth Plumley refused to move out of Izzy's head as the one behind all this. The man was pure evil. He had issued his threats and now he had made good on them.

It's all my fault, she thought. I'm sorry, Melissa. I'm so sorry.

Walk through that door now, she willed. Please, Melissa, come through the door and prove me wrong, and then I'll never go near Kenneth Plumley again.

The door didn't open, but her mobile phone rang. She saw that it was Josh. She answered it immediately and said, 'Josh, have you found her? Have you found Melissa?'

'Not yet,' he said. 'But I'd like to discuss a few things with you, if that's okay.'

Even across the airwaves she could tell he was not his usual self. He sounded like he'd just pulled her over for speeding.

'Sure. The café again?'

'Actually, I was hoping you could make it down to the police station.'

'Okay. Now?'

'As soon as you can. Thanks, Izzy.'

He hung up, and she stared at her phone. There had been deep concern in his voice, and she hoped to God that it didn't mean the worst for Melissa.

'Abel,' she said. 'That was the police. They want to ask me a few more things about Melissa. Do you mind if I go over to the police station? I can wait till my lunch break if it's a problem.'

Abel shook his broad head slowly. 'I can manage. You should go.'

There was something in the way he said this, as though he knew more than he was willing to reveal.

'Are you sure?'

'Go. Take as much time as you need. Books are not as important as people.'

She nodded and collected her things, but even as she left the shop she felt that Abel was holding something back.

She walked briskly to the station, wondering why everyone was being so strange with her. When she got there, even the portly desk sergeant didn't seem as jolly as he had previously.

Josh appeared within minutes and ushered her through. She asked him if everything was okay, but he brushed it aside. The vibes coming off him were all business.

He took her directly to the interview room, and although he didn't slip into police legalese, it all felt very officious.

'Josh,' she said. 'What's going on? Have you spoken to Kenneth Plumley?'

'I've spoken to him. His view of things is very different from yours.'

'Okay. Well, I didn't exactly think he'd be falling over himself to confess. In what way was it different?'

'In every way. In particular, he said you had something of a crush on him when you were at school.'

She blinked rapidly. 'A what? Have you seen Kenneth? He's not exactly dish of the day. And have I not already made it clear to you which lane I prefer to drive in?'

'You have, and I put that to him. He said you were a bit more confused about your identity back then.'

'I wasn't confused. In any case, even if I'd been straight as a die, Plummers wouldn't have made it into the reserves on my shag list. What the hell's he going on about?'

'He's claiming that the rejection was the other way. He turned you down and you didn't take it very well. He said you threatened to go to the school head about him, saying that his behaviour was inappropriate.'

'What? That's ridiculous. And even if it *were* true – which it isn't – what's that got to do with what's happening now?'

'His suggestion is that his appearance on television kick-started it again, and that you came after him, saying that you hadn't forgiven him and this was finally your chance to ruin him.'

'Oh, for fuck's sake!'

Izzy brought her fingers to her temples. This was unbelievable. Reality was being turned on its head. Worse, she could tell that Josh was falling for it.

She tried to sound calm, even though her insides were already seizing up. 'Josh, you have to believe me. None of what he is telling you is true. The only reason I've got him in my sights is that nobody else seems bothered about what he's doing.'

'And what *is* he doing?'

'Why are you even asking that? I've told you. He's abducting young women. He's taken three that we know about, maybe more. It's possible that Melissa is still alive, but if you don't move quickly, it'll be too late for her too.'

Josh drummed his fingers on the table. 'When you bumped into Mr Plumley on Saturday morning, was that really just a coincidence?'

A direct yes/no question. Much as she hated to, she was going to have to lie. Anything else would push Josh even further into Plumley's camp.

'Yes,' she said. 'It's not that big a town. These things happen.'

'He's saying it seemed deliberate to him. He said you must have been watching him, following him, and that you even knew what he'd just bought in the shop.'

'That's not true. He's inventing things to make me look like the bad guy.'

She hoped she sounded convincing. Josh might not have her gift, but he had many years' experience of dealing with deceivers, and she wasn't convinced he didn't smell one right now.

'Uh-huh. So what were you doing in town? Shouldn't you have been working in the bookshop?'

'I wanted to do a bit of shopping, so I asked Melissa to cover for me.'

'Do you often do that?'

'No. This was just on a whim.'

'Uh-huh. Then it was a real stroke of luck, bumping into Mr Plumley like that. I mean, the one time you decide your shopping is so urgent that you make yourself late for work, and lo and behold, you run into the guy you think is abducting people.'

'Are you trying to insinuate something?'

'I'm trying to get you to see how it looks to an outsider. Mr Plumley is saying that you have some kind of vendetta against him. All I'm doing is offering you a chance to refute it, and so far you're not doing a very good job.'

Izzy sat back and folded her arms. 'You can believe what you like. I know what he did. You didn't hear how he threatened me in the bookshop. I suppose he denies ever being there.'

'Actually, no, he doesn't. But what he does deny is that he was the one who did all the threatening.'

'What? He's saying it was *me*?'

'His story is that he went to the bookshop to talk things over with you, get you to see sense, but that it had the opposite effect and you went ballistic.'

'Again, not true. He was trying to get me to back off, and because I wouldn't play ball, he took Melissa. Did you even question him about that, or were you too busy coming up with ideas about how best to shoot me down?'

'It wasn't like that, Izzy. And yes, I did question him about Melissa's disappearance.'

'And?'

'He has an alibi. He was nowhere near the bookshop at the time we think she went missing.'

'Really? And you're just accepting his word on that?'

'No. Not just his word. The word of Mrs Vernon too. She was with him at the school.'

'Mrs Vernon? The head of school? Well, isn't that convenient? That's twice she's got him out of trouble. Doesn't that strike you as just a little bit suspicious?'

'Surely you're not suggesting—'

'Why not? I don't know anything about this woman, and neither do you. Maybe she's had a crush on him since childhood the way every other female in this town apparently does. Maybe he's blackmailing her. Maybe she's helping him with the abductions. The possibilities are endless.'

'Izzy, I think we're in danger of straying into the realms of fantasy.'

She waved a hand. 'Whatever. Can I go now? Because this really isn't helping any of those girls.'

'In a minute.'

'There's more? Okay, go ahead. Throw another rock at me.'

'What were you doing between five and six o'clock yesterday?'

She stared at him. 'You've got to be kidding? You seriously don't think . . .'

'I'm being thorough, like you want me to be. Considering all the options.'

'That's not an option. Melissa is my friend.'

'Humour me.'

'I . . . I went home.'

'You drove straight home?'

'Yes.'

'And after that?'

'Nothing. I stayed at home and I made something to eat and I watched television.'

'Can anyone vouch for that?'

'No. I was alone. Andy was at work.'

'Uh-huh. And you left the shop earlier than usual.'

'Only slightly.'

'Why?'

'I already told you. It was to give Melissa some experience with cashing up and locking the shop.'

'But why on that particular evening?'

'No reason. It was as good as any other.'

'You didn't feel the need to stay and supervise?'

'No. I trust her.'

'When's the last time you asked her to lock up?'

'I don't know. A couple of months ago, I suppose.'

'Months, not days?'

'No.'

'So it's a rare event. But you just happened to ask her to lock up on the day she went missing.'

'Yes. It was pure coincidence. I don't see what that's—'

'How were things between the two of you when you left the shop?'

'Fine. We get on well together.'

'Always?'

'Most of the time.'

'You haven't fallen out recently?'

Izzy hesitated. 'Why do you ask?'

'It's true, then? You had an argument?'

She could tell he already had the facts. He had spoken to Abel. That was why Abel had seemed so sheepish earlier.

'Yes,' she said. 'We had an argument.'

'A pretty heated argument, right? So heated it got physical.'

'I wouldn't call it physical exactly. We didn't hit each other.'

'Not with fists, maybe. But books?'

'Okay, okay. We had a fight. Big deal. It happens.'

'What was it about?'

She paused again. 'Nothing. It was stupid.'

'Try me. I've heard all kinds of reasons for violence.'

'It wasn't violence. It was a tiff. And I don't want to go into the reasons for it.'

'Why not?'

'Because it has nothing to do with her going missing. We fell out, and then we hugged and made up again.'

'But you don't want to say what it was about?'

'No, I don't.'

Josh watched her for a few seconds while he drummed his fingers again.

'All right, Izzy, here's where we are. At school you spent a lot of your spare time in the company of the male caretaker. You've admitted that much. Fast forward five years and you're suddenly accusing this happily married man of abducting a student from that school, with no evidence other than your gut feeling—'

'It's not a gut—'

'—and despite the fact that he has a solid alibi. You somehow

184

manage to track him down to where he is innocently shopping in town, where you spy on him and then interrogate him about the missing student. Not long after that, you follow him again, this time crashing your car into his vehicle and making more accusations, even though it turns out that he's just given a girl a lift home like he often does. Oh, I almost forgot, you do some internet searching, find another missing girl from ages ago and blame him for that one too, again with no evidence. Then Melissa disappears. This is only the day after you've had a massive fight with her, for reasons which you refuse to divulge, and on the same day that you ask her to lock up the shop for the first time in many months. And of course you're blaming Kenneth Plumley for that one too, even though he has a concrete alibi yet again and you have none. Does all that sound about right to you?'

Her voice lost its strength in the face of his onslaught. 'More or less,' she whispered.

'So whose story is a jury going to believe? Yours or his?'

'Jury? What do you mean? Am I . . . am I a suspect?'

It was agony while he left her stewing. She was so anxious she couldn't focus on his emotions.

'No, Izzy, you're not a suspect, and you're nowhere near being one. I'm just trying to get you to see how things might look to an outside observer. I have no idea what's going on in your head about Kenneth Plumley, but I do think you've let it run away with itself. You're digging a hole for yourself that's getting deeper by the day. You're not a suspect, but neither is Kenneth. There's nothing to contradict his version of events. I don't even think there's any reason at the moment to connect the disappearance of Melissa with that of Rosie Agutter. Melissa has been mixing with some very dodgy people, not least the boyfriend she only recently dumped, and so that's where we're focusing our efforts right now.'

Izzy just nodded. She felt battered and bruised.

'Go back to work, Izzy. Then go home and relax. This isn't your problem.'

'Will you . . . will you let me know if you hear anything about Melissa?'

'Of course.'

'Thank you.'

She left then. When Josh escorted her out, she wondered if she would ever see him again. She liked him, had really believed at first that he was one of the few people who got her, but alas their working relationship appeared to be at an end.

She started walking, her heart heavy. It had been a long time since she had felt so alone, so misunderstood.

Go back to work. This isn't your problem.

Well, it *was* her problem.

And she wasn't going back to work.

Not just yet.

29

Standing outside the school brought its own melancholy. The passing of time had made it seem a lot more friendly than she remembered. Hemingway was a good school, and for most, a happy school. She regretted not making more of her opportunities when she'd attended. She was bright enough. She could have been anything now – a lawyer, a teacher. Someone with a decent income and lots of friends. Someone who could afford to sip something better than acidic supermarket plonk.

She stepped up to the front door and jabbed the intercom button. An angry buzz came at once, followed by a metallic snap as the door was unlatched. She stepped into a lobby that was exactly as she remembered it: a staircase to her left next to a seating area in which were displayed the creations of some of the talented sixth-form artists; ahead, the doors to the main hall; and across to the right, a beech-coloured reception desk bearing the school crest which was supposed to depict a woman holding the earth in her hands but which to Izzy's eyes always looked like someone playing bowls.

She stepped across to the desk. The woman behind it looked to be in her forties and had a manic wedge of hair that jutted out beyond her narrow shoulders, like the canopy of a tree. There was a tattoo of a monkey on her wrist. She kept her head down, her eyes glued to a screen below counter level.

'Hello,' the woman said. 'How may I help you?'

You can start by looking me in the eye, Izzy thought. Customer Interface Skills 101.

'Hi,' she said. 'I'd like to see the head of school, please. Mrs Vernon.'

Was the tattoo a monkey, or was it a sloth? She decided it was a sloth.

'You'll need to bring in a note from your parents,' the woman said.

Izzy was mystified. 'Why? I'm twenty-three.'

'It doesn't matter, darling. We need it for our files.'

Izzy went silent while she digested this.

Maybe not a sloth. More rotund than that. Winnie the Pooh?

'But what if both of my parents were dead?'

The woman finally looked up. She tapped a microphone running along her cheek, and it was then that Izzy realised she was wearing a headset under all that hair and was having a conversation with someone else.

'No problem, darling,' the woman said to her caller. 'See you soon.' She looked again at Izzy and repeated her 'How may I help you?' line.

'Er, I was hoping to have a quick chat with Mrs Vernon.'

'Do you have an appointment?'

'No, but I used to go to this school, if that helps.'

Not Winnie the Pooh either. An otter?

'Not really. Mrs Vernon's schedule is pretty hectic. Can you tell me what it's about?'

Izzy didn't want to divulge the real reason. They would turn her away immediately.

'I've travelled all the way down from Edinburgh for a funeral. While I was here, I thought I'd drop in to see my old school. I'm going back home this afternoon, and I really want to thank the head for my time here.'

The woman nodded sympathetically, then pressed a button and relayed Izzy's wishes.

'She can see you for five minutes.' She pointed towards a door. 'It's just over—'

'Yes, I remember. By the way, I love your tattoo. What is that?'

'It's Gary Barlow. I've been mad about him for years.'

'Oh.'

Izzy stepped across to the door and knocked. She felt like she'd been transported back in time, a knot of tension growing in her stomach as though she'd been summoned here for some misdemeanour or other.

'Come in,' said a cheery voice within.

The woman who rose from her desk as Izzy entered looked to be about fifty. Her brown hair was compacted into a tight bun that seemed to be putting tension on her face, including a smile that stretched almost to her ears. Izzy didn't like her, but that opinion had been formed way before she stepped through this door.

'Hello, I'm Mrs Vernon,' the woman said, stretching out a hand. 'I'm sorry, I don't know your name.'

Izzy took the proffered hand with reluctance. 'It's Isobel Lambert.'

Mrs Vernon looked puzzled. 'I don't recall—'

'No. I was here before your time. Mrs Singh was the head back then.'

'Ah, I see. Well, take a seat. What can I do for you?'

Izzy sat, wondered how to launch into this.

'I left this school five years ago. When I was here, I got to know the caretaker quite well.'

'Was that Mr Plumley then?'

'Yes. It was. The next time I saw him after that was when he was on television, talking about Rosie Agutter.'

'I'm sorry, I think there's been some confusion. I thought you'd come to convey your appreciation for what the school did for you.'

'That was . . . a little white lie.'

Mrs Vernon's expression became stern; this was presumably her face of discipline. 'I see. Then perhaps you'd like to tell me what this is really about?'

'I happen to know that everything Kenneth Plumley said about Rosie Agutter was a lie.'

'A lie? Or a mistake?'

'A lie. I believe he had something to do with her disappearance.'

'And why do you believe that?'

'It's a long story. I don't want to go into details.'

'Then I don't know how you can expect me to accept what you're saying. If you have some evidence, you should take it to the police.'

'I already have. They told me that you provided Mr Plumley with an alibi.'

Mrs Vernon blinked several times. 'Ah, so that's why they've been asking me all these questions. Because of you.'

'Yes.'

'All they would tell me was that certain allegations had been made. I had no idea who had made them.'

'Well, it was me. Since then, there's been another disappearance. Melissa Sawyer, a friend of mine, didn't make it home after leaving work yesterday.'

Mrs Vernon nodded. 'That all fits. I had another visit from the police just this morning. Your doing again, I suppose?'

'My doing. And yet again you gave Mr Plumley an alibi.'

Mrs Vernon leaned forward in her chair. 'Isobel, I'm not sure I'm happy about where you're going with this. You say that I'm supplying alibis as though I'm selling them from the back of a van.'

Izzy realised she was on the verge of alienating the teacher too quickly.

'That's . . . not what I meant. I'm just wondering if it's at all possible that you were too willing to give him the benefit of the doubt.'

She thought she'd been diplomatic, but Mrs Vernon was already looking irritated.

'Benefit of the doubt about what? Is there any doubt? So far, all you've given me is some vague speculation that casts aspersions on a highly valued member of my staff.'

'It's not speculation. I know for certain that he took those girls. What I don't get is how he's managed to convince you to cover his back.'

'Cover his— Isobel, you're acting as though there's some kind of conspiracy going on here. I can assure you that whatever I told the police was factual. Now, if you don't mind, I think that—'

'It can't be factual. Not one hundred per cent. Something's missing. Something you haven't told the police.'

'And what might that be?'

'I don't know. Please, I didn't come here to be difficult or to wind you up. One of your students has gone missing, and I'm trying to help you find her. My friend is in trouble too. Somebody's got to do something.'

She heard the desperation in her own voice. It wasn't fake, and Mrs Vernon seemed to recognise that. Her words came calmly, as though she might be talking to one of the distressed girls she encountered every day in her role.

'Isobel, I would do anything to get Rosie back. She's a wonderful girl and a credit to the school. I can't sleep for worrying about her. But I can't give you what I don't have. I can't make something up just to fit your narrative.'

Izzy wished she had known this woman years ago, wished that she had been given the opportunity to absorb all of her mannerisms and tics and body language and speech patterns so that she could now reach in and tease out the truth from the lies.

'I'm not asking you to invent things. I just want to know if it's possible that maybe you piled things on a bit thick – to help him out, I mean. Stretching out the time you saw him at the school, or simply accepting what he told you as the truth instead of seeing it for yourself. We all do things like that, don't we? To help out our friends.'

Mrs Vernon shook her head. 'I can't help you. For one thing, I wouldn't class Mr Plumley as a close friend. He's a colleague, he does a lot for the school, but we don't socialise. I don't owe him any favours, and I certainly wouldn't lie to the police on his behalf.'

'Then . . . does he have something on you? Is he blackmailing you? Is that it?'

'Isobel—'

'You don't have to give me details. I won't even go to the police about it. I just need to know. A simple yes, or even a maybe. Just give me something, please.'

Mrs Vernon sighed. 'Isobel, I think you need to talk to someone about this.'

'I have! I keep talking to the police, and—'

'I don't mean the police. I mean a doctor or a counsellor. I think you need help.'

'A doctor? You think I'm crazy?'

'Crazy isn't a word I would ever use. I have no idea what's going on here, but from where I'm sitting it's something very unhealthy. This obsession with—'

Izzy leapt out of her chair. 'I'm not crazy. I don't hear voices, I don't pray to Satan, and I'm not under the influence of drugs. What I've told you about Kenneth Plumley is the God's honest truth. He knows exactly what happened to Rosie, and you're helping him to keep it from the rest of us. You're protecting him, and that makes you as guilty as he is. Think about that.'

She turned and stormed out of the office, tears streaming down her face again as she rushed past the receptionist and barged through a gaggle of alarmed girls, straight out onto the street, wondering how the hell this shitty place had ever managed to pull off the trick of appearing even faintly welcoming.

* * *

Abel was seeing a customer out of the door when Izzy got back to work. It was something she could learn from, she thought, that personal touch, that extra effort to make the customer feel wanted here.

When Abel closed the door and turned towards her, she said, 'I'm sorry I took so long. The police had a lot of questions.'

Abel nodded. 'Do you forgive me?'

'Forgive you?'

'When they came to me last night, I didn't tell them about your fight with Melissa. I didn't think it was important. But all night long it bothered me. I hadn't given them all the facts, and it bothered me. I thought they should know. I'm sorry.'

He hung his head, and she could feel his shame.

'Abel, it's okay. You did the right thing. The police should have all the facts. When they asked me about it, I knew it must have been you who told them, but what does that matter? I should have told them myself, but I was too scared.'

'So . . . it's okay?'

'It's fine. Come here, give me a hug.'

They embraced, for far longer than she intended. But it felt good.

Abel said, 'Perhaps Melissa will turn up later today.'

'Yes,' she answered. 'I hope so.'

30

As he drove home, Kenneth felt that the world was closing in on him. He decided this must be what it was like to suffer from claustrophobia. He was having palpitations, his hands were clammy on the steering wheel, the veins in his head felt ready to pop open.

Taking Melissa had been a mistake. A huge error. It was too close to home, and it hadn't done anything to deter Izzy.

He had spotted her leaving the school this morning, dashing across to the little white Fiat she had crashed into his van. He figured that she must have called in to see Mrs Vernon, to check out his alibi. He'd expected his boss to summon him at some point during the day, but she never did.

What the hell was wrong with that girl? Why was she so convinced he was responsible for any of this? Had he slipped up somewhere? Was she ever going to stop hounding him?

This couldn't be allowed to continue. He was fraying at the edges. Pretty soon he would unravel completely.

As usual, he parked up behind his house. When he climbed out, he picked up the six-pack of lager he had bought on the way home.

On entering the house he could hear the television. A quiz programme. Polina and Michael calling out dumb answers and laughing when they got it so completely wrong.

He went into the kitchen. Opened up one of the lager cans and set his Adam's apple bobbing as he took a long swig.

Polina came into the kitchen, closely followed by Michael, because wasn't he always there, wasn't he always in her shadow, within touching distance, inhaling her musky scent, whispering his nasty, divisive thoughts into her ears, her easily persuaded brain?

'Kenneth!' Polina said, as if surprised that he should be here, in his own home. 'What are you doing?'

'Drinking,' he said. 'I needed a drink, so I bought some beer. Is that okay with you?'

He saw the shock on her face and took another swig.

'Of course,' she answered. 'But we're getting hungry. We were waiting for you.'

'Is something on the table?'

'On the table? No, Kenneth.'

'In the oven then? I can't smell anything.'

'No. There is nothing. I don't know what you are saying.'

'What I'm saying, my darling wife, light of my miserable life, is that you could have started cooking something without waiting for me. You could even have eaten before me if you're as starving as you say you are.'

'But . . . but we always wait for you. You do the cooking. You make such nice food.'

He shook his head. 'No, I don't make nice food. I make things that are easy. I make spaghetti Bolognese and burgers with chips and macaroni cheese and sausage casserole. Stuff anyone could knock together. Even you.'

'Well . . . okay. But now that you are here—'

'I've eaten.'

'What, Kenneth?'

'I've eaten. I called into McDonald's on the way home. I had nuggets, fries, Coke and an Oreo McFlurry. And now I'm having a beer.'

'But where is *our* food? For me and Michael.'

'You can cook something. I won't be needing any. I'm full.'

Polina stared at him. 'You are in a very strange mood tonight.'

'My mood is fine.'

To Kenneth's annoyance, Michael decided it was his turn to speak; the man dared to think it was acceptable for him to interfere in a domestic discussion that was none of his concern. He came out from behind Polina, his eyes on the cans of lager.

'Sounds like you've already found some Dutch courage there, Kenneth. Are you sure there wasn't some whisky mixed in with that Coke you had earlier? I think it might be a good idea for me to lighten your load before you go overboard.'

He got to the counter, picked up a can.

'Put that down,' Kenneth told him.

'What?'

'You heard me. I said put it down. That's my beer. You want beer, buy your own.'

'Kenneth,' Polina said.

Michael simply smiled. Then there was a pop and a hiss as he pulled back the tab.

Kenneth was on him in two strides, slapping the can out of Michael's hand and sending it spinning across the counter, beer spurting from it like a garden sprinkler.

Kenneth heard his wife yell his name again, but his attention was on Michael. He hadn't been in a fight for a long, long time, but he was ready for one now.

Michael showed his palms and stepped back, but there was still a mocking smile on his face, and that hurt more than any punch.

Polina took hold of Kenneth's arm and started to drag him away, but Kenneth pulled free. He picked up the rest of the unopened cans and took them with him out of the kitchen.

He went into the living room, sat down on the sofa, not the

armchair, because the sofa was his rightful place, then grabbed the TV remote and turned the volume way up to drown out the murmuring in the kitchen and the noises in his head.

Polina appeared shortly afterwards. She sat down next to him, and when she uttered his name he had to force himself not to turn towards her like an obedient puppy.

'Kenneth. What is wrong with you? You are acting very strange.'

'Nothing's wrong. I'm absolutely fine.'

'No. You are not. You spoke to Michael very badly. You should apologise. He is a guest in our house.'

'I don't want him here. I don't like him taking everything that's mine. We were happy before he came.'

'The problem is not Michael. There is something else going on. You need to talk about it.'

'What I *need*,' he snapped, 'is for everyone to leave me alone. I don't want to talk about my shitty life.'

There was a cold silence, and then Polina said, 'Well, I am sorry to hear that your life is so shitty, Kenneth. I will leave you alone like you have asked me, and you can come and talk to us when you are ready to apologise.'

She left the room and closed the door behind her, and he knew that he would be the hot topic of conversation in his own kitchen, that they would be saying he was going through a mid-life crisis or something, and they might suggest he was having an affair and then they would both roar with laughter at the absurdity of such a notion. But what they wouldn't do is care; they wouldn't have any sympathy for him in his moment of need.

Fuck 'em, he thought. I don't need their sympathy.

He told himself that he had absolutely done the right thing. He had stood up for himself, acted like a real man, and perhaps now they would show him some respect and have food on the table for when he got home and keep their hands off his fucking beer and off each other.

But really, he didn't feel strong, didn't feel any more masculine. In fact, he felt utterly alone. Sitting here with just an orange-faced quiz show host for company, he felt so empty, so miserable. And what he also knew was that at some point in the evening he would offer the apology that Polina had said he owed; he would go crawling back on his hands and knees and beg for their forgiveness. Because he was always in the wrong – that was the law in this house.

He sat and continued to sup, but his beer had lost its attraction, had become just a foul-tasting gassy fluid. A part of him hoped that Polina or Michael would make the first move, that they would come into the room and ask him if he was okay, which would be enough of a prompt for him to cast aside his dignity and tell them how utterly sorry he was for his unacceptable behaviour.

But they stayed away. Left him to stew, as if they wanted to punish him, humiliate him. He could picture them in the kitchen, quite happy with whatever processed food they had found in the depths of the freezer, chatting and laughing, the radio on, singing along. He desperately wanted to be a part of that, but it would always evade him.

A fear took hold that they would leave him here all night. They would go up to bed, perhaps the same bed, and he would have to make do with the sofa, but he wouldn't get any sleep because that never worked if there were things left unsaid. He would probably hear them upstairs, the rhythmic thumping of the bedrail and then their contented snoring, and meanwhile his guts would be churning and his head would be pounding and regret would be eating him up.

But that wasn't it. Not really. It wasn't simply about making up over a stupid can of beer or an unprepared meal. The problem ran much deeper. The reason he had come home in such a bad mood in the first place was because his whole life was spinning out of control.

He needed to get things back in order. Apologising to Polina and Michael wouldn't be enough; it would be like putting a bandage on a cancer. He had to start acknowledging the elephant in the room.

He stood up and went back to the kitchen. Polina and Michael sat in front of empty plates, drinking a bottle of wine they had dredged up from somewhere. They looked at him in surprise and expectation, waiting for him to come back to the fold.

Well, they would have to wait a little longer. He had more important things to worry about.

'I'm taking Barclay out for his walk,' he announced.

He caught their exchange of glances, their raised eyebrows. It was clear they hadn't planned on him holding out for so long, and that tiny victory over them felt exhilarating.

He put the lead on the dog and left the house. When he climbed into the van, he could see the faces looking back at him through the French doors, Polina concerned and Michael still wearing a sardonic smile. He wanted to flip his middle finger at them, but he wasn't that brave. He would allow himself this moment of triumph, but there were boundaries he couldn't overstep.

He drove away, the expressions of the people he had left behind still imprinted on his mind.

He didn't even notice the dark blue Peugeot parked down the lane.

31

Izzy hunkered down in the Peugeot as Kenneth Plumley's van drove past. Peering over her steering wheel, she got a clear view of Kenneth at the helm. She started her own engine, performed a three-point turn, and went after him.

The Peugeot belonged to Andy, who had been picked up for work by her ambulance colleague. It was seven years older than Izzy's aged Fiat, and seemed to be held together with luck and a dollop of hope, but the Fiat was too well known to Kenneth, especially now it had a big dent in its side. Izzy had already decided she wasn't going to tell her partner she had borrowed her car.

Stalking Kenneth again hadn't been on her to-do list originally. Following her discouraging and depressing encounters with Josh and Mrs Vernon, her plan had been to write the day off as a disaster and seek refuge in a good book. But then she got to her empty flat, and in the oppressive silence the monster of conscience came after her and demanded to know why she was just sitting there doing nothing when she was the only one in the world who had the power to save her friend Melissa, the only one who could prevent more girls from being abducted in the future, and how could she live with herself?

The monster pushed her out into the cold dark evening, made her get into Andy's car and drive all the way here to the lane leading up to Kenneth's house. She expected nothing to come of it; she expected to sit here until midnight, trying to stay warm and awake and not thinking about her desperate need to pee, while Kenneth and co sipped hot chocolate in front of a roaring log fire.

But lo and behold, the monster was right. Because here she was, once again tailing her nemesis, hoping that this time he had made a big mistake and was about to lead her to his captives, whom she would release and become the big local hero and be granted the freedom of the town, when in fact what Kenneth probably had in mind was a trip to the pub for a nightcap before bed.

As she had done before, she kept her distance behind the van, especially since the roads were so quiet now. It led her back towards town, but it was only when she saw that a couple of pubs were passed that she became more confident she might actually be on to something.

A few minutes later, a car turned out in front of her, which was fine except that it was going at the speed of a tortoise. She considered overtaking but knew that would only cause Kenneth to examine her in his rear-view mirror. There was every chance he would be more cautious about pursuers after what had occurred previously. Anyway, this was working fine.

Until it wasn't.

She saw the temporary traffic lights at a crossroads ahead. They were green, and Kenneth was indicating to turn right. She had a sinking feeling about what was going to happen.

'Speed up,' she told the driver in front of her. 'Faster!'

Kenneth took the turning. The lights were still green.

'Go, go, go! You can get through if you hurry up.'

And then the amber light came on.

'Put your fucking foot down!'

It was too late to overtake now: she was too close to the junction. The lights went red and the car in front of her slowed and came to a leisurely stop. Izzy came right up behind it and tried to peer round the corner, but could no longer see the white van.

'Shit!'

She put the car into reverse, backed it up, started to go around the other car. A horn screamed at her as a truck thundered past in the opposite direction, a string of smaller vehicles in its wake like its offspring.

'Where the hell did they all come from?' she asked nobody.

The road went quiet again but the lights seemed almost begrudging in granting her permission to proceed. When they relented, she roared around the corner. Kenneth's van was nowhere to be seen.

She kept driving. There wasn't much along this road: warehouses, car dealers, the old swimming baths. No reason for him to stop here. She drove on. Her surroundings became more crowded with buildings, and there were any number of turn-offs he could have taken.

A mile or so later, she gave up and pulled the car over.

'Shit!' she said again. This was the second time she had lost Kenneth in a pursuit; it always looked so easy in television dramas.

She thought about going home, then changed her mind. Kenneth would have to retrace his steps eventually. It was still possible that he might call in somewhere else on the way back to his cottage. And even if he went all the way home, she could follow him there and snoop around the property like she had done before. She wasn't afraid of being caught by that bastard now.

Except that she *was* afraid. Terrified, in fact. She felt way out of her depth. She knew about books, and that was all. It hardly qualified her to go chasing alone after vicious criminals. She didn't know how to operate in a world of violence and abduction and murder. Some of the stories that Andy brought home about her shifts on the ambulance made her want to puke.

Yes, Andy. What would she be doing right now? And what would she say if she found out her mild-mannered partner was chasing after an evil wrongdoer in the dark, like something out of *Scooby-Doo*?

But I'm here now, she thought. I've come this far. Pass the Scooby Snacks.

She turned the car around and went back to the roadworks, then took a left onto the road she had been delayed on earlier. A couple of hundred yards further on, she pulled into a deserted parking spot and killed the engine.

She decided she'd give it an hour. If he didn't come past in that time, she would drive to the cottage and see if he had taken a different route home. And if so . . . well, she'd work out the details when it came to it.

The wait lasted less than twenty minutes. After the van whizzed past, she started the engine, counted to ten, then set off after it. Twenty minutes wasn't very long, and she wondered what that meant. Had he just popped into an off-licence or something? Was it too much to hope that he had picked up some food or other supplies to take to Melissa? Was that where he was going now?

She felt a surge of optimism. This was going to work out well. It had to.

The route was familiar – an exact reversal of the one coming here. At each turning she hoped for something different, a deviation that meant he wasn't going home just yet.

They hit the long straight road flanked by dense woodland on either side. She realised she was getting a bit too close and eased off the accelerator a little. The van went over a steep incline and its lights disappeared when it reached the other side. It didn't bother Izzy; she knew there were no turn-offs for the next couple of miles.

She came down in gear to cope with the hill. The old Peugeot sounded like it was coughing its guts up with the effort, and that at any moment it would give up the ghost and slip back down again. She was relieved when she reached the summit and could give the poor engine a rest on the way down.

But that was when she realised the van had gone again.

'No, no, no! Don't do this to me!'

It seemed an impossible vanishing trick this time. The road was dead straight from here, and there were no side roads for miles. There were no streetlights, but the air was clear. Even if Kenneth had suddenly decided to put his foot down, it ought to be possible to see his van's rear lights, especially from this elevated vantage point.

So where the hell was he?

Izzy used the downward slope to pick up momentum. She craned her neck forward, desperate to pick out two burning red eyes staring back at her, but she could see nothing. She floored the accelerator and jumped back up through the gears, heedless of the speed limit. Still nothing.

'Where are you?'

She braked, slowed, tried to think. There was only one possibility.

The woods.

Kenneth must have gone off-road, into the woods.

She performed a U-turn and started heading back towards the hill, all the while trying to estimate how far he could have come before leaving the road without her seeing him do so. When she thought she'd probably reached his upper limit, she slowed the car to a crawl and started scanning both sides of the road, which just looked like walls of blackness.

Can't see the wood for the trees, she thought, which should be funny but isn't, because somewhere out there is a lunatic who wouldn't have stopped for a pee so close to home and so is either doing something very dubious or else he's setting a trap for me.

She got all the way back to the base of the hill having seen nothing, so she did another U-turn and began a second sweep. At that point a car came over the hill behind her, its driver rebuking her for her slowness by flashing his headlights and leaning on his horn. She showed him her middle finger as he overtook, then resumed her task.

Still no sign.

He's got to be in there somewhere, she thought. Unless he's been abducted by aliens, he's in there.

She went back towards the hill yet again, ignoring a pair of cars that overtook. She opened both side windows in the hope it would improve visibility, but all it did was sting her eyes with the cold.

There was nothing else for it: she would have to continue the search on foot.

With no idea how the Peugeot would cope with the rougher terrain, she performed a hard left and took the car towards the line of trees. The suspension creaked and bounced her up and down in her seat as if in revenge, but she urged the vehicle on, stopping only when she'd managed to get it beneath the tree canopy. From the road, her car would be difficult to spot here. Any closer to the road and someone might decide to investigate; worse still, Kenneth Plumley might see it.

She got out of the car and started walking along the border between the road and the woodland. It was so dark she couldn't even see where she was stepping, so she switched on the torch on her phone. Each time a set of headlights appeared on the road, she put her phone in her pocket and ducked behind a tree until it passed. She didn't want anyone stopping for her, either to assist or do harm.

She pressed on, shining her meagre light into the woods. Gnarled trees stared defiantly back at her, guarding their secrets, daring her to enter their kingdom. She was afraid to cross that threshold, and a part of her wished that her search would come to nothing and then she could just go home and try to comfort herself with the thought that at least she gave it her best shot.

And then she found the van.

It was the rear reflectors that first caught her attention, like the eyes of some demonic predator crouching deep in the woods. She moved towards them cautiously, her hand shaking as it held the phone in front of her. Other colours began to shine back at her: the yellow of the number plate and the white of the rear panelling. It was definitely Plumley's van, taken much further into the woods than she had dared to drive.

And then a thought occurred to her: What if he's still in the van and he's just seen my torchlight in his side mirrors, or else he's behind a nearby tree watching me coming towards him. What then?

She shoved the phone into her pocket again. Blackness. She had walked only a short distance from the road and already she had been plunged into complete darkness. She blinked furiously, hoping her eyes would adjust, but she saw nothing. She brought her hand up in front of her face and it remained invisible.

Her breath came out in a flutter. Her heart started to go into overdrive.

He could be there, she thought, just feet away, waiting to grab me, to attack me, and nobody will see, nobody will have an inkling. He only drove here because he saw me following, and now he's set a trap, and like the idiot I am, I'm walking right into it.

But then she realised that, even though she couldn't see him, with her torch off he couldn't see her either, not unless he was wearing night-vision goggles like in *Silence of the Lambs*, and let's not even go near Hannibal Lecter right now.

And then she wondered where that left her. Because they couldn't stand here all night, each waiting for the other to make a move.

This is ridiculous, she thought. He's not in the van or next to the van. He had no idea I was following him, and he hasn't set a trap because if he wanted to do that he would have made it a lot more obvious about where he was putting the van, instead of making me traipse up and down for ages searching for it.

She took her phone out again but partly obscured its light with her fingers, permitting only a dim glow to seep through. It was more subtle, but the downside was that it was also more spooky.

She walked slowly towards the van, stepping gingerly to avoid noise but finding herself defeated in that by fallen leaves that insisted on rustling and twigs that insisted on snapping.

She reached the rear of the van and stopped for a breather. She put her ear to one of the doors but could hear nothing inside. She edged around the van towards the driver's side, ready to start running like hell if the door flew open.

She came almost level with the door. Still no sound. No hands visible on the steering wheel. Another step . . .

He wasn't there. The driver's seat was unoccupied. She let out a breath of relief, brought the torch up to the window to see inside.

Something leaped at her, slammed into the window. Izzy yelped, fell back, tripped, went down, began scuttling backwards. She had dropped her phone and now she was in blackness again, helpless, unseeing, knowing she was about to be overpowered.

She turned her eyes downwards, found a chink of light among the leaves. She pounced on it, grasped her phone again, held it up towards the van.

A massive wolf, like the one from 'Little Red Riding Hood', glared hungrily at her, its eyes searing in the torchlight, making very clear in its own language how its razor-sharp gnashers were all the better to eat her with.

Well, okay, not a wolf. But as near as damn it. She had seen it before, at Kenneth Plumley's cottage. Its appetite for her obviously hadn't waned since then.

She got to her feet and moved away from the van, then secreted herself behind a tree and pocketed her phone again. She was worried that the barking would draw Kenneth back to his vehicle.

She waited. The dog eventually stopped its racket without Kenneth's intervention, so she set off again, deeper into the woods.

She didn't particularly like being here. In addition to Kenneth, there were undoubtedly other vile creatures in the vicinity. She could hear them scurrying and darting through the leaves, and it was such an effort not to let out cries of alarm. She prayed for them not to bite her or run up her leg. Could there be snakes here? There were bound to be spiders – big, evil fuckers with a hundred beady eyes, ready to drop into her hair. And everything smelled damp and musty here: the decay and rot of winter instead of the growth and flowering of the warmer months, redolent of fungi and worms and beetles.

She tried singing to herself in a barely audible whisper. 'This little light of mine, I'm going to let it shine. This little light of mine, I'm going to let it shine . . .'

Her little light turned the trees into pale, thin, angular monsters, towering above her, spiky limbs poised to strike. They looked old but not wise; instead they seemed ready to destroy first and ask questions later.

'Let it shine, let it shine, let it shine . . .'

And then there was another light.

She wasn't sure at first. It was so dim, almost drowned by the eerie glow cast by her phone.

She stopped in her tracks and covered her torchlight. It was there, all right, like some mythical shining pot of gold in the heart of the woods.

She allowed herself to be drawn towards the source of the emanation. As she got nearer, she began to hear sounds: the thudding and scraping of metal against soil.

She turned off her torch entirely, relying instead on the feeble light that reached out to her through the trees.

Let it shine, let it shine . . .

Despite the cushioning of the damp earth underfoot, she was aware that she was still making noise. Twigs continued to snap and she frequently stumbled on pale, knobbly roots that had emerged from the ground like bones. Whenever there was a pause in the activity ahead of her, she halted too, pressing on only when the noises resumed.

And then she saw.

She was standing behind a tree, clutching its rough bark to steady herself as she peered around its trunk.

She could see a small clearing, lit up by a lamp at its centre. At the far edge of the clearing, panting and grunting as he worked, was Kenneth Plumley, digging a hole in the soil.

And to one side of the hole, all ready to be consigned to its final resting place, was something wrapped up in dark material.

Something the shape of a human body.

32

Izzy ducked behind the tree, clamped her hand over her mouth. She so wanted to yell, to scream, because that thing out there, that thing with its mouth, its eyes, its nose all tightly covered over – that was probably Melissa. That was what remained of the girl who thought she had turned a corner, who had made a decision to put her mistakes behind her and start again, the girl who not so long ago Izzy had been tightly hugging. And now here she was. Dead. About to be buried under a heavy layer of wet, worm-infested earth, never to be seen again, never to laugh or cry or love again.

Izzy didn't know what to do. She had trudged all this way without the merest ghost of a plan in her head. And that was mainly because she hadn't expected to encounter this, hadn't really known what to expect. Despite her certainty about what Kenneth Plumley was and what he had done, her mind had refused to grapple with the reasons for his need to be away from prying eyes.

But now she had been confronted with an answer that hit her like a brick, and she didn't know what to do with that information. She was here alone. She couldn't challenge him or even reveal her presence, not in these circumstances. He would stove her head in with that spade and bury her along with Melissa.

She had to get out of here, to summon help.

That was if anyone would listen.

Proof, she thought. Josh keeps telling me I need proof.

She opened the camera app on her phone, made sure the flash

was off. She edged around the tree again. Kenneth was still hard at work. She raised the phone in front of her, centred the camera lens on the terrible scene. It was too far away. Izzy tried zooming in, but the phone struggled with the dim light, wildly altering its focus in order to lock onto something it understood. She zoomed out again, took a deep breath, thumbed the capture button.

To Izzy, the artificial shutter noise was almost deafening. She had remembered to cancel the flash but in her anxious state she had totally forgotten about sound.

Kenneth abruptly stopped his labours. His face snapped towards Izzy, and she ducked behind the tree again.

No, she thought. Surely he can't have heard that? Not over that distance. It's pure coincidence.

She held her breath. Kenneth did not resume his work.

He's taking a break, she thought. Dig, you fucking maniac, dig!

And then her nerve broke and she was pushing herself away from the tree and running, bouncing off trees and tripping over roots and slipping down slopes, her heart in her mouth, choking off her need to scream for someone, anyone, to help her, to believe her, to stop this madness only she ever saw. She fumbled awkwardly with her phone, desperately struggling to get the torch back on now that she was once more enveloped in blackness, and thinking, Don't drop it, don't lose the only thing you've got to get you out of here. And when the light finally did reappear, she started to worry about how much battery power it was consuming, that it was probably going to die soon, which meant that she would probably also die soon, and her stress levels suddenly ramped up and now she really did want to cry and pray for divine intervention because, please God, she didn't want to end up like Melissa, under several feet of mud and insects and squirrel shit, and he might even bury her alive, he might do that just for fun after how she had dared to go up against him. And if that were not bad enough, it also occurred to her that she had no idea where she was going – every direction looked exactly the same and she hadn't laid a trail of breadcrumbs like in that other happy children's story about the kids who get shoved into the old lady's oven or whatever. She was lost, and she had no sense of direction at the best of times. Andy was always laughing at how she never knew where to go to find the exit of department stores, but this was no shop with bright sweaters and crystal glass and heady perfume, this was a fucking forest full of lethal critters and the wolf with the teeth that were all the better to eat her with, and the mad axeman who any minute was going to jump out in front of her and say 'Here's Kenny!' This wasn't funny, it was the least fun she'd ever had in her all-too-brief existence, and why did every tree have to look like every other fucking tree?

And then there was light.

Not her light, not the light from the phone that was about to burst a blood vessel with the effort it was putting into squeezing out some energy. No, this was other light, some distance in front of her, and what she could only hope now was that it wasn't Kenneth's light, that she hadn't run round in a circle like some headless chicken, and that she really wasn't about to end up headless. But there was a noise, too. A heavenly noise. Not singing angels, because she was happy to wait several decades before hearing them, but instead something even more welcome: the rising drone of an engine!

The light grew, the sound grew, and then it was filling the air, assaulting her senses. It arrived and then left in an instant, but now she had direction, she had an objective, and she kept her focus on that, kept going towards that point with a determination that was enough for her to knock down any tree that dared stand in her way.

And then she exploded out from the woodlands, free at last of the dankness and the smells and the threat. Here was the open road again, her salvation. She ran along it, towards the hill, back to her car, and if someone else was to stop for her now, she wouldn't care who it was, she just needed to be with another human being, someone who wasn't Kenneth fucking Plumley.

But then she found the car, its little blue butt poking out from the trees, and she cried with joy at the sight of it. She threw herself inside, located her ignition key, fired up the engine, and then she put it in reverse, revved and revved, but the damn thing wouldn't move, it couldn't get its creaking old bones past a root or a stump or whatever, and she started crying again as it felt as though the engine might burst into flames any second now, and once again death was breathing down her neck.

She had left the handbrake on.

She took it off too hastily and it was like the car had been shot out of a cannon onto the road. She slammed on the brakes, spun the wheel, shifted into first, and then she was roaring back up the hill, willing the car to get to the top like The Little Engine That Could, all the while checking her mirrors for any sign that Kenneth was coming after her.

She drove like a maniac back towards town, breaking all the speed limits and probably the car too. She needed to be surrounded by people again, to see lights and traffic; it was only when she got these things that she felt safe enough to pull into a pub car park, and even then she left the engine running.

She picked up her phone from the passenger seat, her hands trembling, then hesitated. A call to 999 was the obvious choice, but she could imagine how it would go. *Hello, I've just followed a guy into the woods, and . . . No, I don't make a habit of doing that, but that's not the point. He's burying a body . . . Well, I didn't actually see the body, but I saw something wrapped up that looks like a body and he's definitely digging a hole, and it's the same guy who abducted the woman who works in my bookshop, and . . . Hello? Hello?*

There was only one other option she could think of, and so she made the call.

'Hello, Izzy.'

Josh Frendy sounded tired and a little bit like he knew he was going to regret answering this call.

'Josh, I need your help and I need it now. It's Kenneth Plumley. He's burying a body.'

The pause was worryingly long. 'What?'

'Plummers. A body. Probably Melissa. He's burying her in the woods. You need to get here right now.'

'Izzy . . . Izzy, what is this?'

'I'm serious! I followed him. I saw him. He's digging a hole right now. Please listen to me. You can catch him red-handed if you hurry.'

'Izzy, I'm at home. I've had a long day. If you really want to make another complaint about Mr Plumley, you should call the police station.'

'You know as well as I do that they won't do anything about it. They'll fob me off.'

'You think? A hot tip like this, I'm sure they'll send out every car at their disposal.'

'There's no need to be sarcastic. Look, I know I've been a pest, but this time you can check it out for yourself. I have proof. Wait, I'm sending you a picture.'

'Izzy . . .'

'Wait.' She launched the photograph across the airwaves. 'Have you got it?'

'No.'

'Give it a second.'

'Okay, it's here now. What am I looking at?'

'You see it? That's Kenneth, digging a hole.'

'Looks like a black cat in a coal cellar to me.'

'I know it's not great, but it's the best I could do. Please, Josh, you need to hurry. I'm sure he's still there.'

'Izzy, this is ridiculous. Why are you even doing this, after all that's happened?'

'Because . . . because I can't let it go, okay? I can't. He's putting my friend Melissa into a hole. You have to catch him before he leaves.'

There was a long silence and then a heavy sigh.

'Where are you?'

33

Every minute she waited felt like an hour. She could hear voices and music from within the pub, people enjoying themselves, not knowing what she knew, not aware of what was going on in their community.

A dark Audi entered the car park, slowed, then pulled into a bay. Josh Frendy got out. Izzy left the Peugeot and went across to him.

'Josh, thank you. Thank you for believing me.'

He grunted, and she knew he was saying he hadn't gone as far as admitting he believed her.

'I hope this isn't another wild goose chase, Izzy.'

'It's not. I promise.'

He gestured towards his car. 'Get in.'

She opened the passenger door and lowered herself onto the plush leather seat. This was so much swisher than her Fiat or Andy's Peugeot. Josh pressed a button and the engine purred into life.

She started giving directions. When they reached the quieter part of the road she said, 'You might need help. He's dangerous.'

Josh seemed unconcerned. 'Let's just check it out first, shall we?'

He's still not convinced, she thought. That's why he's not worried about Plummers. He still thinks I'm making this up.

'Can't you put your foot down?' she asked.

He gave her a glance that said, *I'm a police officer. I obey the law.*

They eventually reached the wooded road. Izzy felt her stomach churn with anticipation.

'There's a big hill up ahead. Plumley is just on the other side of it.'

The car sailed over the hill with no noticeable increase in effort.

'Here! Pull in here.'

Josh stopped the car and put on his hazard lights before getting out. 'Now what?'

'Have you got a torch?'

Josh stared at her, then opened the boot and took out a massive black torch with a rubberised case.

'Along here,' she said. She rushed ahead, beckoning to him to keep up. She found the spot where she had come off-road with the Peugeot, then started jogging.

'It's around here somewhere. Keep up. I need more light.'

Josh picked up the pace behind her.

'There!' she said. 'Tyre tracks. See them?'

She headed for the trees, waiting for the colours of the van to jump out at her as they had before.

'Can I take the torch, please?' she asked.

Josh handed it to her and she kept going, scanning the trees and the ground. She was getting a bad feeling about this.

'It's not far now, I'm sure of it.'

But then the tyre tracks came to an end and she realised the van had gone.

'Shit!' she said. 'He's escaped. We took too long!'

'Izzy—'

'He was here! Can't you see the tyre marks? I wasn't lying.'

'Izzy, those tracks could have been caused by any vehicle. They—'

'Except they weren't caused by any vehicle. Most people don't drive into the woods, do they? It was Plumley's van. I saw it.'

She started moving deeper into the woods.

'Izzy, where are you going now?'

'I'll prove it to you. I'll show you where he buried Melissa.'

She heard Josh mumble something under his breath, but he followed her nonetheless. She only wished she knew exactly where she was going. The way ahead was much clearer with this powerful torch, but none of it seemed familiar.

'Izzy, do you know where we're going?' Josh asked.

'Yes, of course,' she lied. 'Did you bring a gun?'

'A gun? No, I didn't bring a gun. This isn't America.'

'You should have brought a gun. A truncheon might not be enough in a situation like this.'

'Well, that's fine, because I haven't brought a truncheon either.'

'What kind of cop are you?'

'A gullible one, apparently.'

'That's uncalled for. This is serious shit, Josh. Plummers was right about . . . *here!*'

More by chance than design, she had found the clearing. But there was no sign of Kenneth Plumley.

'This is it?' Josh asked, his tone noticeably lacking in excitement.

'Well, what did you expect? Fireworks and a big neon sign? He was here. I was behind that tree when I took the photo.'

While Josh began to trace the perimeter, Izzy approached the spot where she had seen Kenneth working. She started scraping leaves aside with her foot.

Josh said, 'There's no sign of anyone having been here, Izzy.'

'No? Then what do you call this?'

She kept the torchlight fixed on the ground while Josh came and stood next to her.

'Look,' she said. 'You see how the soil has been freshly turned over underneath these leaves? The way it forms a mound?'

'I see it.'

'And then there's this . . .'

She crouched, playing the light across the ground to cast shadows. A large footprint was clearly visible in the damp earth.

'I see that too.'

'So now do you believe me?'

Josh said nothing for a while. Then: 'Come with me.'

'Where are we going?'

'Back to the road. I'm going to need some assistance.'

Izzy wanted to punch the air. This was it, the proof she needed. This would nail that bastard.

This is for you, Melissa, she thought. I was too late to save you, but I can get you justice now. He's going to pay for what he did to you.

They got back to the car, and Josh told her to wait inside while he walked away and made some phone calls.

'Help is on its way,' he said when he returned.

'Thank you,' she said, and a tear ran down her cheek.

'You okay?'

She nodded. 'Grateful tears. You listened to me.'

'That's always been my downfall.'

'What do you mean?'

'Nothing.'

'Do you mean your wife?'

He nodded. 'I listened to her when she said I should ask her to marry me. I also listened to her when she said it was time to end it. I should stop listening to women.'

'Women are always right.'

'So they keep telling me.'

'I was right about this, wasn't I?'

He ducked the question. 'You're an idiot.'

'Rude.'

'You are. If Kenneth Plumley is what you say he is, then you've been taking huge risks with him.'

'I . . . I don't see it that way.' Even as the words came out, she knew she was rejecting the truth. She had been terrified for her life in those woods, her pulse rate still high now.

'Well, maybe you should,' Josh said. 'Real life isn't like all those books you read. You could get hurt.'

A wave of emotion hit her. A wave of caring, of concern. It squeezed her heart.

'You're a good man, Sergeant Frendy.'

'No. I'm an idiot too. I need to stop listening.'

'Never do that. Never stop caring.'

He went silent then. After a while, he turned on the car radio, and while the music played they chatted about trivial things.

Eventually, two cars pulled up in front of them. Two uniformed police officers climbed out of a marked estate, while a bald man in a puffer jacket got out of a dark saloon car.

'Here comes the cavalry,' Josh said.

'Who's the bald guy?' Izzy asked.

'My boss. I don't have the authority to green-light a search like this. Wait here.'

Josh got out of the car and went to join his colleagues. She watched them chat, Josh gesturing in her direction and then towards the trees.

A minute later, a large van with 'Scientific Support Unit' written on it drew up. A man and a woman in plainclothes got out and entered into discussion with the others, then they opened up the rear of the van and began donning protective suits and dragging out equipment.

Izzy gulped. She had seen plenty of real-life crime scene investigations on television, but the magnitude of the response here was still mind-blowing.

When it seemed everyone was ready, Josh beckoned to Izzy to leave the car. She walked up to the group, feeling like she was going on stage in front of an audience of hundreds. Josh invited her to lead the way.

Finding the clearing was easier this time, the route now imprinted on Izzy's brain. When they arrived, Josh told her to remain at a distance with him and the other police officers while the forensics people worked on uncovering what was beneath the mound of earth.

It wasn't long before they discovered something.

'It's some kind of plastic sheeting,' the woman said. 'Like a tarpaulin or something.'

Izzy's heart was hammering in her chest.

'Keep at it,' Josh's boss said.

As the excavation continued, Izzy couldn't prevent herself from letting out a whimper. Josh turned to her, then grabbed her arm and started to lead her further away.

'You don't need to see this,' he said. 'Stand over here and—'

She didn't know what the commotion was at first. She heard heavy footsteps and rustling and scrambling and then there were voices, loud voices, and then she saw him.

Kenneth Plumley.

He thundered into the clearing and he was yelling something at the police, and there was something dark and angular clutched in his hand.

'*He's got a gun!*' Izzy screamed.

Josh was suddenly running, racing towards Kenneth, who stood looking confused as officers descended on him. He shouted something and raised the thing in his hand, and Josh launched himself, seemingly covering a vast distance in his flight before smashing into his target. The two landed heavily and rolled on the ground, and Izzy could no longer see the gun. She didn't know why, but she found herself moving towards them, her eyes wide with fear and the need to find the weapon.

The other police officers piled in and Kenneth was quickly sub-dued, but still he kept telling them to stop, that they shouldn't, that what they were doing was wrong, and Izzy kept walking, scanning the ground.

And then she found it.

It wasn't a gun.

It was a cross, crudely fashioned from two pieces of wood screwed together.

She held it out in front of Kenneth, now pinned beneath the officers.

'You sick bastard,' she said. 'You came back to mark her grave. Why would you do that?'

'No,' he said. 'I mean, it's not what you think. I—'

'Keep at it!' Josh's boss called to the crime scene investigators. 'I want to know what's in that tarpaulin.'

'Please,' Kenneth said. 'You have to stop. You can't do this.'

Izzy continued to stare at him, stunned by his boldness, his arrogance.

A minute later, the woman in the protective over-suit returned. 'We've got something.'

'A body?' Josh asked.

The woman glanced at Izzy before answering. 'You'd better come and see for yourself.'

Izzy watched them go. Josh and his superior stood over the burial site as one of the investigators crouched and lifted a flap of material. Izzy winced, even though she couldn't see what they were staring at. She looked at Kenneth again. He was stretching an arm out towards the grave he had made, and tears were running down his cheeks.

Too late for your remorse, she thought.

Josh came back to her, his head low. She felt pain from him, a heaviness that came with death. She let out a cry.

'It's her, isn't it? It's Melissa.'

Josh nodded at the uniformed officers guarding Kenneth. 'Let him up.'

Izzy watched in disbelief as they released their hold on Kenneth and allowed him to stand.

'What are you doing?' she said. 'That man's a killer.'

Josh breathed out harshly. 'It's a dog.'

'What?'

'The body. It's a dog.'

Her eyes darted in search of a more acceptable truth. 'No. It can't be.'

Kenneth staggered across to them. 'I told you. You had no right. It's my dog. Barclay. I made a cross for him.'

He pointed to the object still in Izzy's hand. She raised it, flipped it over. Fastened to its other side was a metal dog tag, the name 'Barclay' engraved on it.

'No,' she said. 'I followed you. The dog was alive. It was in your van.'

'My dog was hit by a car earlier. I brought him here to bury him because it was his favourite place. He loved it here. He . . .'

He choked back a sob. Izzy wanted to vomit.

'I thought he needed a marker. A cross,' Kenneth said. 'So I went back—'

'LIAR!' Izzy yelled at him. 'You made a switch. You saw me watching you, and so you killed the dog and swapped the bodies. Where's Melissa? What have you done with her body?'

'Izzy—' Josh said.

'No! It wasn't the dog. The dog was fine when I was here earlier. Take a closer look at it. You'll see the damage wasn't caused by a car.'

'Izzy—'

'Check out the tarpaulin. And the van. Take it to your labs. There'll be forensic evidence. They'll prove I'm telling the truth.'

'ENOUGH!'

The single word ricocheted through the woods.

'Enough,' Josh said again, more quietly now. He addressed Kenneth. 'Mr Plumley, please accept my apologies. I'm sorry we've disturbed you at this upsetting time.'

Izzy stepped forward, her mouth open to speak again, to let it be known that this was so wrong, such an upside-down view of the truth. But then she saw the hardness in Josh's eyes and she remained silent.

'I'm afraid that you won't be allowed to re-bury your dog here,' Josh continued. 'It's against the law. But that doesn't excuse the way you've been treated tonight. Please accept my assurances that it won't be allowed to happen again.' He turned his eyes on Izzy as he said this, driving the warning home.

Kenneth gestured towards the burial plot. 'I can't take him home. Not in that state.'

Josh thought about this for a few seconds. 'Would you like us to dispose of him properly for you? It's the least we can do.'

Kenneth nodded dolefully.

While Josh went back to his boss, presumably to issue another grovelling apology, Izzy kept her gaze fixed on Kenneth. He stared back at her in the gloom, the glint of torchlight reflected in his eyes and the wetness on his cheeks, and she detested him, hated him more than anything she had ever hated in her life. She wanted to leap at him, to claw that light from his eyes and match them to the dull lifelessness that was already in his heart. He was coldness, he was ice, he was death personified.

And when Josh came back and took her by the elbow and she went to protest and he told her not to say another word as he led her away, she looked back one more time and she saw Kenneth Plumley raise a palm in a goodbye gesture.

And on his face was a smile.

34

She tried to talk. Tried several times to explain, to justify.

He was having none of it.

Didn't even bother to reply.

He just drove in silence.

She could see his answers, though. Clear as day. They hung on him like a written sign. *We're finished*, they said. *I don't want to hear from you ever again.*

It made her sad. Made her cry.

When they pulled up in the pub car park, she made no attempt to get out of Josh's Audi, and he made no immediate attempt to eject her.

'Josh, I want you to know . . . I want you to know that I wasn't messing you around tonight. And not just tonight. Kenneth Plumley is much cleverer than I thought. He—'

'Izzy—'

'Okay, you don't want to hear about Plumley. I get that. After all I've put you through, I get it. What I'm trying to make you understand and believe is that I've been honest with you all along. But it hasn't worked out as I wanted it to, and I'll just have to accept that.'

'Yes, you do need to accept it. There can't be a repeat of this.'

'No,' she said. And that should have been it. She should have accepted defeat and got out of the car and gone home. But instead she added, 'I'm not wrong about him, though.'

It was the mistake that opened a steam release valve in Josh. 'Jesus!' he said. 'Will you listen to yourself? You *are* wrong. You've been wrong all along. *That's* the thing you need to accept. I don't know why I'm even here tonight. I should have listened to my instincts, because they seem to be a damn sight more accurate than yours.'

'So why did you come out tonight?'

'God only knows! I must be a glutton for punishment. I have just made myself look a complete idiot. I'll be the talk of the force for years to come. And all because of you.'

'I said I was sorry.'

He rounded on her. 'Actually, no, you didn't say you were sorry. Not once have you apologised. You just keep telling me why you're right and everybody else is wrong, including me.'

'Do I do that?'

'Yes, you do.'

'Then . . . let me apologise properly. Let's go into this pub and I'll buy you a drink and I'll tell you—'

'*I don't drink, Izzy!* I've told you that before. Do you ever listen to anyone but yourself?'

The strength of his outburst shocked her, and she stopped talking.

'I'm sorry,' Josh said. 'I shouldn't have shouted at you. I shouldn't get angry at you. It's unprofessional. But damn, you have a knack of pushing my buttons.'

'It's one of my many talents,' she said, but he didn't smile.

'Izzy, I think you need to talk to someone about this.'

'That's what I've been doing. That's what keeps getting me into trouble.'

'No, I don't mean the police. I mean a doctor. I think you've got a problem.'

'Oh, God, not you as well. You're the second person today who's—' She stopped herself.

'What? Who else has said that?'

'Nobody.'

'Izzy. Who?'

Shit, she thought. Might as well aim for a clean sheet now, ask for all my other offences to be taken into consideration.

'Mrs Vernon.'

'Mrs Vernon? The head of Hemingway School?'

'Yes, that Mrs Vernon.'

'You spoke to her? Today? When? Right after I told you to go back to work and forget about your private investigating?'

'Possibly then.'

Josh threw his hands up in the air. 'Oh, for f— Why do I even bother?'

'Because you like me?'

'No, not that. I don't like you. You give me stress and sleepless nights and indigestion. How could I like someone who does that to me?'

'I could show you another card trick, if you like.'

'I'll pass.' He sighed. 'Look, Izzy, I'm serious. You are treading on very thin ice here. If Kenneth Plumley decides to make life difficult for you, we'd have to throw the book at you.'

'Which book?'

'The one that has chapters on wasting police time, harassment, stalking . . .'

'Plummers won't do that. He won't push.'

'What makes you so sure?'

'Because if he went on record, you'd have to open a formal investigation, and that means you'd have to look at him a lot more closely. That's the last thing he wants.'

'Or maybe – hear me out here – maybe he just wants a quiet life. Maybe he's just an ordinary guy going about his ordinary business, walking his ordinary dog that tragically got killed by an ordinary car on an ordinary road, and he just wants to be left alone to get on with his ordinary life. He did his duty in coming forward about a crime, and now he's regretting it because someone with a grudge has decided they want to make his life a misery.'

'I don't have a grudge. Or at least I didn't before he started killing young women.'

'Well, that's not what he says. And right now, I know which way my sympathies are leaning.'

She stared at him. 'You can't be serious. You believe his nonsense?'

'What nonsense? All the nonsense has been one-way, as far as I can see. Every accusation you've made about him has proved to be unfounded. You keep making a fool of yourself, and it needs to stop. Get some help, Izzy, and *stay away from Plumley.*'

The final four words were hammered home with a force that left Izzy almost shaking. Her vision clouded over, and she turned her head away from Josh to hide her tears.

'Izzy, did you hear what I said?'

She blinked, faced him again, nodded. 'I heard. And you'll be happy to know I'll be taking your advice.'

He looked surprised. 'You will?'

'Yes. I promise. I can't do this anymore. It's eating me up. I can't stand the disappointment. I can't stand feeling so shitty when everything I try goes tits-up. I've had enough. It's over to you now. There are at least three dead girls out there, and I hope for everyone's sake that you catch whoever did it. Because I'm out. I'm going back to my books and my partner and my life, and I'm glad I met you, Josh, because you're a lovely man and a good police officer, and I think now I'll say goodbye.'

She got out of the car then. Got out and closed the door behind her on Josh's words. Walked quickly away before Josh had time to think about coming after her, but why would he do that anyway?

Why would he want to waste his time following up the ridiculous accusations of such a loser? Why wouldn't he be happy to eliminate the unfathomable complication in his life that was a twenty-three-year-old bookseller called Isobel Lambert?

35

Kenneth wore a broad grin as he drove home.

Another victory. He'd fooled them all.

Yes, it had been close. That Izzy was a fiendish bitch. She'd almost had him this time. If he hadn't caught sight of her in the woods . . .

But he had. He was alert, clever, adaptable. It was like playing chess. For every pathetic attack she mounted, he responded with a combined defence and counter-attack. She couldn't win. She just kept making herself look desperate and obsessive and a little bit unhinged.

So that was why he was smiling.

And also now crying.

He stopped the car at the side of the road. He could no longer see where he was going.

Barclay.

He'd got him as a puppy. A rescue. They'd been together a long time. He thought they'd have at least a couple more years together.

But look what he'd done.

He didn't think he was capable of such an act, not with something he loved. And there were few things in this world he truly loved.

She had driven him to this. Izzy Lambert. What alternative did he have? Like chess, sometimes you have to make sacrifices to come out on top.

But Barclay . . .

He wept until his chest ached.

Simon says stop crying like a little girl.

This would have to be an end to it, he decided. He couldn't carry on like this. He needed to take more control of his life. Try to make it something close to normal. Keep the past in the past.

He went home. Parked around the back as usual. Glanced at the passenger seat before he got out, saw that Barclay wasn't there, shed another tear.

He walked into the house without his trusty pet at his side, and he knew they wouldn't even notice. Might even be a whole day before they realised he wasn't around, and even then they wouldn't be especially upset about it. One less mouth to feed.

There was no sign of Polina. Michael was at the kitchen dining table, a chessboard and a glass of beer in front of him.

'Where's Polina?' Kenneth asked.

'She had a migraine. She's gone up to bed.'

Probably blames me for that, Kenneth thought. All the stress I caused her earlier.

He stared at Michael. Ask me, he thought. Go on, ask me about the dog.

'This isn't your beer,' Michael offered instead. 'In case you were wondering. I went out and bought some more. Thought we could have a few together. Maybe play a game or two.'

I could do that, Kenneth thought. I could sit down and play and chat and act like nothing happened.

But that would be going backwards. Like putting on yesterday's dirty clothes.

He went to the fridge and opened it. Michael's beers were lined up neatly on the shelf. Kenneth ignored them and pulled out one of his own cans. He turned to face Michael and popped the tab in an act of clear rejection.

'I'm going to watch TV,' he said.

He started towards the door, then turned.

'I want you out.'

Michael stared back at him.

'I want you out of my house,' Kenneth said. 'You've got till Sunday night to find another place to live.'

And then he went and found his spot on the sofa, in front of his television, his feet up on his coffee table, and he drank his beer and remembered his dog.

36

Sometimes the genie shouldn't be let out of the bottle, the three wishes shouldn't be used up. There are some things that are so powerful, so uncontrollable, that mere humans shouldn't be allowed anywhere near them.

This was how Izzy felt on Thursday morning. Her gift was her curse. It had never brought her or others happiness. It created only misery. If there was a surgical procedure that could remove it, she would gladly go under the knife.

And the funny thing was that she had only ever tried to use her insight for good. Okay, not so funny. More ironic. Like helping an old lady across the road, who then beats you up because she didn't want to go there. It stops being funny when you lose count of the times you've ended up with those bruises.

Izzy longed to be normal. And yet she didn't even know what it was like to be normal. How sweet it must be to live in such blessed ignorance, to move among others without being bombarded by their emotions, battered by their deceits.

'Are you okay?'

This from Abel, staring with concern at her over the top of his spectacles.

She knew she should shrug off her mood. Paste on a smile and say she'd just been lost in thought. But the shroud she wore was too heavy, and she was too tired. She didn't have the energy to concoct the lies that jumped so readily to the lips of others.

'Actually,' she said. 'I'm pretty down today.'

'Are you thinking about Melissa?'

It was a good question, and in truth the answer was no. Melissa was dead. Izzy was the only one who knew that for certain, and so her thoughts had broadened. But at the same time, and to her shame, she realised that her spinning plates of thoughts had been entirely about herself. She had been absorbed in self-pity, that most destructive of sins.

'I'm thinking about lots of things. Sometimes the world doesn't seem very fair.'

'It isn't fair.' He got up and came towards her. With a sweep of his arm he gestured towards his packed shelves. 'You know why people like books?'

It seemed such a non-sequitur, and with no succinct answer – a whole dissertation would be required to do it justice. And so she stared at him blankly.

'Because books are the only place in which one can find a fair and just world. Not every book, I admit; just go to our friend Will Shakespeare if you want a story where everyone dies. But if you want the detective to catch the criminal, the pauper to marry the prince, the loser to win, the sad person to find happiness, you can find all that in books. People need these views of the world. They need to be told that the good will be rewarded and the bad will be punished. Books give them that when the real world lets them down.'

'I want life to be like it is in those books,' she said. 'It hurts too much.'

Abel looked at her for a while, and then he said, 'Wait here.'

He disappeared into the back room, and was gone for several minutes. In that time, no customer came or went, as if they knew better than to disturb this moment.

When Abel returned, he was carrying two mugs.

'What's that?' she asked.

'The cure for all sadness.'

He set a mug down in front of her, and she took in all its colours and its perfume and its sweetness.

'Hot chocolate,' she said. 'With whipped cream and marshmallows!'

'Guaranteed comfort in a mug.'

'I've never seen you drink this. Where have you been hiding it?'

'I don't have it very often.' He patted his paunch. 'At my age I have to be careful. But today I had to buy it. Today is special.'

'Why? Why is it special?'

'Today is the anniversary of the death of my Zara. Whenever either of us were sad, we would make hot chocolate just like this. It always made things better. This is the first time I have made it for anyone else.'

'Oh, Abel.' She threw his arms around him.

'You're beginning to make a habit of this,' he said. 'But I'm sure Zara won't mind.'

'You're making me cry.'

He pushed her gently away. 'Stop it or you'll shrink my cardigan.' He paused. 'I couldn't stop my Zara dying. Nothing worked, not even prayer. Sometimes we have to accept that there are things we cannot change.'

'That's what I'm finding difficult. There's something I've tried to fix, but I haven't been able to do it.'

'Did you try your hardest?'

'Yes. I think so.'

'Then that's all that matters. Now drink.'

Izzy picked up the mug, and her lips fought through the fluffy marshmallows and cloud of whipped cream to get to the shock of the sweet heat below.

'Nice?' Abel asked.

'Wonderful.'

'Feel better?'

'A little.'

He laughed. 'Sometimes it takes a while. I'll tell you what: why don't I give you the afternoon off?'

'Oh, Abel, you don't need to do that. I can't leave you here to cope by yourself.'

He nodded to the emptiness around them. 'Dealing with all these customers, you mean? I think I'll manage. And I think you have better places to be. Someone to share your troubles with.'

Izzy thought about Andy. Tonight would be her last late shift. Knocking off early would mean being able to see Andy properly before her own work began. They could talk. She so needed to talk.

'Has anyone ever told you that you're a very wise man, Abel?'

'Frequently.' He pointed heavenward. 'Just don't tell Zara. She thinks I'm a schmuck.'

* * *

She drove home as though the weight lifted from her enabled her little car to breeze through town. Josh was right: she needed to step down from her self-appointed role as righter of wrongs; she wasn't suited to it. Abel was also correct: she needed to stop beating herself up, accept what she couldn't change, and get on with her life. Everyone else was right, she was wrong, and that was just how it was, next patient please.

Andy would be up and about now, with several hours to go before her evening shift. Izzy planned to use that time to confess everything, to clean the slate. She was going to tell Andy how stupid she'd been, how obsessed, but it was all at an end now, and all she wanted to do was spend every minute she could with the love of her life. She knew Andy would forgive her, because that was the sort of person she was. She'd call Izzy a complete dickhead and a few other choice phrases, but it would all be good.

She could hear Andy's music even before she came through the front door. 'The Imperial March' from *Star Wars*. It felt ominous.

Just bad timing, Izzy told herself. The next track will be from *Frozen* or *Mary Poppins* or whatever.

She called out to Andy, but could hear nothing over the music. She turned it down, went back out to the hall, called again. Still no reply, but she could hear noises coming from the bedroom.

Something was wrong.

Izzy moved cautiously down the hallway.

'Andy? You there?'

Nothing.

If that's Andy, Izzy thought, then why isn't she answering? And if it's not Andy . . .

She was beginning to wish she'd picked up a knife from the kitchen.

She reached the bedroom door, pushed it open, stepped inside . . .

Andy didn't even look up. She was busy packing a bag. She was also busy radiating a force that rivalled anything Darth Vader could produce. A force driven by anger and hurt.

'Andy? What are you doing?'

'What does it look like I'm doing?'

'Why are you packing?'

'Because I won't be coming back here after my shift tonight. I'm taking my car – which, by the way, is full of twigs and leaves and shit, and I'd quite like to know why – and then I'm driving straight to my mum's house.'

'I can explain about the car. I needed—'

'Izzy, this isn't about the car. It's about you and me and what I thought was a relationship built on trust.'

Izzy stared as Andy stuffed a sweater unceremoniously into her bag. She could feel the raw emotion, but had no idea what lay behind it.

'Andy, I don't know what's going on here. Have I done something wrong?'

'It's what you *haven't* done. Christ, Izzy, I always thought we told each other everything.'

'We do. And I've been wanting to talk to you properly for ages, but we've hardly seen each other. It's okay now, though, because I'm over the Kenneth Plumley thing. That's all in the past now, and I thought we could—'

'What are you talking about? This isn't about Kenneth fucking Plumley. Just for once, can you stop making things about *you* and concentrate instead on *us*?'

'I am. I do. I just ... I don't know what I've done to upset you like this.'

'Well, why don't you just read my mind, like you do with Kenneth Plumley?'

It was a cutting remark, and Izzy sensed the regret as soon as it left Andy's mouth.

'Andy, please. Whatever it is, tell me and I'll do my best to fix it.'

'You can't fix this one. Nobody can fix this.' She grabbed a top from a hanger in the wardrobe and made a hash of folding it up.

'That's going to come out creased. Do you want me to help?'

Andy suddenly stopped packing and lowered her head. Izzy knew there were tears.

'You knew,' Andy said. 'You've known all along.'

'What about?'

Andy raised her head, aimed glistening, accusing eyes. 'About my mum.'

Izzy had trouble getting her jaw to work. 'Andy, I ...'

'You knew, and you kept it from me.'

'I wasn't sure. I—'

'You were sure. When it comes to people you know, you're always sure.'

'I don't know your mother all that well.'

Andy shook her head. 'Don't bullshit me. You know her well enough. Better than that Percy and Ethel couple.'

'Who?'

'The old couple. In the bookshop. The other day.'

'Ronald and Edith.'

'Whatever. A couple of brief chats with them and you were able to come up with a complete medical diagnosis. What's so different about my mother?'

'It . . . it wasn't a diagnosis. I just knew Ronald was lying about his health.'

'And my mum?'

Izzy hesitated. 'All right. Look, I knew she wasn't being wholly truthful about her reflux, but she—'

'No buts. You knew. You knew, and you kept it from me.' Andy opened one of her drawers and started manically pulling things out of it and dropping them on the floor like they never should have been there in the first place.

'Wait a minute. Who was it who said I should let Ronald and Edith live their life the way they want to live it? Who was it who said Ronald had every right to tell a few white lies so that his wife wouldn't fall apart? Oh, that's right, it was you.'

'That's different.'

'How is it different? Because this time it affects you?'

'Yes! Because I'm not going to fall apart. I'm a paramedic, for Christ's sake. I have some medical training. I can't fix my mother, but I can at least give her advice and make sure she gets the help she needs. And I could have done that a lot sooner if you hadn't kept the truth from me.'

Izzy watched Andy continue to turn the bedroom into a dumping ground. 'What are you looking for?'

'That brown leather belt for my jeans.'

Izzy pointed to the bag. 'It's there. You already packed it.'

Andy checked, clucked in irritation, and then zipped up the bag. 'What's she got?' Izzy asked. 'Your mum.'

'Cancer. Stage four. It's everywhere. Inoperable now.'

Izzy thought she detected a slight emphasis on the word 'now', as though there was a suggestion that earlier action on her part might have saved a life.

'I'm sorry,' she said. 'I was—'

'I can't believe I was taken in by her. Acid reflux, my arse! I've spent years seeing through the stories given me by drug addicts and stab victims, and I couldn't even tell when my own mother was hiding the biggest secret imaginable. You, on the other hand . . .'

She let it lie there, but Izzy could feel the anger bubbling under the surface.

'Andy, I'm really sorry. I don't know what else you want me to say. I was trying to respect her wishes. You don't understand how difficult these things are for me – when to say something and when to let people hold on to their privacy.'

Andy picked up the bag. 'That's just it, isn't it? You still haven't learned. Izzy, you have an amazing gift. You can see things that nobody else can. You have to stop pretending it doesn't exist and start putting it to good use. Sometimes that's going to mean making tough decisions, but you need to have the guts to do what feels right.'

Andy started towards the door.

'When will you be back?' Izzy asked.

'I don't know. My dad hasn't taken the news very well; he's worse than useless at the moment. My mum needs me around for a few days. I'll ring you.'

And then she went. Not even a kiss or a hug. She was just gone.

In a daze, Izzy wandered back to the living room and turned off the music. The place dropped into an eerie silence.

She realised it was their first real row. Like most couples, they'd had disagreements aplenty, but nothing on this scale. She felt torn and battered.

She thought about the charges Andy had levelled at her, and at first she thought they were totally unwarranted. She hadn't done anything maliciously; she had merely allowed someone to hold on to what was theirs. What right did Izzy have to shatter confidentiality without any attempt at consultation? Wasn't that as bad as delving into someone's diary or reading their love letters or listening in on their phone calls and then revealing all their secrets to the world? How the hell could Andy expect her to justify such a grubby intrusion?

But then the precision of Andy's comments punctured her indignation, and regrets began to flow.

It *was* different from Ronald and Edith, wasn't it? The two cases weren't the same at all. For one thing, Ronald had made it crystal clear that he didn't want his dear wife to be crushed by the knowledge of his imminent demise, whereas Andy's mum had made no such request. Izzy had made assumptions on her behalf, when it was perfectly possible that, on the inside, and despite her cover-up, Andy's mother was crying out for someone to offer her a helping hand.

And for another thing, Andy wasn't Edith. She wasn't fragile. As she had pointed out, she was a medically trained professional who might just have something useful to contribute to the well-being of her own parent.

So why hadn't Izzy seen that? Why had it fallen to her distraught partner to highlight these things when she should have been able to see them for herself? Why had she not foreseen the drama that would naturally have flowed from her rash decision-making?

Well, that brought her to the bigger issue.

She was immature.

Too many of the issues that life threw her way were too big for her to handle. And so she ran away. She buried her head in the sand. She knew all this. Knew exactly why she always dressed in black and worked in a bookshop and didn't socialise.

She was afraid.

And it was all because of her gift. She had allowed her super-power to make her less powerful than everybody else.

Use the force wisely, Andy had joked. But there was a serious message there, hammered home in the argument they'd just had. Izzy wasn't like most other people, and what she needed to do was embrace that rather than try to pretend she was 'normal'.

She needed to grow up.

37

Twice she found his name in her contacts, and twice she closed it down again without ringing.

Come on, she told herself. What's wrong with you? You've just given yourself a stern lecture about being such a wimp, and now you can't even make one simple phone call? Come on. Fortune favours the brave, and all that.

She tried again. Her finger hovered over the call icon for a few seconds, and then she held her breath and tapped it.

Done. You're committed now.

The phone rang for ever.

He's seen it's me, and he's not going to answer, she thought. He doesn't need any more grief from me, so why would he answer?

He answered.

'Hello, Izzy.'

She expected more. Sarcasm, maybe. *What is it this time, Izzy? Plummers hide something under your floorboards?* Something along those lines.

She was glad he hadn't gone down that route. He still sounded less than pleased to hear from her, though.

'Hi,' she said. 'How has your day been so far?' That's it. Be friendly. Normal. Someone he wouldn't mind chatting to.

'You want to know how my day has gone?'

'Yes.'

'My day has been shit. My day has involved trying to find two women who have gone missing and having no success whatsoever. As I foretold, it has also involved trying to explain to my boss yet again why I thought it necessary to drag him away from his wife and kids to help me dig a hole in the woods.'

'Oh.'

'Yes, oh.'

'Sorry about that. But you'll be glad to know that I'm not ringing you up to ask you to do anything like that.'

'Well, that's nice to hear, because I was looking forward to another fruitless excursion to take my mind off a day in which I haven't even managed to have lunch yet.'

Ah, she thought. The sarcasm at last.

'Three o'clock and you haven't had lunch?'

'No.'

'Well, that's good.'

'That's your definition of good?'

'Yes. No. What I mean is, you should have lunch. With me. I'll buy you lunch.'

There was a long pause. 'I don't think that's a good idea, Izzy.'

'It is. It's a very good idea. The best idea.'

'No, Izzy, it isn't, and you know it.'

She knew nothing of the sort, but she let it ride. 'Coffee, then. And cake. We could go to Claudette's, like when we first met. For old times' sake.'

'Old times— Izzy, you're acting like we've known each other for years.'

'Feels a bit like that, to be honest. In a good way, I mean. Like, I really think we understand each other now.'

'I'm glad one of us feels that way.'

'Yes, well, anyway . . . Can we do that? Meet for coffee?'

'No, Izzy. I appreciate the offer, but I'm really too busy.'

It was a brush-off. He wanted nothing more to do with her, and it made her sad.

'Then . . . can we at least just meet up for a few minutes? Carrick Park is just around the corner from your station. We could meet there.'

'Izzy . . . what's this all about?'

'It's just . . . I don't like the way we left things. You think I'm a nut, and I get that, I understand why you feel that way, but . . . I want to say goodbye properly.'

'You want to say goodbye?'

'Yes. Properly. I'm not going to bother you again after today. Not ever. Not even with inside information on a plan to rob the bank on Dunster Lane.'

'There's going to be a bank robbery?'

'No. At least I don't think so. That was just an example. My point being that nothing will compel me to contact you after today. Not if you let me say goodbye. We need closure.'

'Closure.'

'Yes. I like things to end properly, like they do in books. Life is messy enough without leaving shoelaces untied.'

'That's a great saying.'

'I think so. I just made it up. Now will you meet me? Please?'

A heavy sigh. 'All right, Izzy. I'd hate you to go around tripping over your shoelaces. What time?'

'Say fifteen minutes? Carrick Park. I'll see you on the first park bench when you reach the lake.'

'I'll do my best.'

Izzy said goodbye and hung up, and then found to her surprise that her heart was pounding furiously, like she'd just been sprinting. She wondered why, and then she realised it was because this was important, and she had to get it right. It would be the most crucial test she'd ever had of her ability to use her gift wisely.

***

Twenty-five minutes later, he still hadn't showed up. She was freezing her arse off on an ice-cold bench, wondering how it was that the ducks in the water didn't seem to feel the cold, but also thinking that Josh had found more important things to do. Because, let's face it, spending his time with a crazy woman in a park was probably not too high on his list of priorities right now.

He could at least have let me know, she thought.

She checked her phone, in case she'd missed a message. An emoji, perhaps, or an amusing GIF. Anything that would suggest he hadn't blown her off completely.

There was nothing on her phone.

She thought about ringing him again, then decided it wasn't worth it. She'd prefer not to have the let-down spelled out for her like she was an idiot.

'Hey,' said a voice from behind.

She turned. It was Josh. Good old dependable Josh. How could she ever have doubted him?

'Sorry I'm late,' he said. 'Had to deal with a couple of things.'

She wondered what it was like to be so busy all the time. Must be exhausting. At the bookshop she found it stressful enough coping with a line of more than two customers at the till.

'No probs. Have a seat. Hope you've got your thermals on, though.'

'It's okay. I've got tights on under these trousers.'

'Really?'

'No, not really. I only wear women's underwear on my days off.' She placed a brown paper bag next to him. 'I got you something.'

'Victoria's Secret?'

'Better than that. A coffee and a piece of that cake you like. Did you know Claudette's does takeaway? Coffee might be a bit on the tepid side now, though.'

'I'll take anything. I feel like somebody's put a nil-by-mouth sign on my back.'

She doled out the food and drink, pointing out that she'd opted for the lemon drizzle again. She hoped the nostalgia might help to soften him up a little.

'So,' he said when he was halfway through his coffee and cake, and all the perfunctory stuff was out the way, 'I can't spend long here, Izzy. They need me to solve all their cases.'

Meaning, *Get on with it already.*

'Does that include Rosie and Melissa?'

He gave her a look that told her the remark was uncalled-for.

'I'm sorry,' she said. 'I didn't mean . . . What I was trying to say, what I was trying to ask was whether you'd made any progress on the missing person cases.'

'Some. None. Depends how you look at it. There are lots of things we've ruled out, not so many we've ruled in.'

'So you still don't know where they are or what happened to them?'

He shot her the look again.

'Oh, shit,' she said. 'I'm ballsing this up already. I'm not having a go, honestly. I was just hoping there might be something. Melissa was my friend.'

'Was?'

She didn't bother changing it to 'is'. This wasn't a time for wishful thinking; it was a time for facing up to hard truths.

'I'm sorry,' she said again. 'I had a whole speech prepared, and I've already strayed off the page.'

'A speech?'

'Don't panic. It won't take hours. There are just some things I need to say to you.'

'You're making me nervous.'

'Not half as nervous as I am.' She took a deep breath. 'The first thing I want you to know is how hard it was for me to come to you in the first place. I don't make a habit of these things. In fact, I pretty much do everything I can to avoid it. People are problematic for me, and their emotions are even more problematic.'

'Well, I suppose that people and their problems are what keep me in a job.'

'Don't get me wrong. Some people are lovely. My partner Andy is lovely, and you're lovely too.'

'Thank you.'

'You're welcome. But generally, I shy away from getting to know people too well because of all the baggage they carry. I've lost count of the number of times that I've tried to use my gift for good and it's backfired on me. You remember I told you about my dad?'

'I remember.'

'Yeah, well, there was also the time I tried to help a girl at school who was being abused. She ended up taking her own life.'

'But not because of what you did.'

'Debatable. Anyway, I've got lots of stories like that. I dropped out of university because I kissed a girl who fancied me.'

'That sounds like a bad reason to drop out.'

'This girl didn't know she fancied me. To be more accurate, she didn't want to admit to herself that she fancied me. She was brought up a strict Catholic, and homosexuality wasn't allowed through the door. Cut a long story short, she turned against me and started spreading nasty rumours. I was already pretty isolated and that just made it worse, so I packed my bags and came home.'

'That was a pretty shitty thing for that girl to—'

'And then there was my first real job. Before I went to the bookshop, I worked in a shoe shop. Just a sales assistant, nothing fancy, but I liked it.'

'So what happened there?'

'I went to the boss and told him that one of the other assistants was a foot fetishist.'

'And was he?'

'Oh, yeah. But only I could see how he got turned on every time he went near someone's pinkies, even though I wanted to barf at some of the feet I encountered. It was his word against mine, and the boss decided to believe him – who, by the way, was a friend of the boss's family – so I was fired.'

Josh raised his eyebrows and shook his head. 'Again, another tough—'

'So you see what I'm up against. When I try to fix things, I break them even more. It got to the point where I'd just stopped trying.'

'And maybe that's for the best. Maybe—'

'Until Kenneth Plumley decided to go on television. He changed things. I could have ignored it. I could have just carried on with my life and pretended it was none of my business. And you're right: maybe that would have been the easiest thing both for me and for you.'

'Well, I won't argue with—'

'But it wouldn't have been the *right* thing, would it? I had to try. I had to tell you what I knew, even though my stress levels were through the roof.'

Josh went silent for a moment, as though he was starting to feel uncomfortable.

'Izzy, you told me. You got it off your chest, and I investigated, and that's it. It's behind us now.'

He was ready for the goodbyes. Practically ushering them in.

'The other thing I want you to know is that I'm not nuts. Not even mildly eccentric. This thing with Plumley hasn't worked out for me, I accept that, but it's not because it's all in my head. The gift I have is real, and it's not just about card tricks. I know things.'

'We've had this discussion, Izzy. What you know and what you can prove are two different things. I hope you agree that I've listened to you and I've acted on everything you've told me, but it didn't pan out, did it? We have to move on. *You* have to move on.'

'Yeah, that's what I told myself. And you're right. I promised you that I would stay away from Plumley, and I'll stick to that promise. There's nothing more I can do.'

'No.'

'But *you* can.'

'I can what?'

'Earlier on, I asked you about the missing women. Rosie and Melissa. You admitted you're getting nowhere with it. I bet the same is true for that other girl, Heather Cunliffe. You still haven't arrested someone for that, have you?'

'Izzy, I don't think we should carry on with this. You told me this was about saying goodbye.'

'And it is! But just hear me out. Please. You're getting nowhere because you're looking in the wrong places and at the wrong people. It's Kenneth Plumley. He's your man. He took all three women, maybe more, and he killed them and he hid their bodies.'

Josh's discomfort had nudged into the irritable stage. 'Okay, Izzy,' he said. 'I've come here and I've listened. Thank you for the coffee and the cake. It's been nice knowing you.'

He stood up, on the verge of exiting her life forever.

She made her move.

'How did your wife die?' she asked.

He was stunned for a couple of seconds, then attempted a recovery.

'I never said she died. I said we were no longer together.'

Izzy shook her head. 'She died, Josh. And you were devastated.'

'I . . . Who told you that?'

'You did, Josh. Even if the fact that you keep photographs of her on your desk wasn't a big enough clue, I read it in you when you spoke about her. I know you now. I know how you feel about things. You miss her terribly. What you said was true, but I could tell it wasn't the full story. And when you told me that you listened when she said things had to end between you, you weren't talking about your marriage, were you?'

Josh turned visibly pale and had to resume his seat on the park bench. He said nothing for a while, and then: 'She . . . Her name was Emma. She found out she had a brain tumour. What they call a glioblastoma. There was nothing the experts could do for her. When she said it was time to end things, she was in a hospital bed and I was holding her hand. She was talking about withdrawing from treatment, about ending her life. We'd only been married two years.'

His pain came at Izzy with agonising force. 'Oh, God. I'm so sorry.'

'If anyone who doesn't know the story asks about her, I dodge the question. It's easier. Their pity brings it all back. Even now I find it difficult to cope sometimes.'

'But at least you've stopped drinking.'

He stared at her again. 'How . . . ?'

'Your reaction last night when I talked about going for a drink. I'd felt it before from you, but last night I was certain. There was a hatred there, but also a regret and a hope that you'd never go there again.'

He nodded. 'After the loss of my wife I became an alcoholic. There's no other word for it. When it started interfering with my job, I went to AA meetings. I'm nearly six months sober now.'

She smiled. 'Congratulations. That's huge.'

'I haven't told anyone about that. How did you know?'

'I told you. I'm not a crazy person and I'm not just a card magician. I can pick up on these things.'

He nodded, but she could tell there was still some doubt there, some suspicion that she must have done some digging around and unearthed the truth about him.

It was time for the final revelation.

'There's something else I know about you.'

'What's that?'

'The real reason you've been so helpful to me, so willing not to dismiss me as just another nut-job.'

He said nothing. Just waited.

'What is it, Josh? What is it about me that reminds you of Emma?'

His eyes glistened. 'I ... I don't know. Something about you. Your smile, maybe. Your voice. I don't know. It was ... I'm sorry. It was stupid of me.'

She reached out for his hand. 'It's not stupid at all, Josh. We all want to hang on to things from our past. I wish I could bring her back for you. I wish that was my gift.'

He looked down at her hand, then back up again. 'I miss her so much.'

'I know. But you're strong. It'll get easier.'

They stayed like that for a while, hand in hand, and then Josh suddenly cleared his throat and stood up.

'I should get back.'

'Yeah. I ... I didn't mean to keep you here so long.'

'That's okay. I learned a lot today. Mostly about myself.'

She laughed. 'I wish I knew myself better.'

He nodded. 'So we got to it eventually.'

'What?'

'The point of all this. The bit where we say goodbye.'

'I suppose we did. Is it okay to give a police detective a hug?'

'Not usually, but I think I can make an exception on this occasion.'

They embraced. Izzy wrapped her arms around a collection of

confused emotions, but amongst them was the bitter-sweetness of one final hug with his wife.

'Goodbye, Izzy,' Josh said.

'Goodbye, Josh.'

He walked away slowly. She let him get a few metres before she found her parting words.

'He'll go back.'

Josh turned. 'What?'

'Plumley. I don't think he'll have gone back to the woods last night, after what happened. He'll have been too spooked. But he will soon. Tonight, tomorrow night, but definitely soon. They're in those woods, Josh. The girls are in there somewhere.'

He didn't answer, but resumed his weary departure. When he was out of sight, Izzy sat back on the park bench and cried copiously – tears of remorse for the way she had manipulated Josh, but also surrogate tears for the man who had fought so desperately not to shed them himself.

38

She had made two promises to Josh, both of which she intended to keep. One was to stay away from Plumley. The other was to seek help.

Which was why she was here.

At Plumley's house.

He wouldn't be at home; he'd still be at the school. So that was the first box ticked. His wife might be home, though. And okay, by a strict interpretation, that might not have been the sort of help Josh meant, but words are flexible, aren't they? The beauty of the English language relies on that fact, so there.

This wouldn't be easy, but since when had any of this been easy? When had any point in the whole of Izzy's life been easy?

She imagined, but had no evidence for it, that wives are usually ferociously protective of their husbands. Which was scary. Izzy didn't know anything about the woman except that she was a Russian internet bride, but somehow that made her seem even more scary. Dangling yourself on a line in cyberspace in the hope of attracting an adoring mate while avoiding all the sharks and other creepy denizens took some guts.

As she had done when all this began, Izzy left her car on the lane and walked up to the house. She stopped for a while on the driveway and stared at the property, taking it in, wondering what reception she might get. What do people do when you tell them their spouse abducts young women, kills them and buries them in the woods?

She approached the door, hesitated, rang the doorbell. It was opened within seconds by a woman with ice-cold eyes and a sliver of a mouth.

'Hi,' Izzy began. 'Mrs Plumley?'

'Yes,' Polina said cautiously.

'I'm sorry to bother you, but I was wondering if I could have a few minutes of your time.'

'What is it about?'

Direct and to the point, Izzy thought. 'It's about your husband. Kenneth.'

'Kenneth? What about Kenneth? Has something happened to him?'

'No, not at all. It's . . . God, this is difficult to talk about.'

'What is so difficult? Who are you?'

'My name's Isobel Lambert. I was a student at Hemingway School a few years ago. I got to know Kenneth very well.'

Polina's eyes narrowed. 'How well?'

'No, not in that way. We were friends. But now . . . well, I think Kenneth is in a lot of trouble.'

'What kind of trouble?'

Izzy looked behind her. There was nobody around, but still it didn't feel right to have this discussion on a doorstep.

'Do you mind if we go inside to talk?'

Polina recoiled. 'I think I should phone Kenneth first. I don't know what is happening here.'

Izzy put out a hand. 'Please, Polina, don't do that. Not before you hear what I have to say.'

'How do you know my name?'

'I . . . Kenneth told me. He said you were from Russia and you met on the internet.'

'When did he tell you this?'

'Saturday. We went for coffee in town. He didn't tell you about it?'

She could tell from the shocked expression on Polina's face that he hadn't, and that was a good thing. If she wasn't being let into his confidence, it made it more likely that she wasn't acting as his accomplice.

Now it was Polina's turn to survey the surrounding area, as though checking for nosy neighbours.

'You can come inside,' she said.

Polina led Izzy through to a kitchen, and invited her to sit at the dining table.

'What is this about, please?' Polina asked.

'Last week, I saw Kenneth on the television, talking about Rosie Agutter, the missing schoolgirl.'

'Yes. So what?'

'He said he witnessed the abduction.'

'Yes. He is hero. He helped the police.'

'No. He didn't help, and he's not a hero. He lied.'

'Lied? What are you talking about?'

'This is going to sound crazy, but your husband took that girl himself.'

Polina stared at her for some time. 'You are right. It is crazy. Why are you saying these things? Why would he take this girl?'

'I don't know why. Maybe he's ill. You know him much better than I do. Does he find it difficult coping with women?'

Polina stiffened. 'That is very personal question. We love each other. There is no problem.'

'Like I say, I don't—'

'Why are you talking to me now? Why don't you go to the police if you know these things?'

'I've been to the police. They tell me I need proof. That's why I'm here.'

'For proof? You want proof from me? Then you are wasting your time.'

'Polina, please. I'm not trying to upset you or make you angry, but I know that Kenneth has been hiding things from you.'

'This is not true. Kenneth tells me everything.'

'Did he tell you about having coffee with me? Did he tell you about the time when my car crashed into his van and we had an argument on the street? Did he tell you about coming to the place where I work to warn me to stay away? Did he tell you about what he does in the woods?'

Polina was starting to look more uncertain. Izzy felt she just needed to keep chipping away.

'What do you mean, in the woods?'

'It's where he takes the girls. He buries them there.'

'Girls? Now it is more than one?'

'Yes. He took my friend Melissa. He warned me to stay out of his business, and when I didn't, he took her and he killed her.'

Polina waved her hands, as though to shoo Izzy away. 'Now you are saying he is murderer? This is ridiculous. I think I have heard enough about this.'

'Polina, did he tell you about the dog? About Barclay?'

'How . . . how do you know the name of our dog?'

'I was there when Kenneth buried him. Did he tell you what happened to Barclay?'

'He said he ran out onto the road and he was hit by a car.'

'That's not true. Kenneth killed him. He was burying Melissa, but he didn't know I was watching. When I went to fetch the police, he killed Barclay and buried him there instead. Here . . .' She found the photo on her phone. 'I took this last night.'

'This is not very clear. It could be anyone.'

'It's not. It's Kenneth, and that's a human body. Look at him closely. You know that's him.'

Polina stared at the screen for a while, then pushed the phone away. 'No. You are creating fantasy. I do not believe any of this.'

'Did Kenneth tell you about the police last night? About digging up Barclay's body? About being questioned by a detective? He didn't, did he? If he's so innocent, why didn't he tell you any of that?'

'I—'

'He disappears, doesn't he? Kenneth goes missing sometimes in the evenings or at night. Do you ever wonder where he goes?'

'He takes dog for long walks. Sometimes he goes to pub.'

'Really? Do you know that, or is that just what he tells you?'

'I believe him. He tells me, and I believe him. Why would I not?'

'Because he's lying to you! His whole life is a lie. He hasn't told you about any of the things he's been doing or the people he's been seeing, including me and the police.'

'But maybe it is you who is liar. I have never met you or heard of you. Maybe for some reason you want to hurt Kenneth. You want to hurt me too.'

'No, Polina. I really don't want that. I promise you.'

'Then what do you want from me? What am I supposed to do with this information?'

'I ... I don't know. I thought that maybe you could help me. Kenneth is a sick man. He needs to be stopped.'

'Kenneth is my husband. He is not sick. He would do anything for me. I trust him.'

'You shouldn't trust him. He's dangerous.'

Polina raised her voice. 'Dangerous? My Kenneth? No, not possible. How do you know these things? Who told you this about Kenneth?'

Izzy had given careful prior consideration to this question. She knew she couldn't start talking about her gift; it would sound as wacky to Polina as it did to others, and she needed Polina to take this seriously. But at the same time, she couldn't concoct a story that would be easily disproved.

'Nobody told me. I just know him well. I know when he's lying. And I bet you do too. I bet that, deep down, he has told you things that you know are lies, about where he goes and what he gets up to. I think you know he has some problems, even though you don't know how bad they are. You're absolutely correct: I could have been wrong about him at the start, but since then he has threatened me and warned me and he has repeatedly lied to me and the police, so I know I'm right. I just can't prove it.'

There was a silence between them, and Izzy knew it signalled a tipping point. Polina would either veer towards kicking her out or demanding to know more.

'This is too much,' Polina said finally. 'I don't understand. I don't know what you want. Are you trying to get money from me?'

Izzy sat back in her chair. 'I don't want money. The only thing I want from you is the truth. There must be something you know about your husband that would confirm what I'm telling you. Something you've found that would prove he took those girls. On both occasions he said he was at the school at the time. Maybe you know different.'

Polina seemed to be turning things over in her mind, but then she shook her head. 'There is nothing like this. Kenneth is a good man. He works hard and he looks after me. That is all.'

Izzy held back a sigh of frustration. This was going nowhere. Whether out of loyalty or sheer ignorance, Polina seemed to have little to offer.

A thought occurred to her. Memories of another figure visible through the French doors in the kitchen.

'Is there anyone else who lives here apart from you and Kenneth?'

'We have lodger.'

'Would he be able to answer any of my questions?'

'No. Michael is not here now, and anyway he is not close to

Kenneth. I do not want him to know about any of this. I do not want you to say these things to anyone.'

Izzy appreciated her objection. The last thing anyone would want is someone spreading rumours that their partner had a penchant for stealing young women off the streets. But now Izzy felt she had exhausted all her options.

'I'm going to leave now, Polina. I won't come back, not unless you want me to. Can I give you my phone number?'

'Wait,' Polina said. She rose from the table, fetched her mobile phone from the worktop near the sink, then returned. 'You can give it.'

Izzy recited her number as Polina tapped it in.

'I know this is a lot to take in,' Izzy said. 'We've never met, and so you have no reason to trust me. I understand that. But please think about what I've said. I'm not making it up. If anything comes to you, or you just want to discuss it further, please call me.'

Polina didn't say she would or she wouldn't, but she seemed pensive as she escorted Izzy out of the house.

Walking down the lane, Izzy breathed a sigh of relief. It could have gone much, much worse, and what that told her was that her accusations hadn't seemed completely off-base to Polina. It was as if they slotted in neatly with things she already knew.

Izzy could do no more. She had planted seeds of doubt in both Polina and Josh. Her only hope was that one of them would come to fruition.

39

Polina hadn't thought it possible, but her life here in England had turned out much crazier than it had been in Russia.

She had been born and raised in a run-down town 400 miles east of Moscow. Decent jobs there were scarce, and the landscape as far as relationships were concerned was equally bleak. Polina's father was a drunkard who assaulted her mother on a regular basis, almost by appointment, and she quickly came to realise that many of the other men she encountered were of a similar mindset, with little imagination for their young spouses crossing the boundaries of the kitchen or bedroom except when doing the daily shopping. Her father explained to her that her fate was sealed in that way because the female mind was wired differently, the two halves of the brain being unable to communicate efficiently enough to permit thinking on the same higher plane as that of the male.

The solution for some of the women she knew was to turn their eyes to the West. Or at least to convince those in the West that they could be saviours, this appeal to their vanity often convincing them to part with large sums of cash.

It usually began on a small scale. You would post some pictures of yourself on the internet, along with some made-up shit about your interests and experience, and declaring your desire to find a like-minded male with whom to interact. If your looks fell somewhat short of the stunning mark, then Photoshop was your friend, or else you simply used downloaded images of a random model. Judicious use of skimpy lingerie was a key ingredient, but not to be overdone lest you appear sluttish.

Once you hooked a mark, work could begin in earnest. This is where you entertained, you flattered, you beguiled, you entranced. And then you mentioned the possibility of meeting up.

And then you mentioned money.

Getting a visa in Russia is difficult, you would say. And difficult meant expensive – sometimes hundreds of dollars, that being the preferred currency in these transactions. And then there was the cost of flights and other transportation, clothes of course, suit-cases, make-up . . .

When the money arrived, that's when you pulled the plug. Polina knew girls who sometimes had dozens of men on the go simultaneously, all at different stages of the process. It could get very complicated. And also very lucrative. Which is why the Russian Mafia often lent an expert hand, invited or not.

The idea of earning so much money was attractive, but Polina wanted more than this. She wanted to escape and start a new life elsewhere, and Russia wasn't full of likely elsewheres.

She was honest with her online photographs – well, they were a few years old and taken when she was several pounds lighter – but she wanted potential suitors to know what they were getting. She didn't want to step off a plane only to be turned around and pushed back on for the return journey. It made it more difficult to stimulate interest – she had long ago faced up to the depressing fact that she was no looker – but then along came Kenneth Plumley, and the rest, as they say, was history.

Kenneth was no great catch himself, but beggars can't be choosers. She didn't have to think long and hard about whether to marry him, even though it meant taking on a stupid old dog. All she wanted was stability and a home and freedom – not such unreasonable asks really.

It quickly became apparent that Kenneth was a weak man, and she fell into the role of dominating him without giving it any conscious thought, although she did occasionally experience pangs of guilt at the ways she took advantage of her power over him.

She had no real desire to leave Kenneth. She'd have preferred someone with a bit more money and a bit more oomph, particularly in the bedroom, but he worshipped her, and that made up for many of his shortcomings. Besides, the arrival of Michael on the scene had helped to scratch an itch, and so she felt no great compulsion to roam more widely.

But now there was this.

This was completely crazy. That girl Isobel had arrived like a tornado, tearing Polina's life apart and leaving her to pick up the pieces.

But only if she was telling the truth.

What she had said didn't seem likely at first. Kenneth kidnapping girls? Killing them? Burying them? No, not Kenneth. Not this spineless, impotent caretaker.

But then how well did she really know him? What did she know about any Western men? In Russia she had been told repeatedly that the West was full of perverts and predators, totally lacking in morals and decency. Exaggerated, surely, but perhaps containing a grain of truth?

She had been married to Kenneth for less than three years. The only facts she knew about his life before that time were what he had told her. What if it was all just a story? He had found her on the internet after all, so what if his philosophy was no different from that of the women in Russia who posted online about their entirely fictitious lives?

She felt suddenly scared. Was it possible that she had married a monster?

The more she thought about it, the more concerned she became.

What was certainly true was that Kenneth had recently started disappearing for unusually long time periods – substantially more than he used to when walking the dog. She hadn't minded because it had given her more opportunities to fool around with Michael, but now it seemed odd. Why had he taken so long?

And what had really happened to Barclay? She had never liked the mangy animal, but it was obedient and it was slow on its feet. It would never go running out into the road. Could Kenneth really have killed it? And to cover up the burial of a body? The photograph on the girl's phone – that could easily have been Kenneth.

Isobel had mentioned a crash, too, and she had noticed the dents on the van, but when she questioned Kenneth he told her that he'd accidentally nudged a low wall. It had seemed strange to her at the time because he was normally such a careful driver.

And then there were the secrets he was keeping. Why had he not told her about going for coffee with Isobel if it was such an innocent meeting? And if it was true that he had been questioned further by the police, why keep that to himself?

His behaviour had certainly been strange lately. Not himself. That argument with Michael about the beer was completely out of character.

Polina paced the house for at least an hour, these thoughts racing around her head. Now that they had been planted there, she didn't think she would be able to act normally when he got home. She would be constantly observing him, studying him, probing him with questions. He would become suspicious.

Unless it was all nonsense, of course. Could Isobel have a motive for making this up? What would that motive be? She could hardly be a jilted lover, given Kenneth's malfunctioning equipment, so what else? Coming to a stranger's house to warn them about their husband's activities took courage and conviction. There had to be some basis to what she was claiming, even if she had read too much into it.

There was only one way to find out.

She picked up her phone and called her husband. He answered almost immediately.

'Hello, love. What's up?'

'Something very strange,' she said. 'I have just had call from police.'

She listened to the pause, and in her mind it seemed full of meaning.

'The police? What did they want?'

'They were talking about last night, about digging up a body in the woods. I didn't understand what they meant.'

'A body? You mean . . . Barclay, right?'

'Yes, of course,' she said, but she'd already heard the unease in his voice. 'What was he talking about, Kenneth?'

'Nothing. It's . . . the driver, the one who hit Barclay, he called the police. They wanted to confirm it.'

'Why?'

'I don't know. Maybe they have to, in case a crime has been committed.'

'But the man on phone was detective. Why would they send detective for this?'

'I told you I don't know. I don't know much more about the police than you do. They came to the woods, checked it out, and it was all fine.'

'Then why did they need to dig up the dog again?'

'In case it was anything suspicious. I suppose digging a grave at night in the woods would make anyone suspicious.'

He tried to laugh it off, but there was definite nervousness there.

'You said the driver had already told them it was a dog.'

'Yes. He did. They were just doing their job. It was nothing. Stop worrying about it.'

'And the woman?'

Another lengthy pause. 'What woman?'

'The detective mentioned there was a woman there. Isobel or something.'

Kenneth sighed over the phone. 'There's a crazy woman. She used to be a student at the school here. She keeps phoning the police about me. It's a long story.'

'Why does she phone police? What have you done?'

'I haven't done anything. I told you, she's crazy.'

'Kenneth, why are you saying this now? I have not heard any of this before. You have not mentioned the woman. You did not say anything about the police in the woods.'

'Because it wasn't important. It was just a mix-up. And don't forget I wasn't in a very good mood last night. I haven't felt like talking to anyone. I'll tell you all about it later, okay?'

'Okay.'

'Are you sure?'

'Yes.'

'Because it really is nothing important.'

'Okay.'

But she wasn't satisfied. All that this conversation had done was to make her even more convinced that something was going on. Something bad.

'So what was the phone call about?' Kenneth asked.

'I'm sorry?'

'The phone call, from the detective. I assume he wasn't calling just to tell you everything that was going on in my life, which he shouldn't be doing anyway.'

Polina hadn't prepared herself for this question. 'Oh, he called about the woman.'

'You mean Izzy?'

'Izzy?'

'Isobel.'

'You call her Izzy?'

'That's beside the point. Was that who he was calling about?'

'Yes. He . . . he said the same as you. He also thinks she is crazy. He phoned to say he had spoken with her and she would not bother you again.'

'That's why he phoned?'

'Yes.'

'But he also happened to mention all the other stuff about the dog and the woods and so on?'

'He. . . he thought it was funny and ridiculous. He was laughing when he told me.'

'I see. Well. . . that's good. Because it is funny and ridiculous. I'll tell you what, why don't I buy a bottle of wine for later, and we can have a good laugh about it ourselves? How does that sound?'

'That sounds nice.'

'Good. Then that's what we'll do. So you'll stop worrying about it now, yes?'

'Yes.'

'Great. I'll see you later, then. Love you.'

'I love you too,' she said, and the line went dead.

Polina put down the phone and looked around her kitchen. She didn't know what to do. Michael had gone out on one of his long walks, but even if he were here, she couldn't discuss it with him. As intimate as she'd been with him, he wasn't family.

Everything Kenneth had said confirmed the girl's version of events. He knew her well – well enough to call her Izzy. Why had he been keeping so much from his wife? What was going on here?

Polina felt frightened and confused. Her world had suddenly been flipped, and now everything appeared upside-down.

But perhaps it still wasn't as bad as Isobel had said. Perhaps there could still be an innocent explanation.

She set to work.

She searched the whole house. She went through all the pockets of his clothes. She emptied out bags, suitcases and hampers. She removed drawers, tipped them out, looked underneath and behind them. She checked the laundry basket for possible bloodspots or other evidence on his attire from last night. She examined all his documents, including the phone bills for suspicious activity and bank statements for unusual payments. She went through the internet history on the computer. She even checked notepads for indentations made from writing on pages now torn out. The KGB would have been proud of her.

It took a long time.

And she found nothing.

Mentally and physically exhausted, she put the kettle on and made a mug of tea, then forgot about it while she wandered around the kitchen again.

She picked up her phone, found Isobel's number in her contacts. She sent a message: *I would like to speak with you again tomorrow.*

The response came back quickly:

Have you found something?
    No. I just want to know more from you.
I can call you now?
    No. Kenneth will be home soon. I will call you in the morning.

She put her phone down and returned to her mug of tea, only to find it was disgustingly tepid. She poured it into the sink and stared out at the garden. It was already shrouded in darkness, and the men would soon be home. She worried that she wouldn't be able to act normally in front of Kenneth. Would she be able to listen to his tale about the girl without throwing accusations at him? Would she ever be able to trust him again?

And then she realised what she was looking at. It was right in front of her.

The shed.

Kenneth spent a lot of time in that shed. He regarded it as his domain. He called it his 'man-cave'. He didn't like Polina going in there, claiming that she would 'mess up his system', and she had never been inclined to defy him.

Until now.

She went to the understairs cupboard and pulled a tin down from one of the shelves. She took it back to the kitchen and opened it. It was full of keys. For some reason, Kenneth owned a million keys.

She carried the tin outside with her, together with a torch. She examined the padlock on the shed, then began rifling through the keys for a likely match. There were literally dozens of candidates. She knew that Kenneth carried a shed key on his person, along with his other house and van keys, but surely there had to be a spare here somewhere?

Several minutes later, she was ready to give up. All the keys she had tried lay in a pile at her feet. The rest didn't look right. She swirled them around in the tin.

There was one more.

She took it out and held it up to the torchlight. Could it be?

She pushed it into the padlock. It fitted perfectly, like the glass slipper in that stupid fairy story. And then it turned, and the lock sprang open.

Polina entered the shed and snapped on a light switch. An old fluorescent light flickered into life and cast a dim yellow glow over the interior. The shed was huge but still crammed with things. There were boxes and drawers everywhere. It would take a month to search this place properly.

She made a start on one side of the shed. She found tools; she found a million screws and nails; she found various lengths of wire and cord and chain; she found bottles of lawn feed and weedkiller and white spirit; she found cans of paint and varnish; she found vehicle parts.

What she didn't find was any evidence that her husband had done anything wrong.

She turned and faced the other side of the shed. A wooden workbench ran the length of it. What surprised her was how much stuff had been crammed underneath it. Plastic crates and full refuse bags had been stuffed in there haphazardly, in contrast to the orderliness elsewhere, and then large items like the lawn mower, scarifier and hose reel had been lined up in front of them, as though in a weak attempt to screen the untidiness.

Polina slid the equipment out of the way and crouched down. She dragged out one of the crates. It was empty, but the movement caused a cloud of flies to bloom out towards her, along with an unpleasant odour of damp earth and decay that reminded her of the time she found a dead badger in the field behind the house.

And then she heard the noise.

Kenneth's van, coming up the drive to park behind the house.

At first she panicked. Kenneth would have seen the shed door open. He would know she was in here. It was too late to go back to the house.

But then she told herself she had every right to be here. It was her shed too, even if she never used it. And if Kenneth had nothing to hide, there wouldn't be a problem.

She pulled out another couple of crates, then started on the bin-bags.

She heard the van door open and slam shut. Footsteps coming towards her.

'Polina?' Kenneth called. 'Is that you in there?'

She said nothing. Just continued to move the junk.

He appeared in the doorway. 'Polina, what are you doing?'

'I was looking for something.'

'What are you looking for?'

'The sink plunger. The bathroom sink is blocked again and I can't find it anywhere.'

'It's not here. It's in the understairs cupboard. Come away from there.'

She ignored him and pulled out another bag. Below it she could see a layer of tarpaulin. Flies danced around it.

'Kenneth, what is this? It smells.'

'It's nothing. Just rotting compost.'

'This is not compost. Why would you put compost here?'

She grabbed another bag, started to pull.

'Polina, you're making a mess. Please stop.'

The whine in his voice angered her, driving out any trepidation. She was more determined than ever to get to the bottom of this. She freed the next bag, reached for the tarpaulin . . .

'NO!'

The yell from Kenneth and the sudden flurry of movement behind her made her heart leap in her chest. She turned and caught a glimpse of a raised hand holding a hatchet.

The first blow neatly separated the hemispheres of a brain that had dared to build dreams of a better life in the West.

40

Some days were a struggle.

Actually, Josh Frendy thought he'd had far more than his fair share of difficult days. One of the biggest, of course, was the day his wife was finally taken from him by a malign mass of cells wreaking havoc in her brain. Josh had lost count of the number of times he'd offered his soul to prevent that outcome, but the powers that be had never considered it a worthwhile proposition.

That day had been merely the first in a long series of unbearable days – days in which it seemed the agony would never fade. Alcohol offered a convenient escape route, the only saving grace during that dark period being that most of the suffering did not stay in his consciousness. Huge chunks of time were lost to him forever. But not nearly as lengthy as the time that had been stolen from Emma.

Today had been especially difficult for a number of reasons.

First of all, it was their anniversary.

It struck him how much the death of a soulmate changed the calendar. Days that had once been causes for celebration – birthdays, anniversaries, Christmas, New Year – were now sources of foreboding and sadness. They were constant reminders of how much he had lost.

He had worked damn hard today, as he did every day, partly as a distraction. It had been his recognition of the power of the job to do this that made him give up the booze and become a workaholic instead. But now he was home, and he was alone, and it was his wedding anniversary. He made a prawn korma, because it had been Emma's favourite, and he sat at the table with a white cloth over it and candles and a crackled stem vase with a single red rose in it, and he drank sparkling water because alcohol was no longer allowed in the house even though days like today seemed to whisper to him to start drinking again, and he raised his glass and made a toast to the woman who had been everything – was *still* everything – and he cried as he pictured her opposite him in that lacy red dress he'd always loved on her, raising her own glass and smiling that heart-breaking smile and telling him how she would never leave him, not ever, and he wished with all his might that he could see her in the flesh again, just one last time, to hold her, to kiss her, to tell her all the things he wished he'd said while she was alive, because that's the only chance any of us ever has, and he'd wasted it like the fool he was.

After the meal, he played some episodes of *Friends* on the television. They'd always enjoyed *Friends*; it never got less funny, and they often reminded each other of their favourite moments. Josh remembered how the pair of them had once blasted the competition out of the water that time they took part in a quiz based on the programme.

Good times. Happy times. The memories made him smile. But then he picked up a framed photograph of Emma, taken when they were on holiday in Egypt, when her tan emphasised the whiteness of her eyes and her teeth, and the waiters kept hitting on her because she was so extraordinarily beautiful, and she made him dance constantly, and she proved how much faster she could swim, and she nursed him when he got food poisoning, and it all made him cry again.

God how he missed her.

He wondered what it was about Izzy that reminded him of

Emma. He wasn't sure he could pin it down. Something in the voice, maybe, or that slight downward slant of her eyes; he wasn't sure. She'd hit the nail on the head, though. How had she done that? How had she been able to tell him something that he hadn't fully admitted to himself, which was that it wasn't so much her crime-solving potential that had endeared her to him but rather that she had the uncanny effect of bringing Emma alive again?

And that wasn't the only uncanny thing Izzy had said at the park. She knew that Emma was dead, and she knew that he had turned to drink. Was all that really based on just a few throwaway remarks he had made? Was Izzy that good?

And if she *was* that good, what did that say about her opinions on the fate of the missing women?

Because that was another crappy thing about today. Working like a demon is one thing, but when you have nothing to show for it despite your best efforts …

The investigations had hit a dead end, both for Rosie and Melissa. Not to mention Heather. Those three aside, he had an exemplary record in tracking down 'mispers', as police jargon would have it. But a string of failures like this was beginning to make him think he'd lost his touch, and he hated that self-doubt. The work was all he had left, which is why he detested days off, and tomorrow was his day off, not through choice but because his boss had insisted on it. Josh had been told that he needed to take a break before he burned himself out, which was probably meant as it was said, but which Josh, sensitive soul that he was today, took to mean that he simply wasn't up to it.

So today was a struggle.

They're in those woods, Josh. The girls are in there somewhere.

What if Izzy was right? What if the answer to all this had been right under his nose all this time? She had been right about so many other things today, so why not that?

Made no difference. He was home now. No work tomorrow either. Let someone else find those women. Someone more capable.

He looked at the photograph of Emma again and thought he saw Izzy looking back at him.

I don't think he'll have gone back to the woods last night . . . But he will soon. Tonight, tomorrow night, but definitely soon.

It couldn't wait, could it? If Izzy was right, something had to be done about it now.

It wouldn't do any harm, he thought. A bit of surveillance on my own time. Why not? It's either that or sit here wallowing in misery.

About half an hour later, he was sitting in his parked car on Kenneth Plumley's road.

He was still sitting there when it turned eleven o'clock, which is when he started wondering why, yet again, he had allowed Izzy to persuade him to go on another wild goose chase. He actually laughed when he realised that it probably had something to do with the fact that he would have done the same for Emma, especially when she was adamant, and especially when she believed she was right, which was always.

He was tired, but there'd be plenty of time for sleep tomorrow, it being the day off he didn't want. He'd done stakeouts before, knew how deathly dull they could be, particularly when you didn't have a partner with you to talk about crap. The difficult part was staying awake and alert. A colleague of his had once slept through the emptying out of a whole house by burglars while he was sat in front of it on surveillance.

Josh was rewarded for his diligence at 11.30. Kenneth Plumley's white van pulled out onto the lane and headed directly towards him. He lay down across the front seats of his car until it went past, then started up his engine, turned the car around, and began following.

As he drove, he felt the adrenaline kick in. This was an odd time for anyone to go out on a drive. He felt in his bones that Kenneth was up to something.

He kept his distance, the red tail lights of the van mere dots ahead of him, but if Izzy was right, then he knew where Kenneth was going.

They reached the road with the woods on each side. There was hardly any other traffic.

'What's it to be, Kenneth?' Josh muttered. 'Are you stopping or not?'

The van kept going, past the point at which they'd begun their search for a body last night.

'Come on, Kenny. Prove Izzy right. Go off-road.'

And then brake lights.

Josh slowed down his own vehicle. 'Oh my God. You're doing it. You're actually doing it. No dog as an excuse this time, Kenny.'

He pulled his car onto the verge and killed the engine and lights, then waited, his eyes focused on the point where he thought Kenneth had come off, even though it was pitch black out here and seeing anything was almost impossible.

He waited a few minutes, giving time for Kenneth to get involved in whatever it was he was doing. Like burying a body, for example.

When he thought an appropriate amount of time had passed, he started the car again and drove at a crawl along the road. He kept the headlights off to avoid alarming Kenneth, relying on the car's running lights to guide him. When he thought he was close enough, he turned into the woods and parked.

From his glovebox he took out a torch and a police extendable baton, then he got out of the car and started walking. It didn't take him long to find the van, its big white backside wedged between the trees. He approached cautiously, baton at the ready. There was no sign of life, but he was taking no chances. He risked a peek through the driver's window and saw that it was empty. The door was locked. Kenneth Plumley was out and about and quite possibly up to no good.

Josh plunged into the woods. The words of a song came to him as he trekked:

If you go down in the woods today, you're sure of a big surprise.

Yeah, except it was going to be Kenneth getting the big surprise on this occasion unless he had a damn good story to tell.

The woods thickened, became difficult to penetrate. Josh began to wonder if he'd come the right way. He pressed on, alert for sounds.

He pushed through into a clearing, but there was no sign of Kenneth, and from here there were about a dozen trails into different sections of the woods.

He cursed under his breath, wondering what the chances of finding his quarry were if he simply chose a path at random. He stood silently and listened for clues, but could hear nothing. He even switched off his torch for a few seconds and turned on the spot, his eyes straining for any residual light from Kenneth's own torch finding its way through the branches. He realised it was a bad idea when he switched his torch back on and was unable to pick out the way he'd come into the clearing.

He cursed again.

The sound he heard next wasn't the one he was hoping for.

Kenneth's van was being started up.

More expletives escaped Josh's lips as he raced towards the sound. How had Kenneth completed his task so quickly? Had he just dumped a body and covered it with a few leaves instead of burying it properly? Or had Izzy got it wrong about him again, and there *was* no body?

He prayed that Kenneth might just sit in his van for a while, perhaps getting warm or listening to his favourite song that had just come on the radio or contemplating his success at outwitting the police or any damn thing that might keep him there a minute or two until Josh got to him.

Using the engine noise as a homing beacon, Josh moved as swiftly as he could, ignoring the branches that clawed at his clothes and his skin. Knowing he'd be covered in a multitude of scratches when he got there, he thought, This better be worth it, Izzy, this better not be another of your ridiculous errands. If I appear out of the blackness in front of Kenneth and he asks why the hell I've just followed a man who was on a perfectly legitimate journey, then I am going to feel like the biggest arsehole in the world, and you, dear Izzy, are going to feel the force of my wrath even if you do remind me of my wife for some reason I haven't quite yet pinned down.

But then he heard revving, and he knew he wasn't going to make it. The van whined in reverse gear, then sputtered as it accelerated away.

Shit.

By the time Josh broke out of the woods again, there was no sign of the van, either in the trees or on the road. His mind struggled to formulate an alternative plan. Go after Kenneth or stay here and search for whatever he might have dumped?

He decided he could always come back here and search later. Right now it might be worth trying to catch up with the van in case it wasn't going straight home. Get back in the car, floor the accelerator, and he might just be able to get on Plumley's tail again.

He ran along the road to where he'd hidden his car. He jumped behind the wheel and slammed the door. He started up the engine, checked his rear-view mirror.

He wasn't expecting the face that stared back at him.

But by then it was too late.

The cord was whipped over his face and pulled into his neck. Josh felt instant pain, and his fingers reached up in reflex, clawing to save him, but all they found was a furrow where the cord had already bitten deep into his flesh, and so his nails tore at his skin, trying to find and stop the invader that was slicing into him, cutting off his air, the blood supply to his brain. He opened his mouth to scream, but he could find no noise, no breath, and then he began to flail instead, his arms lashing out wildly, his legs kicking and stamping. And then sparks began to flash across his eyes and all sound disappeared, and knowing it was dying, knowing it could carry out only one more act, his brain gave him the most precious gift it could find, which was Emma, and he saw her smile and heard her laugh and was ecstatic beyond belief that he was finally getting his wish to be with her again.

41

I will call you in the morning.

That was what Polina had said in her text message. It was morning now, but morning was a long time. Technically, morning stretched out till noon, and Izzy didn't think her nerves could endure waiting that long.

But then again, was there any point in getting excited about the promised call? In the same conversation, Polina had said she hadn't found anything incriminatory about her husband. She had also said she wanted to learn more from Izzy. That sounded like it was very much going to be a one-way flow of information, with Izzy simply going over ground she had already covered. And if anything new and startling had come to light since that exchange of messages, Polina would surely have let her know by now.

Which was disappointing to say the least.

And the same went for Josh. No contact from him either. Okay, officially they had said their final goodbyes, but final didn't have to mean final, did it? Not when she had left him reeling from that humdinger set of revelations that must have knocked his socks off. She hated to admit it, but she had harboured a slender hope that Josh might have slipped her a subtle hint that she had just helped him achieve the biggest investigatory success of his career.

She had been relying on either Polina or Josh to come through, but it seemed that both had let her down, that neither had taken her seriously enough, which made her feel crap. What made it worse was that this wasn't something that could be put at the bottom of a to-do list. Kenneth Plumley couldn't be permitted the time he needed to cover his tracks.

At just after ten o'clock, when she had put a smile on Abel's face by selling a complete set of ancient encyclopaedias, she sent a message to Polina: *Are you still going to call me?*

She didn't expect an immediate answer, and she didn't get one. In fact, she'd still heard nothing when it came time for the morning coffee break. While the kettle boiled, she fired off another message: *Polina, please get in touch. I'll tell you anything you want to know.*

She knew it sounded a little desperate, but she was clutching at straws now.

At a minute after twelve, with the morning dead and gone and still no answer from Polina, Izzy tried once more: *OK if I call you?*

She had already decided that, even if a reply was forthcoming, she would have to wait for her lunch break to make the call. This wasn't something for Abel's ears, and she didn't want to leave the shop before then after all the time off he had given her yesterday.

But then lunchtime arrived and her messages sat unanswered on her phone. She checked with Abel that it was all right to go out for her lunch, then she put on her coat and headed towards the town square. As soon as she reached the end of the road, she halted and phoned Polina's number.

It went straight to voicemail. Not even a ringtone.

She tried a few more times in rapid succession. Same result.

Polina doesn't want to talk to me, she thought. She found nothing on Kenneth and then she slept on it and decided I'm a kook, and now she's blocked my number on her phone.

Izzy resumed her walk. She reached the Old Square and paced the periphery, glancing in shop windows but not really seeing what was there. She sat on a bench and tried Polina's number again. She got voicemail, and this time she left a message:

'Polina, it's Izzy. Please call me back. I promise you that everything I told you was true. I will answer any questions you have. Please ring me.'

She hung up, then stared at the list of people she had called recently. Josh was high up on that list.

No, she told herself. You can't call him. Not after yesterday.

But wouldn't it be nice to know that he was at least considering what she had said about Kenneth, even if he hadn't done anything about it yet?

She began to prepare a little speech that would go something like, *Hi, yes, it's me, sorry, I know we said goodbyes, but I was just wondering if, possibly, you might have done some thinking about me, and, well . . .*

That's as far as she got before hitting the call button for Josh.

Voicemail again.

'What the f—' she exclaimed, stopping herself as a stern-faced old lady glared at her.

What was wrong with people? All this mobile phone technology and nobody could be arsed to make use of it. They needed to answer. They needed to let her know what was going on.

Angry and frustrated, she marched into the nearest sandwich shop, bought a limp-looking tuna on white, then headed back towards the bookstore.

The impulse grabbed her and pushed her across the street before she had time to think about it. Took her to her car, bundled her in and ordered her to drive.

But what about Abel? was her question.

This is too important. Drive.

So she drove. Hang the consequences. She needed answers.

She got to the Plumley house in record time, her forgotten tuna sandwich warming nicely on the passenger seat. Kenneth would be at the school, she reasoned, and hopefully the lodger would be out doing whatever it is the lodger did. Just me and Polina again, she thought. Woman to woman. She'll talk to me, I know she will.

She walked up to the front door and knocked. It was about a minute before she heard footsteps from within. The door opened. Izzy readied herself.

A man opened the door. The lodger, she realised. She racked her brain for the name Polina had mentioned. Michael – that was it.

'Hello,' she said. 'Sorry to bother you. I'm looking for Polina.'

Michael seemed surprised and also a little sceptical. 'Polina? I'm afraid she's not in at the moment. Can I take a message?'

Izzy's shoulders slumped. 'Do you know where she is?'

'I don't. Actually, I haven't seen her since yesterday.'

'You haven't?'

'No.' He paused. 'Sorry, but who are you?'

'Sorry. My name's Isobel Lambert. I was a student at Hemingway High, which is where I got to know Kenneth.'

'You know Kenneth as well? I see.' Another pause. 'Look, I'm just a lodger here – name's Michael – so I don't know everything that goes on in this house, but to be honest, I'm a bit concerned.'

'Concerned? Why?'

He scanned the area behind Izzy, exactly as Polina had done. 'Would you like to come in?'

She nodded, and he showed her through to the living room. Near the door was a small table holding a chessboard. He invited her to sit, and she hoped he wasn't planning to ask her to play.

'I often go for long walks round here,' Michael said. 'I went on one yesterday. When I got back, it was already dark – it gets dark so early now, doesn't it? Polina wasn't here, but Kenneth was. He said they'd had an argument and she'd stormed out of the house.'

'Did you believe him?'

'Sort of. Put it this way, I had no reason to disbelieve him. But it's not like them to have massive arguments like that, and then she didn't come home at all last night.'

'So you haven't seen her at all since you went on your walk?'

'No.'

'Did you see Kenneth this morning?'

'Yes, briefly. He looked very upset but wouldn't talk about it. I asked him if he was going to make it up with Polina, and he just said he'd have to see about that.'

'So . . . what do you think happened?'

'I don't know. It all seems very odd. And the other thing is that I've tried ringing her and her phone goes straight to voicemail, like it's switched off or something.'

'Yes, it did that to me too.'

'When did you last see Polina?'

'Yesterday, when you were out on your walk.'

'Did she seem all right to you?'

'Yes. I think so. Look, I'm going to tell you something, okay?'

Michael looked concerned. 'What is it?'

'There's been something going on with Kenneth. A police investigation.'

'You mean . . . something criminal?'

Izzy hesitated. She didn't know how much to say, but she couldn't just walk away now.

'You heard about the missing schoolgirl, Rosie Agutter? And the young woman from the bookshop, Melissa Sawyer?'

'Yes. What about them? Surely you don't think Kenneth has anything to do with that?'

Izzy nodded. 'I'm afraid so.'

'No. That's ridiculous. I've got to know Kenneth well while I've been living here.' He gestured to the board in front of them. 'We play chess. We have a beer together. He's not that sort of man.'

'I'm afraid he is. And now that Polina's gone missing—'

'Wait. How do you know all this? Are you with the police?'

'No, but I've been working closely with a detective. There's no doubt. Kenneth has been doing some terrible things.'

'So then why hasn't he been arrested?'

'Because we haven't been able to prove it. Polina was helping us, and now I'm worried that Kenneth must have found out about it.'

Michael shook his head in disbelief. 'No, that can't be right. Not Kenneth. He's so, well, timid.'

'You said yourself that he's been acting strangely. Maybe you don't know him as well as you think you do.'

Michael sat back and put his hand over his mouth while he considered this. 'I . . . I don't know what to say. This is quite a shock. If you're right about Kenneth . . .'

'I am. I promise you. And now I need your help. We need to find Polina. She's probably in great danger.' She didn't add 'if she's still alive', but she thought it.

Michael opened his mouth to speak, then changed his mind.

'What is it?' Izzy asked.

'It's . . . This morning, Kenneth was doing something at the back of the house.'

'What do you mean?'

'Normally, he just gets in his van and goes to work, but when I came down to breakfast, I saw him carrying something from the shed and loading it in the back of his van.'

'What was it?'

'I don't know. It was dark out there, but I could tell it was big and heavy. I opened the kitchen door and asked him if he wanted a hand, and he slammed the van doors closed like he didn't want me to see what was in there. I asked him what was going on, and he just said it was some stuff he needed for the school.'

Izzy stared at him. She knew they were both thinking the same thing.

'Will you come with me,' she asked, 'to talk to the police?'

'But I don't know anything.'

'You've seen enough to convince them to search Kenneth's van, and probably the shed as well. If you could tell them what you've just told me . . .'

'I . . . I don't know.'

'Please. It won't take long. For Polina's sake.'

He deliberated for a while longer, then nodded. 'All right. I'll do it. Let me get my jacket and keys.'

He left the room. Izzy stared down at the chessboard. She had a sinking feeling that she was too late, that Polina was already dead. But maybe now, with Michael on her side, she could finally persuade Josh to take her seriously. Maybe there was still hope that Kenneth could be stopped.

She heard a noise behind her and went to turn.

The hands were on her neck too quickly. They were strong, powerful hands.

He's come back. Kenneth has come back!

She tried to prise the fingers away from her throat, tried to call out. She heard the noise of the table and chairs overturning, the chess pieces scattering, laboured breathing from behind her.

He's killing me!

Someone help me!

But nobody came, nobody stopped it.

And then the sounds became nothing and she accepted her fate and the world was switched off.

42

Life.

She was still alive.

But the continued darkness . . .

She could not see. Yet she could hear. Tearing, ripping noises. The sound of . . . yes, tape being unwound from a roll. She realised there was tape over her eyes and her mouth. She tried to cry out, but produced only weak, muffled sounds. She tried to move, but her ankles and wrists were also bound.

More lengths of tape were put in place around her limbs and around her face, even across her ears, and then she could just about make out the sound of footsteps receding and a door being closed.

She lay there, unable to do anything else. She had no idea how long she'd been unconscious, and dreaded to think what might have been done to her in that time. She didn't even know where she was. Was this still Kenneth's house? And what had Kenneth done with Michael?

More time passed, her fear mounting with the seconds. Her mind conjured up all kinds of terrible endings, including being buried alive in a grave in the woods. She prayed that wouldn't happen. If I'm to go, she thought, let it be quick. Please don't let him torture me.

She tried shuffling along the floor, with no idea of where she was going. What if I'm not in the same room? she thought. What if I'm on the edge of a set of stairs or something, and I'm about to send myself falling down them?

She found solidity. A wall or a door. Rolling onto her back, she raised her legs and kicked out. She heard the bang through the tape. She tried again and again, and it wouldn't break, but she wasn't about to give up, because maybe somebody would hear her, maybe—

Her feet found only air, and she thought at first that she'd had some success, but then she felt something slam into her side, and then her abdomen, and she realised she was being punched or kicked, punished for her defiance. The blows rained down on her until she thought she would die.

They stopped suddenly. She lay still, her whole body throbbing with pain. She wondered if any bones had been broken, any organs ruptured. She wondered if this was just the start, a warming up for the real suffering to come. She wanted to pass out again and never wake up.

He came back for her eventually. Hands landed roughly on her, picked her up. She was thrown over his shoulder like she was a sack of potatoes.

She felt the steady bounce as he walked with her, carrying her. A door was opened and cold air prickled her skin. More doors, metallic this time. Kenneth's old white van. She was tossed roughly inside and then the doors were slammed shut. Seconds later, the engine was kicked into life and they were moving.

The whole van seemed to shake and rattle. She winced at every pothole, as though her battered body was being pummelled further. Tears leaked from her eyes, forming a cold film beneath the tape. Although her nostrils were exposed, her crying was blocking them and it was difficult to get enough of the diesel-laden air into her lungs. She thought she was on the verge of a panic attack.

The journey seemed to last hours, but was probably only

minutes. The van jerked to a halt and the engine cut out. She heard doors being opened and closed, then silence. Shortly afterwards, the rear van doors were opened and she was grabbed and manhandled out, before being carried again. She knew she was outside, and she really hoped it wasn't the woods, but then the air changed, the dimmed sounds changed, and she knew she was indoors once more.

She was carried for some distance. Kenneth's breathing became heavier, his steps louder as if on a hard surface.

Finally, he put her down on a cold floor. She heard a slight snicking sound near the side of her face, and then the tape being sliced through and pulled away from her mouth. She breathed the air in greedily.

'Thank you,' she said. 'Please, don't hurt me. I promise I won't tell anyone about this.'

She got no answer. The tape covering her eyes and ears was peeled away, but left hanging from her hair. She blinked.

Kenneth stared back at her, like a scientist studying a new animal species. He was holding a craft knife, its razor-sharp blade glinting.

She looked left and right, trying to work out where she was. A huge, sunken chamber. A warehouse? No, not a warehouse. A . . . a swimming pool! She was at the bottom of an empty swimming pool!

The only light source was a set of flickering candles dotted at even intervals around the edges of the pool. It was cold here, so cold.

'Kenneth, whatever it is you're planning to do to me, you don't have to do it. If you let me go now, I won't tell. I swear.'

Kenneth said nothing. Just continued to stare, the candlelight dancing in his eyes.

'You know me,' she said. 'We were good friends at school.

Remember those times? Remember how we talked about books all the time, and how I read to you?'

She wasn't certain, but she thought she saw tears fill his eyes. Was it working? Were her reminiscences bringing out his humanity again?

'I know something must have gone wrong for you, but it can be fixed. We can get help for you. You don't have to—'

'I'm sorry, Izzy,' Kenneth said, and now she was convinced he really was shedding tears.

'Don't be sorry. It'll be fine. Just untie me, and—'

'I'm sorry. I can't do that. You've caused this yourself. I tried to warn you, but you wouldn't listen. Why wouldn't you listen? Why couldn't you have just stayed out of my life?'

She shook her head. 'I couldn't, Kenneth. You know I couldn't. What you did to those women, to Heather and Rosie and Melissa. And to Polina too? Is she . . . is she dead?'

Kenneth nodded slowly, his head seemingly heavy.

Something opened up inside Izzy. She wanted to wail her heart out.

'Did you have to kill her? Was it really necessary? She was your wife.'

Kenneth looked directly into her eyes. 'I didn't kill her,' he said. 'I didn't kill any of them.'

The shock of his words stunned her so badly she was convinced she must have misheard, or that the beating she had received must have confused her radar.

But no.

She was certain. As certain as she'd ever been.

Beyond a shadow of a doubt, she knew that what Kenneth had just told her was the truth.

43

It seemed impossible. It didn't make sense. She had asked him directly, hadn't she?

Or maybe not.

Thinking back, she realised she had never asked Kenneth outright whether he had killed the women or even abducted them. She had caught him out in a number of lies, and it was clear that he was involved – why else would he be here with her now if he wasn't involved? – but the one thing she hadn't done was pin him irrefutably to the most heinous acts.

'Kenneth,' she said, 'what's going on? Why have you brought me here? What happened to the others?'

'I didn't hurt them,' he said. 'I'm not like that.'

Again, truth upon truth.

'Then . . . who?'

She got her answer in the form of footsteps clanging on the metal ladder that led down to the bottom of the pool. She looked to her right, saw the figure of a man in the gloom. He turned and approached, came into view.

It was Michael. The lodger.

'You look so confused, Izzy,' he said. 'What a mess you've made of things.'

'You? You took the girls? You killed them? Why?'

He seemed genuinely surprised by the question. 'Why? I don't really know. It just kind of . . . happened. When we were playing our games. I like to play games, you see. Simon Says is my favourite. But I also play a lot of chess with my brother.'

'Your brother?'

'Yes. Oh, sorry. There's still a lot you don't know, isn't there? Yes, Kenneth here is my older brother.'

* * *

Izzy watched open-mouthed as Michael walked over to Kenneth and put his arm around his shoulders. While Michael grinned, Kenneth looked afraid of him.

'Lovely to be back with the family again,' Michael said.

'You don't look anything like each other,' Izzy said.

Michael looked a little crestfallen. 'No, well, different genes you see. When Kenneth was born he wrecked our mother's womb or something, so she couldn't have any more kids naturally. I was adopted. Second-best. Still, better than nothing, eh?'

Izzy sensed real hurt there. An inferiority complex that had been there since he found out the truth about his origins, gnawing at him.

'I'm sure your parents didn't think of you in that way. They must have loved you both the same.'

Izzy was willing to try anything to get on his side, to understand what he was going through in the hope of turning this around.

'Oh, yes, they did. But then our father left, pissed right off, and our mother found a new man. She married him. His name was Simon. Simon liked to play games, which I suppose is where I get it from. Funny how your upbringing can influence you like that.'

It crossed Izzy's mind to ask what kind of games, but she thought she knew the answer.

Michael gripped Kenneth's shoulder more tightly and shook him. 'Not with Kenneth here. He didn't like to play games with

Kenneth, oh no. Possibly because he's an ugly little sod. But me, yes. He'd play with me every single opportunity he got. He pretended it was fun. Kept telling me we were having a great time. Best time ever. Couldn't tell Mum, though. Couldn't tell anyone. Simon said we couldn't, and we had to do what Simon said.'

He was starting to sound hysterical now, Izzy thought. Her mind worked desperately on ways to calm him down.

'I'm so sorry, Michael. But that was—'

'DON'T!' he said. 'Don't try to make me feel better about things. You don't get to do that. That's Kenneth's job.' He turned to his brother. 'Isn't that right, Kenneth? You were always there for me when we were little, just like you are now.'

Izzy could sense the fear in Kenneth. She saw how he wanted to pull away, release himself from the shackles of loyalty Michael had placed on him.

'Because that's what brothers do, isn't it?' Michael said. 'They look after one another. Except Kenneth didn't. He didn't look after me. HE DIDN'T LIFT A FUCKING FINGER! While our stepdad was molesting me, Kenneth here just sat and watched. He didn't move. He didn't say a thing. I'm surprised he didn't get out the popcorn.'

Michael suddenly pulled away from his brother and came towards Izzy again.

'I can't blame him, though. Simon could do anything he wanted. Give him his due, he was pretty inventive. Those games of his became quite elaborate as time went on. He told us he would kill us if we said anything, and we believed him. I JUST WISH . . . I just wish it hadn't been *me*, you know? That he hadn't decided that I'd be the lucky one out of the pair of us. But what's done is done, eh? No use griping over spilt milk, as our dear old mother used to say.'

'I don't understand,' Izzy said. 'Why were you pretending to be a lodger at Kenneth's house?'

'Ah, that. Yeah. Some people looking for me, you see. I was a wanted man down south. Did a few naughty things. Descriptions of me being circulated.' Michael barked a sudden laugh, making Izzy flinch. 'Should have seen the look on Kenneth's face when he came home and found me there. We hadn't seen each other for about ten years before that moment. I think he was ashamed of me. Didn't even tell his wife he had a brother! I only found out he'd got married when I searched for him online and came across wedding photos his missus had put on a social media site. Anyway, when I needed a place to lay low, I saw the adverts Polina had posted for a lodger, and I thought why not? Perfect timing, perfect hiding place. So I became Mr Danvers – the latest in many identities I've had recently. I usually go for a different first name too, only I knew my slow brother would've blurted out my real name by mistake.'

She looked at Kenneth. 'You took him in? Knowing what he was doing?'

Michael jumped in before his brother could answer. 'Oh, he didn't know the full story. Not at first. He knew it was shady, and he wasn't happy about that, but he gave me a bed. Or two.' He winked at Kenneth as he said this. 'That's what family do, isn't it? Blood is thicker than water, and all that. He owed me, see. He had to make up for things, for not doing what big brothers are supposed to do.'

'And the girls? Why the girls?'

Michael actually shrugged and smiled. 'I like girls. One thing that Simon didn't manage to screw up for me. Girls like me, too. I'm a handsome devil compared to this pug here, don't you think? Got more lead in my pencil, too, if you know what I mean. Kenneth here struggles a bit in the bedroom department, don't you, Ken?'

She felt Kenneth's humiliation. Like he wanted to drop to the floor and curl up in a tight ball.

'The first girl. Heather. She *was* the first, wasn't she?'

'The first to die, you mean? It's okay, you can talk plainly here. This is all between friends. Yeah, what about her?'

'How . . . how did you find her?'

Michael looked upwards as though trying to recall. Izzy couldn't understand how such an outrageous act could not always remain at the forefront of someone's consciousness.

'It wasn't planned or anything. Fate, I suppose. I was driving along, minding my own business. It was lashing down. Bit of a storm. I saw this girl with a heavy bag. She was running towards the bus stop, but the bus pulled away before she got there. She looked drenched. I stopped the car, asked her where she was going, did she want a lift, and . . . well, that's it unless you want all the sordid details.'

'You brought her here?'

'Yeah. Good venue, don't you think? Courtesy of Kenneth. He likes keys, you see. Always has done, ever since we were kids. He collects them. At the house he's got this biscuit tin full of them. He showed me his prized possessions one dull, boring night. Took great delight in telling me what they were for. Seemed to drag on for hours. Anyway, one of the things that did stick with me was that he had the keys for this place. Used to work here, see. So I borrowed them and had copies made. Thought they might come in useful one day.'

'So you *were* making some plans, then?'

He thought about this for a few seconds. 'Yeah, I suppose I was. Funny how the mind works, isn't it? The way it makes preparations for stuff you don't even know you're going to do.'

'So you brought Heather here. You killed her. What then?'

Izzy was trying to keep him talking. If she was to have any chance of using her gift to get out of this, she needed to know him better, even though the notion of doing so sickened her.

'Needed to get rid of the body, didn't I? That's where Kenneth stepped in. Well, not stepped in, exactly. He was more sort of dragged in. I told him what I'd done, and that I needed his help. Simple as.'

She looked at Kenneth again. 'Was it that simple, Kenneth?'

He opened his mouth, started to shake his head, but again Michael interrupted. 'He had no fucking choice, did he? I already told you. He owed me. Still owes me. You have no idea what I went through as a kid. He does. He watched every single second of it and did nothing. This was his chance to make amends. To be honest, I don't think it was asking all that much.'

Izzy marvelled at the curious and dysfunctional relationship between the brothers. A bond forged through guilt and remorse. Kenneth, clearly the weaker of the two despite being the eldest, doing what he could now to make up for what he hadn't done before. And Michael, arch manipulator, exploiting Kenneth's subservience to the extreme.

'So then along came Rosie Agutter. Why her?'

Michael sighed heavily. 'Well, I'd tell you, but I'm getting bored shitless of this now. I think we need to start the game.'

'Please. I want to know. If I have to play your game, then fine, but at least let me know why it is I'm playing. Make me understand why we're doing this.'

Michael licked his lips. 'You want to understand. YOU WANT TO FUCKING UNDERSTAND? You'll never understand. Nobody will.'

'I bet Kenneth does.'

Michael glanced at his brother. 'Not even him. Seeing is not the same as doing. And the thing is, I didn't even know when I was doing it right. Simon fucking says! You have to remember to listen out for the "Simon says" bit or it gets even worse for you. All that shit going on and you still have to treat it like a game, like it's entertaining.'

'Did Rosie play your game?'

'She did. She was pretty good at it, actually. Lasted a long time before . . .'

'Before what?'

'Before she broke.'

Izzy thought she detected a hint of regret, but she wasn't sure whether it was in Michael's voice or something being emanated by Kenneth, whose body language made him an open book she could read even in this dim, quivering light.

'Again, why her?'

'Another spur-of-the-moment decision. Saw her walking home, stopped to chat to her. She was a bit more sensible. I had to get a bit physical with her to get her to cooperate.'

'And Kenneth's TV appearance? That was your idea too?'

'God, no. It was that idiot.' He stabbed a finger towards his brother. 'Got it into his stupid head to try and throw the police off the scent. That worked well, didn't it?'

'It was my school,' Kenneth protested. 'I had to—'

'You didn't have to do anything, dimwit. It was all in hand. Get rid of the body – that's all I asked you to do. Simple enough, but oh no, you had to go and complicate things. See what happens when you try to think for yourself, you cretin?'

Kenneth clammed up again and looked down at the pool floor. Izzy shivered in the atmosphere that suddenly seemed massively chillier.

'And then along came Melissa,' she said. 'But she was for my benefit, right?'

'Hmm, kind of.' He paused. 'There was a little mix-up with that one. I thought it was you.'

The revelation was like a punch to the stomach. 'Me?'

'Yeah. Blame this pathetic loser here.' Again he indicated Kenneth. 'Started acting like a girl when you got on his back.

Panicking about getting caught because of the things you were saying and doing. I told him not to worry, but I could tell he was losing it. I had to do something for both our sakes. Only, he didn't give me the full details, did he? He told me where you worked, but that was about it. So naturally, when I saw a young woman locking up the bookshop . . .'

Oh my God, Izzy thought. It was supposed to be me. Melissa died in my place.

She couldn't stop the tears flooding down her cheeks.

'Hey,' Michael said. 'No need to cry. She was actually a lot of fun as it happened. You've got a lot to live up to.'

'You bastard. You didn't have to do that. Melissa was a good person. She had nothing to do with any of this.'

'Well, like I say, you know who to blame for that one. I can only work with what I'm given, right? And speaking of blame, you're not exactly in the clear here, Isobel. I mean, everyone after Rosie is dead because of your interference. Have you thought about that? About the cost of sticking your nose in where it's not wanted?'

'Don't even go there, Michael. You killed them, not me. And I'm guessing Polina is one of your victims too, isn't she?'

'Yeah. More collateral damage from this battle you started. She was acting on your advice, you know. That's what got her into trouble. You're a terrible influence, young lady.'

Izzy turned to Kenneth. 'She was your wife! How can you just stand there and listen to this crap? How can you defend him?'

'Don't talk to him,' Michael said. 'You'll get more sense out of the bodies he buried. When I came home yesterday, I found him standing with her in the shed, just watching while she unwrapped poor Melissa's corpse. I mean, what does that tell you about the kind of idiot he is? I was the one who had to put the ugly Russky bitch out of her misery, because he certainly wasn't going to.'

'Kenneth! Are you listening to this? He murdered your wife! Are you going to let him get away with it? He's not even sorry.'

Kenneth continued to look at the floor, but his shoulders began heaving, and she knew he was sobbing silently.

'He doesn't care,' Michael said. 'She used him just to get into the country. She wasn't even good-looking like some of the internet brides you see. No wonder he couldn't get it up for her. Have to admit, even I struggled a little with that one. Still, helped to pass the time when there was nothing on the telly, I suppose.'

The coldness of Michael's heart was stinging. It held no empathy, no compassion. Not even for his own brother.

'You can't get away with this, Michael. If I disappear, they'll come for you. The police know what I've been saying about Kenneth all along. They'll come to the house, and then it will be over for you. There's too much for you to hide. I should have been back at work now. They're probably already looking for me.'

'They? You mean your little detective friend? I don't think he'll be looking for me any time soon. In fact, I don't think he'll be doing much of anything from now on.'

'W-what do you mean?'

Michael smiled and lowered his voice. 'He's in the woods, Izzy. Dead to the world.'

'No. You're lying.'

'We played a nice trick on him last night. He thought he was clever following us like that. He didn't know we were on to him. You should have seen the surprise on his face when I squeezed the life out of him.'

'No! Kenneth? Is he telling the truth, Kenneth?'

Kenneth lifted his head. Nodded almost imperceptibly. It was the only confirmation she needed.

'NO!' she cried. 'Not Josh! Please, not Josh!'

'Your fault,' Michael said. 'Melissa, Polina, Josh. All dead because of you, Izzy. That's a pretty good record you've got there.'

Grief overwhelmed her. She wailed uncontrollably, the sound reverberating around the pool. At the forefront of her mind was the last image she had of Josh as she said goodbye to him in the park. That final goodbye.

She knew now that her situation was hopeless. Michael killed without mercy. Enjoyed it, in fact. Nothing would stop him from experiencing this latest pleasure. Certainly not Kenneth, the spineless brother who had acted as a willing accomplice through- out. She had been so wrong about his part in the abductions, the killings, but that didn't absolve him of guilt.

Yes, Abel would grow concerned about her failure to return, and at some point he might decide to follow it up. Or maybe Andy would try ringing her and wonder why she couldn't get an answer. But without Josh to drive things, it could take an age for the police to join the dots and start looking in Kenneth's direction for answers. By then, it would be over. She would probably have joined the others in the woods. Michael and Kenneth would be long gone, perhaps even out of the country. Or perhaps Michael didn't even care about that. Maybe he knew his end had arrived and he was going out with a bang.

Either way, Izzy's fate seemed sealed.

Michael was obviously thinking along the same lines.

'Well, that was fun,' he said. 'But the preliminaries are over. Let the games begin.'

44

As Michael approached, Izzy shuffled back until she was up against the hard tiles. Michael squatted before her.

'So,' he said. 'The game is Simon Says. You know that one, don't you?'

She nodded.

'Good. To make it interesting, you'll pay a forfeit every time you get it wrong.'

'W-what type of forfeit?'

'We'll make it up as we go along. Sometimes it's nice to be impulsive, don't you think?'

He held a hand out to his side. 'The knife, Kenneth.'

She watched as Kenneth slowly neared and slapped the craft knife onto Michael's outstretched palm.

'Thanks, bro. You can step back again now. Give me room to work.'

Kenneth did as he was told, and then Michael said, 'Flip over on to your stomach, Izzy.'

She stared back at him. 'No.'

'No? You don't get a choice in this. Lie on your fucking stomach!'

She shook her head. 'No.'

He moved his face closer, until she could feel his hot breath and his spittle and his hatred landing on her. 'NO? NO? WHY THE FUCK NOT, IZZY?'

'You . . . you didn't say Simon says.'

Michael glared. Then he smiled. Then he laughed.

'You're good. Very good. I can see why you outwitted my brother here. Not that it's much of a compliment to outwit an imbecile like him. Eh, Kenneth?'

Kenneth didn't answer.

'Okay, we'll try again. Simon says lie on your stomach.'

She still didn't want to obey. Turning her back on a lunatic with a knife in his hand did not feel like the wisest of moves. But what choice did she have?

She slipped down the wall and rolled over. Waited for pain.

Michael cut through the tape around her wrists and ankles. She could move again.

'Simon says get up.'

She pushed herself off the floor. Got to her feet. Michael was facing her, Kenneth behind and off to one side.

Something caught her eye. The knife. Michael had left it on the pool floor. She had to force herself not to stare at it.

Michael said, 'I think we'll start with the usual. Swimming. Can you swim, Izzy?'

'A little. Not very well.'

'That's okay. The water's pretty shallow today.' His smile was reptilian. 'Come on, then. Show us what you can do.'

'You . . . you want me to swim? On the floor?'

'Well, unless you know how to hover, that's exactly what I mean.'

So this is how he gets his kicks, she thought. By degrading his victims. Humiliating them. Making them less than human.

She got down on the floor again. Began to simulate a breast stroke. She had never felt so small, so alone, so worthless.

The kick connected hard with her ribs. She screamed, then clutched at her chest as she rolled around on the floor.

'YOU'VE FORGOTTEN ALREADY, IZZY! WHAT IS THIS GAME CALLED?'

'S-Simon . . . Simon Says.'

'Exactly. And did you hear the magic words?'

'N-no.'

'No. You didn't. So let's try again, shall we?'

She blinked. The shapes above her were blurry and indistinct, but still she could detect Kenneth's extreme discomfort, his fervent desire to be anywhere but here.

'Simon says swim!' Michael commanded.

Izzy resumed her position and repeated her movements. Her ribs were on fire, and she wondered again if they were broken.

'Look at that, Kenneth,' Michael said. 'Poetry in motion. Actually, it's probably a bit more like a frog. Wait a sec . . . Simon says go *ribbit*.'

Izzy made the noise, her voice breaking. Above her, Michael laughed crazily, and she felt herself slipping further and further down in his estimation, so that she would soon become nothing to him, a bug worthy only of squashing.

'Okay,' Michael said. 'I think we've had enough of the amphibian impressions. Simon says stand up.'

She got to her feet.

'It's cold in here,' Michael said. 'I think you need a bit more warming up. Maybe a bit of dancing. You don't look much of a dancer, but I'm sure you could manage the twist. You could do that, couldn't you?'

Izzy said nothing.

'Simon says do the twist.'

She started moving, but tentatively, the pain in her ribs intensifying.

'That's shit. Simon says put your back into it. Come on!' Michael began snapping his fingers and singing 'Let's Twist Again'.

Izzy grimaced but did her best to comply. Tears streamed down her face, but Michael seemed to care nothing for her distress. He was relishing it. Behind him, Kenneth had lowered his eyes in shame.

'It's better, but something's missing.' He paused. 'I know! The fingers across the face, like Uma Thurman in *Pulp Fiction*. Anyone ever tell you that you look a bit like her? Simon says do that.'

She performed the moves. Michael continued to sing out of tune. He started to do his own dance. He began to turn away from her, lost in his insanity.

She pounced.

The knife was right there on the floor, her only chance, the only thing that could give her an edge. She went straight for it, fully intending to use it without hesitation, to maim, to kill, to strike at the monster again and again and again.

The whirl from Michael was almost balletic. It put power behind an outstretched palm that slapped into her face with a whipcrack noise, sending her reeling backwards and then falling and smacking onto the unrelenting tiles.

'NO!' Michael yelled. 'Did Simon say go for the knife? No, he did not. Bad girl. Bad fucking girl.'

Izzy's ears were ringing, her whole face on fire. She shook her head to clear it. Michael had closed in on her again. He sat on his haunches in front of her.

'Bad girl,' he whispered.

And then he reached out and grabbed hold of the duct tape that was still attached to her hair, and he yanked on it as hard as he could, and she felt the hair and the skin being ripped from her skull, and she let out a long scream that reached nobody beyond these four walls, and she knew that she had been set up, that the knife was bait and Michael had expected her to go for it, and now all was lost, all was lost.

Michael stood up and examined the tape in the candlelight. 'You could make a wig out of this, Kenneth,' he laughed. 'Here!' He tossed it to Kenneth, and then he reached down for the knife and threw that to him too, and Kenneth almost caught it before realising that the blade had not been retracted, and he did this odd little dance as he tried to avoid its path.

'Haha! Pick it up, you big girl. Jesus, you're lighter on your feet than Izzy is.'

Then Michael turned back to Izzy.

'All right, so you remember what we said about forfeits, yes? Well, now things start to get more interesting.'

45

Kenneth Plumley prayed silently.

He wanted God to know that he wasn't all bad. He had done some terrible things, but he wasn't evil. He hadn't killed anyone. Hadn't directly hurt anyone. It was all his brother's fault. If anyone deserved punishment, it was him.

Kenneth had tried to do what was right, hadn't he? He had provided shelter for his brother when he needed it. Wasn't that the Christian thing to do? And yes, he had buried bodies, but they were already dead. They hadn't died at his hands. Hadn't even suffered at them.

Except for Barclay, of course.

That had been hard. Killing his beloved dog had been so, so hard.

But he wasn't given much of a choice, was he? Izzy had seen to that. She had backed him into a corner. He did what he had to in order to survive, and to protect his little brother. Surely he could be forgiven for that?

He never witnessed what Michael had done to the girls; he saw only the aftermath, the broken bodies.

But Polina . . .

They had been happy before Michael made a reappearance in his life. Well, maybe not happy, but at least content. Their relationship had worked after a fashion.

She didn't deserve what Michael gave her.

He could still see her face as that first blow of the hatchet parted her skull. It seemed almost unbelievable now. He would never get that image out of his head.

There were too many terrible images in there now. Too many bodies. Too much death.

This was even harder. He didn't want to watch what Michael was going to do to Izzy. Michael had made him do enough watching of him in bed with Polina. She had loved it, but it had been Michael's sick idea, all to make up for the times he had watched him with their stepfather.

Simon says look at us, Kenneth. Look at the fun we're having.

Yes, he had looked. He had watched. He had felt the damage done to both of them on each occasion.

And afterwards he had hugged Michael and rocked him gently and told him that everything would be okay.

But it never was.

And these were the consequences. All because Kenneth had never done anything about it when he should have.

There could be no forgiveness for that.

* * *

Izzy sensed death coming. It was getting closer, almost as if it were a figure standing somewhere in the shadows of the empty pool, moving stealthily forwards, step by ominous step.

Michael said, 'I know it's cold here, but you should be fine after all that strenuous activity. I think it's about time you took some of those clothes off.'

She had dreaded this. She had contemplated dying, but not violation. That was too much for her mind to take.

'So come on, then, Izzy. I think Kenneth here is itching to see what you look like naked. He's got a bit of a thing for you, and

I don't mean what's in his trousers.' He laughed uproariously again.

Death. Another step nearer. Izzy was beginning to welcome its approach.

'Take your top off, Izzy.'

She didn't move.

'Did you hear me? I said take your fucking top off. Kenneth wants to see the goods.'

She shook her head. 'No.'

Michael smiled. 'Clever girl. You remembered this time. But I'm not letting you off the hook. Simon says take your top off.'

Izzy still didn't budge. Her pulse was racing, her breath ragged, but she was not going to take part in this game any longer.

Death shifted forwards, became a stronger presence. She had never felt anything like this before. It was almost palpable. Hairs rose on her flesh.

'No,' she answered.

Michael snorted. 'No? Did you actually just say no?' He turned to Kenneth. 'Your girl's got spirit. She's actually going to put up a bit of a fight.'

Death took a step backwards.

Wait, she thought. What's going on here? Why am I suddenly in less danger? Why has Michael suddenly become less threatening to me?

And then she realised something.

She didn't know Michael well enough to read him. She didn't know what he was feeling or when he was telling the truth.

Which meant . . .

'You're a pervert,' she said loudly.

Michael stared at her in disbelief. She felt Death find its power again.

'You heard me,' she said. 'You're a pathetic, cock-sucking pervert.'

The only reason you're doing this is because you can't cope with women in the real world.'

Michael showed her a smile, but it seemed weak. Death grew in stature.

'I think you should have asked Polina about that.'

'What, your brother's wife? You call that the real world? That was just revenge on Kenneth. You let your own stepfather abuse you, and now the only way you can get a hard-on is when you can hate at the same time. Isn't that right, Mikey?'

A twitch took hold of Michael's lip. He seemed flustered.

'You really want to see what hatred looks like?' he asked. 'You want to be on the sharp end of all the hatred in my body?'

Izzy edged sideways, causing Michael to turn with her, blocking Kenneth from her view.

'What have you got, big boy? That iddy-biddy knife? Yeah, that's you all over, isn't it?'

Michael put a hand out to his side. 'Give me the knife, Kenneth.'

Izzy held her breath. Prayed that she'd been right.

Death listened. Death loomed.

'*Give me the fucking knife!*'

Death clamped a hand over Michael's face. Brought the other to his neck. The act was swift and merciless, the blade slicing effortlessly right around, severing the major veins and arteries.

Izzy watched in horror and fascination as Kenneth sank to the floor, pulling the jerking figure of his brother down with him. He cradled Michael in his arms, rocking gently as the steaming blood spurted over both of them.

'It's all right now,' Kenneth said. 'I'll look after you. Nobody can hurt you anymore. I've stopped it, like you wanted me to. I'll take care of you now.'

46

TWO MONTHS LATER

The Handmaid's Tale.

A good choice, Izzy thought as she rang it through the till. Nothing like a cracking bit of dystopian fiction.

But that's not why the woman's here, she thought. She might never even read the book. She's come to see the monkey in the zoo. She keeps sneaking enquiring looks at me, and she's desperate to ask me about it.

It had been like this for weeks now. The shop was doing a roaring trade. Many were like this woman, keen just to get within touching distance of someone with local celebrity status. Others were less inhibited about saying what was on their minds: *What was it like? How did you find him? Did he try to kill you? Did you kill him? How did you do it?*

Mostly she gave little away. She told them that she just happened to get dragged into it and was extremely lucky to get out of it. Some were satisfied with this mundane account, others not so much, but she didn't care. Whatever she said, the community and the media added their own embellishments, turning her into some kind of superhero – exactly what she had assured Josh Frendy that she wasn't.

The woman took back her debit card and the book, then smiled and said, 'I just want you to know, I think you're incredibly brave.'

'Thank you,' Izzy said, 'but I'm really not.'

The woman gave her a knowing look. 'Modest too. The world needs people like you.'

And then she left.

Izzy watched her go. She didn't regard herself as brave. She'd survived, and that was it. What had happened to her had scarred her for the rest of her days.

She had watched a man die. She had looked on as his body spasmed and his lifeblood pulsed out of his neck. It wasn't like the movies. Despite what Michael had done to her, to people she cared about, seeing life leave him was the most horrible thing she had ever witnessed.

She had watched another man who had lost everything. His dog, then his wife, then his brother. Kenneth had changed from someone she despised to someone for whom she felt incredibly sorry. She saw him now as a man who, in his own warped way, had tried to step up and do the right thing for a brother he had repeatedly failed in the past. And then, when it came to it, he had accepted that there was only one right thing to do.

And then there were the others. The ones who really kept her awake at nights. Melissa, Polina, and above all, Josh. All three of them involved because of what Izzy had said to them. And all three now dead because of that. She had attended three very different funerals within the space of one week, and had not needed her gift to feel the devastation caused to those left behind.

It was the guilt that had hit her hardest. It nearly drove her to a breakdown. She was receiving counselling because of it. And Andy, her beautiful Andy, was always there for her. Andy's mother was still living, but even the prospect of losing her hadn't prevented a full reconciliation with Izzy once Andy became aware of what she had been through – although she did call Izzy a fucking idiot when she found out.

Those who were really on Izzy's side, and not just nosy onlookers, pointed out repeatedly to her that she had stopped a serial killer. She had achieved what nobody else could – not even the police. Many more might have died had it not been for her intervention. She had nothing to feel guilty about.

They were still just words. She tried to believe them, and maybe one day she would.

She missed Josh.

Their encounters had been few and they had been brief, but there had been a genuine connection there. Nothing sexual or sordid. Each had discovered something in the other that they needed, and that was a rare and precious thing. She cried about him often.

'Fancy a coffee?'

This from Jamie, a young assistant recently taken on by Abel. Ever eager to please, he didn't ask too many questions about what had happened. Izzy thought he was lovely, but she was wary of getting to know him too well. The baggage that came with that intimacy was too off-putting. Perhaps one day she would let him in, but not yet.

'If you don't mind,' she answered.

'Right-ho!' he said. It was a quaint affectation of his.

While he disappeared into the back room, Izzy began to tidy some of the shelves. She had barely begun when she heard someone enter the shop. She rushed back to the counter.

It was Edith. And she was without Ronald. And there could be only one reason why she was without Ronald.

'Hello, dear,' Edith said.

Izzy was already filling up.

'Edith . . .'

'I just popped in to tell you something.'

'Ronald.'

Edith didn't seem surprised that she should jump to that conclusion. 'Yes. He passed away last month.'

Izzy reached out for Edith's hand. 'Oh, Edith, I'm so sorry. You made such a lovely couple.'

'Thank you. He had a good, long life. I thought you should know because you've been so kind to us. I've read all the books we got from here.'

'I didn't really do anything, but I'm so glad you enjoyed the books. I hope . . . I hope that you'll still keep coming.'

'You're a good girl. I wish I could, but I'm moving down south to live with our son. I'm afraid this will be my last visit to this wonderful shop.'

'That's such a shame. I'll miss you both.'

Edith nodded. After a lengthy pause she said, 'I knew, you know.'

'Knew what?'

'About Ronald. About his condition. Although not at first. He told me the doctors had given him the all-clear, and for a while I believed it. We never lie to each other, you see. But later I just knew. He didn't come right out and admit it, but I knew. I just let him believe he was protecting me.'

Izzy smiled through her tears. 'I can see why you stayed together for so long.'

'Yes. He didn't know about our gift, did he, dear?'

'Our gift?'

'Yes. What women can do. Men always think they're the stronger ones, but they don't know about us. Even when we tell them, they don't believe us. They don't realise that we can see right through them. We know their deepest thoughts, even when we don't admit it to ourselves. They have no secrets from us. No secrets at all.'

ACKNOWLEDGEMENTS

Getting the words down is only the first part of writing a novel. Much of the work comes in the editing phase, and for *No Secrets* I've had an amazing editing A-team to help me. Miranda Jewess, Therese Keating and Hayley Shepherd have, at the various stages, provided me with superb feedback and suggestions, saving my literary bacon many times over. My heartfelt thanks go to all of them, as well as to the rest of the Viper/Profile team and the external proofreaders, designers and consultants who have had a hand in the final product.

Thanks as always to Oli Munson and his colleagues at A M Heath. It's such a comfort to know they have my back.

It's been another funny old year, and I'm really looking forward to getting back to the literary festivals, not least to thank in person the many authors who have read my books and provided blush-inducing quotes. I also need to thank the many bloggers and reviewers who have offered such kind support and encouragement.

A silver lining of the pandemic and other recent events is that it has brought my immediate family much closer together, and not merely in a spatial sense. Through much laughter and tears, the strengthening of our bond has been almost palpable, and I will be eternally grateful to Lisa, Bethany and Eden simply for being who they are.

It is no accident that the protagonist in *No Secrets* works in a bookshop. It's my way of thanking anyone who reads books, collects books, sells books or has anything to do with books. That includes you, you wonderful person!